UNKNOWN

By

ASHLEE MISHAEL SNELL

First paperback edition February 2021

Hardback ISBN: 978-1-7366980-0-6
Paperback ISBN: 978-1-7366980-1-3
Ebook ISBN: 978-1-7366980-2-0

Edited by Chersti Nieveen
Cover art by Doug Hoppes
Edited by Halleigh Thompson

Author Website:
www.AshleeSnell.com

My Sunshine's.

I love you big, big like the sky!

Chapter 1

Blackness. It is what surrounds me while my eyes try to adjust. The forest is hauntingly beautiful, but I must remember to not get lost in what is fiction. It just seems so real. The trees are so close to one another it looks as if they would offer complete support. It makes me believe that if one tree fell, they would all follow suit. The tops create the canopy of darkness I stand under. I hug my shoulders as a cool midnight breeze wraps around me.

I reach out to touch the branches that hang down with a sense of sadness. Smelling how their dead leaves create the musty, wet layer of debris underneath my feet. My bare toes crinkle at the slimy feeling of mush I seem to be standing on. Wondering where my shoes would be a normal question, but I know I didn't go to bed with them on.

UNKNOWN

The sinister silence I hear is almost inviting as I start to take a step forward. My body becomes hesitant when I look ahead of me and it seems as if the forest will swallow me whole. The murkiness, as eerie as it seems, pulls me in like the tide of the ocean. I feel myself swaying back to safety and then being pushed into the unknown. The moment my determination sets in and I move forward, dozens of black birds come rushing near me. I can feel them beckoning me with a warning not to move. I should heed the recommendation, but it is like I am compelled to ignore it. My feet start shifting through the thick heap of forgotten leaves even though in the back of my mind I know that it is probably not a good idea. It always ends up the same, no matter what I try to change.

As I push my way into the grove of trees, I notice that I have no idea where I am going even though mentally, I should remember this part. Each dream is the same. My body seems to work on autopilot, even though my mind is foggy. I slowly start to feel like this is just a normal stroll in a park I have spent years exploring. Once I am deep into my journey, I allow myself to feel the magnitude of being so small in an area that is so vast.

My body goes on high alert once the weight of being lost consumes me. A feeling of dread accompanied with a handful of knots form in the pit of my stomach. The hairs on the back of my neck stand tall and goosebumps raise along my arms. Before I make the conscious effort to move, my body bites the bullet and I begin running at a dead sprint. Running. Faster than humanly possible. I push past trees and underbrush not caring that my clothes are being ripped.

My arms and legs feel like they have been torn to shreds. The stinging on my skin begging me to stop, if only for a moment. Do you think I listen? Not a chance. My mother's voice comes through my mind, "Do you always have to be so stubborn?" I allow my laugh to echo throughout the stillness ahead. It is almost exhilarating to watch the trees pass by in a blur.

I run for what seems like miles when my body betrays me and stops. I double over and fling my hands above my head trying to catch my breath. I concentrate on the sounds around me. Twigs snap and brush rustles with movement, but I am unsure of which direction it is coming from. This strange sense of foreboding comes to me as I push forward trying to receive answers. Trying to grasp on to reality in a world full of fantasy.

I stop moving and concentrate on making my breathing as quiet as possible. Trying to seem invisible to lure out whoever is hiding. After some time, a figure steps out of the night. I continue to make myself as still as possible, but as soon as I almost have my answer, I feel the rush of wind and my view turns sideways.

I try to catch myself from falling but my arms betray the rest of my body. My head pounds from where it made contact with a rock. Spots cloud my vision and there is a high pitch ringing in my ears while my lungs feel like they are stuck together. I roll over coughing, struggling to sit up and mentally curse myself for blowing my cover. Nothing. I see nothing around me. The calm is almost unnerving until I finally pick up on a figure in the shadows.

I try to speak, but my voice seems to be gone. Locked away, somewhere I am unable to reach. I want to scream just to catch the attention of whatever is out there, but not even air makes its way out of my throat. I slowly stop my struggling and focus on observing.

Watching my company as a strange sense of calmness comes over me. The calm before the inner storm. My body tries to go into flight or fight. Both halves waging war on me internally, battling to take control. I want to continue running, not away from potential danger but towards my answers. I want to go back to the start, not for self-preservation, but so I can try to make something else happen beside this repeated illusion.

I catch myself wishing for the person in the shadows to acknowledge me. Deep down knowing if I could have answers it would change the course I am stuck on. My breathing catches in my lungs and my heart skips a beat, when suddenly whoever is there tilts their head up just enough for their eyes to be visible. My breathing halts as I find myself staring into the most beautiful pair of icy blue eyes I have ever seen. They are calling me like a lighthouse calls a boat. My head becomes rattled with the possibility of who is behind those eyes. I become utterly relieved to look into these vast pools of color, so pure they look like fresh snow.

My mind starts to have a thousand questions competing for attention when I unexpectedly smell what seems like pine trees and cinnamon. I want to know who this is- no -I need to know who this is. His emotions seem to swirl with an intensity that could rival the

Starry Night by Van Gogh. They seem to almost glow in this vast, colorless, forest as he takes a small step forward.

My body abandons me as I try to sit up. Refusing to listen to my command as I reach out for the person in my dreams. Those eyes never leaving mine as the darkness swallows me whole. I feel this strange sense of nothingness, almost like floating before a faint beeping is heard. Beep. Beep. Beep. Louder and louder the out of place sound grows when I become jolted awake with an all too familiar feeling of ice-cold water dousing me.

"Really Brina Lee Scott", I yell at my supposed best friend as she stands there with a pitcher nonchalantly in her left hand. I want to curse her because this time I was so close to answers. Closer than I have come in years. This dream felt so real. I throw back my covers and look at my legs. Running my hands up and down my smooth skin. Blinking twice when I can feel the stinging as my hands go across what should be cuts and scrapes even though they are flawless.

What makes this dream different from the others? Never have I felt anything after waking up. My lungs still burn, and I reach for my head due to the pounding sensation that hits me. My senses go into overdrive as the scents of pine trees and cinnamon are still fresh on my nose, as if it were December, instead of August. As I am trying to wrap my head around my dream, Brina's laugh echoes through the empty room. My empty room.

Her voice cuts through my mental anguish and brings me back down to earth. "Adalee, did you really think I was going to let you slide on our morning run? I don't care if it is the first day of school or not!" She said this pragmatically, while swishing her platinum blonde ponytail, which only left me exasperated. I know she heard my alarm going off right before she doused me with water.

She knows I hate to run, but I put up with it out of love for her. I may love her, but that doesn't mean I have to like her all the time. I push up and out of bed, throw my covers off of me with force, and brush past her. Making sure to grace her with my best eye roll full of as much sass as I could muster at five in the morning. "Give me a few minutes to dry off and change."

I reach up to stretch my aching muscles, grumbling as she prances out of my room. I hear her dance down the hall, walk down the stairs, and right out the door before I can even reach my closet. That girl has some nerve to her, she is the only seventeen-year-old I know who loves this time of the morning. No one, and I mean no, one should have that much energy when running is involved.

As I put on my tights and a t-shirt, I think back to my dream. Remembering every detail with a vividness that feels like I could relive it while awake. Like I could just close my eyes and I would still be in that forest that has plagued me for years. "Adalee! Will you hurry up?" I make a mental note to tell Brina later about the latest revelation in my reoccurring dream, unsure of what it means to have had company in my dreams last night. I push all of that out of my mind for a few moments because right now I need to muster all of the strength I can to get through these five miles.

This has been our morning routine for the last couple of years. Brina wakes me up in an uncomfortable way, I grumble and drag my feet while she flounces circles around me. We go for a "light run" as Brina loves to say. Usually at the end of our run I look like I jumped in a lake while she is barely winded.

The corners of my lips turn up ever so slightly as I think about our friendship while grabbing my headphones. I tip toe through my room making sure not to knock down any of the boxes stacked up in piles that litter the floor like a maze. Mentally making a note to work on unpacking. Just the word unpacking causes my shoulders to slump forward. Having to pull out my stuff from boxes once again makes me cringe.

This is the hardest part of moving, in my opinion. Every time I tell myself to start over in a new way. Each new town I think I can reinvent myself. Yet, it always ends up the same. I become the outcast. Labeled as the weird girl who has unexplainable incidents. Unable to tell them the truth. If they could know, it might combat some of the fear, but this is my burden to bare. Brina has such an easier time with the constant change that occurs in our life. I sometimes envy that from her.

I start humming to the melody coming from my headphones as I finally make my way outside. When I step through our screened door, the crisp smell of rotting leaves hits my nose and I cannot help but think of how the forest in front of our house gives off a similar vibe to the one I just escaped from moments ago. A shiver runs down my spine. My attention once again, being held longer than normal by a cluster of trees. Cool blue clouding my vision.

"Gah, you're such a slow poke Ad." Brina's southern bell charm ringing over my music as she draws out the words at an uncomfortably sluggish pace. "Sorry. Just lost in my thoughts."

Usually I would break and tell her everything about what has my

head, but I am not sure I understand it enough to explain. "Where are

we running today?" I answer back flatly as I turn up the volume on

my music, hoping she gets the hint.

I wait for a reply anxiously, but she just starts stretching. I

silently thank her for understanding that I will spill everything when

I am ready. After several stretches, Brina taps me on the shoulder

and I follow her as she takes off slowly. We run the first mile at a

slow pace, but soon we were pushing our legs to propel us faster and

faster through the worn trail behind our house. Running normally

helps clear my mind, but I cannot seem to shake those eyes. Every

turn we take down our path I seem to see them deep in the forest.

Each time I want to stop and examine every detail. Struggling to

keep my body from being pulled like a magnet. It is like I have no

control over where it goes, and I do not like it.

When we get back to the house, I throw myself on the ground

attempting to catch my breath. I pick my head up to look over to my

right and notice Brina's lips are moving. "CAN'T. HEAR. YOU." I

yell, struggling to make my lungs expand. She walks over and pulls my headphones out. "Hey, why did you…" I attempt to spit out before she puts one hand on her hip and one in the air to stop me. "I was asking if you were ready to talk about it yet?" Her condescending mom voice sounding like nails on a chalk board to my ears that are still slightly ringing.

Am I ready to talk about what I saw in this dream that was every bit the same as it was different? Do I want to worry Brina with something I don't know enough about just yet? If I am still unsure, my best bet is diversion. "Just thinking about what to get you for our birthday." I can see her mulling over my statement in her mind. Watching as curiosity and hesitation flashes in her eyes. You can almost physically see the gears spinning out of control. "Adalee, I see what you're doing, and I am only falling for it this time." I give her my best smile, pearly white teeth and all, when I realize she is dropping the subject, for now.

We happen to share our birthday. September 5th is considered a holiday in our household. I think it is one of the many things that makes us connected more like sisters than best friends. Brina adores her birthday and I try to skip the whole month of September to avoid it. They say time heals all wounds. Well, whoever thought that surely did not have a deep enough wound.

Each year, my wound grows larger and more painful.

Before I disappear through my door I stand there for just a

few moments and take notice that Brina's room is already unpacked

and decorated with pastel pink and gold accents. Taking a few steps

closer, I peak in to see if she has her memory wall up yet. It is my

favorite place in each house we have ever lived in. I could spend

hours looking over the memories she usually has covering one entire

wall from top to bottom and left to right. Movie posters, pictures,

restaurant napkins, menus, letters, and other trinkets she had

acquired in our years of starting new all neatly secured.

I look down the hall and notice mom's room is still nothing

but boxes. Curious if she will see us off on our first day. Deep down

I know the answer, but I do not want to accept it. I cannot remember

the last time she was home when we left for school. I practice

plastering a smile on my face. Unsure if people will notice that the

smile does not reach my eyes, conflicted as to why I suddenly care

what other people think. With my favorite white bells from Texas, a

cheetah print top from Florida, and a pair of black toms from

Nevada, I feel as ready as I ever will to take on senior year. Here I come, or better yet, here we come.

As Brina navigates the winding road to Rose Preparatory Academy I just stare out the front window listening to music. Hoping I can master becoming a natural with people and changing situations in the time it takes us to get to school. A school I know has a secret of its own. We have moved more times than I can count in the last ten years of my life. Usually once if not twice during the year. I know it is for safety reasons, but that is all I know. Truthfully, I do not remember if we moved around before the age of seven. That was a super rough year. A year I only remember starting in September. The different psychologists that I have seen off and on throughout the years usually state that the memory lapse is a response to the trauma of what happened that year. A way for my mind to protect itself.

I would like to believe the individuals in their fancy white coats, but I know what I am. I know what my mother is. I know what Brina is. I know we are not normal and that most supernatural creatures don't get memory lapses due to trauma. Witches like my mother and I, or wolves like Brina, usually lose their memory due to a magical cause. A spell, curse, hex, or hoodoo, it's really all the same. Individuals who come from my world learn from an early age that tragedy is something that runs in our blood. It is the only thing connecting each supernatural species. Catastrophe plagues each and every one of us like a curse bestowed from whatever higher power you believe in, in an attempt to cause balance. If I believed that my lack of memories from my early childhood was due to losing a parent, Brina would be effected twice as much.

Our families were best friends. My mom says that they even had family dinner every Saturday night. A week after the funeral my mother took over full custody of Brina and we moved for the first time. Monday, September 20th of 2010 was the day we left our home. The day my memories left me behind like an unwanted object.

I only know this life that I have had with Brina and my mom. I guess in a way it helps with the sadness. Usually, I get this enormous feeling of sorrow, but no memory as to why I am unhappy. Like when I eat rocky road ice cream or when I pick up the hunter green throw blanket off my mother's bed. It is as if my body knows I hold precious memories with these objects that my mind will not let me think about or remember.

At first the lapses in my memory didn't bother me, but as I grew up I started searching for myself and continued to hit hurdle after hurdle. I made a vow a few years back to find out the truth, regardless of who or what may come my way. Nothing will sway me in my ultimate goal of retrieving my memories

Chapter 2

"Adalee, now honey, please do not get down on me today." She demands so much sometimes. I just sigh at her and give her a small half smile. She always knows what I am thinking. It is like she can feel and understand my emotions before I do. I muster up as much enthusiasm as I can, even though it still doesn't make the negative thoughts go away.

I remember that first week without my father as clearly as if it had happened yesterday. I didn't talk, didn't really eat, refused to play with my toys, and hardly slept. My tears were as constant as the rain for that first week. That was the first time I learned about my abilities. I believe, relearned, would be a better word. My mood effected the weather and it terrified me feeling the raw power surge through me. I was a blank slate. Someone who was lost with no recollection of anything before getting in the car to move to Louisiana.

The only thing that was constant in my life was Brina. She was my saving grace. My guardian angel if you will. She should have taken this harder than anyone, yet she has been an example of true grace. Over the last ten years she has never let me down, not once.

"Okay you win. I will give it everything I've got. Just know that isn't much at the moment." I watch as she ponders at my reply then gives me this look of pure trouble. "So tell me, what are you getting me for my birthday? We only turn eighteen once Adalee." I can't with this girl. She used my own tactics against me because she knows I was lying. She can look right through me as if I was made of glass.

I mentally smack my forehead. I look at her, really look and notice she truly has the best smile I have ever seen. "Guess you might find out later. Just promise me you won't snoop through my closet this year." I really owe her a truly magnificent gift. Something about this birthday has always held a special place in Brina's heart.

She has talked about it for years. She thinks that once we turn eighteen our life will do a complete one-eighty. That it magically becomes happy and that our pain will go away. I hope she finds her happy. I admire her for the hopefulness she seems to resonate, but all I feel is dread when I think about this birthday.

Sometime later Brina pulls the jeep into the parking lot and we are both flabbergasted. The pictures online did not do this building justice. The Rose Prep Academy looked almost out of place in this isolated forest. The massive building looked to be three, if not four, stories tall. With stones of varying sizes and shapes giving it a castle-like appearance.

Each stone that makes up the buildings is a contrasting shade of grey. Moss and vines compete for a place on a few of the walls giving it a vintage, earthy, vibe. The witch in me can feel the raw power coming from the campus grounds. "Brina, do you see the tall stone steps next to the fountain? They are stunning." Radio silence. I allow us to both process the beauty of the academy in silence. My eyes wonder over beautiful displays of varying flowers and large trees that scatter the lawn.

Brina reaches over and pinches my arm. "This has to be the prettiest school I have ever seen, Adalee. I wanted to make sure I wasn't dreaming." I continued to gawk at the mesmerizing and vast depth of beauty that surrounded us and felt like for the first time I was at peace with starting somewhere new. I understand why she just did what she did. It was almost like what I imagine being home would feel like. I take a long, exaggerated breath of fresh air and smile. Mentally remembering to keep my fangs in check on the first day of school. Something that has not happened in a very long time.

I continue to rub the spot on my arm that is still red from Brina as we walk into the office. The first thing I noticed was that no one gawked at us like they normally would when we start at a new school. "Don't be such a baby, Adalee. I barely pinched you." Brina usually beams bright enough to draw attention with her larger than life personality.

"You call that barely, Brina? I'll have a bruise for over a week." I tend to stay in the shadows. Being this is probably the fifteenth time to be a new student, I was used to getting those stares. It gave me a sense of relief but left me super curious at the same time to not have everyone watching.

Being supernatural tends to draw in humans, and so my interest peaks thinking about how many other students are like Brina and I. Mother warned us we would be going to a place with both mundane humans and creatures of the night in attendance. I almost wish someone would stare us down instead of every student passing us like we were not even there. "Geez Brina, where's the welcome committee?" Brina just shrugged her shoulders and started dragging me back on track towards the office. "Come on, time for us to get our schedule." She has so much enthusiasm in her voice that I can't help but roll my eyes.

We met with Principle Allen and sat down in front of his desk. He handed us a map, our schedules, and a packet of information about the school activities. Brina giggled and pointed to the first thing she noticed on the calendar. In big bold letters was a Welcome Back Bonfire. It was the same night of our birthday. I just looked at her and nodded towards the principle as if to say silently to pay attention. I really would like to stay off his radar if possible.

"Ladies, please pay attention." Too late. His voice rang with authority, sending a chill down my spine. "This part is important, and I do not take interruptions lightly. At this school, it is of utmost importance to maintain student safety. No fighting under any circumstances. That is all, please make your way to class before you are late." He basically growled his final statement. Great, already on his bad side and wolves tend to hold a grudge. Before we could spit out a thank you, Principle Allen was opening the door and dismissing us with a wave of his hand.

We stop by our lockers and it takes every ounce of concentration I can muster to go through the motions of opening it. My mind not on the topic of school at the moment. The excitement of being here is wearing off, leaving me extra emotional. Brina grabs my shoulder playfully and flashes me a smirk full of wonder and delight.

"Adalee, what's wrong?" Her voice becomes laced with worry and concern when I don't give her one back. "Nothing important." In an attempt to hide my insecurities, I push forward and start walking once more. Hoping to avoid having this discussion with so many listening ears. I know I shouldn't be annoyed with her, but I really don't like how she doesn't mind the fact this year is already so different. I don't handle change well and the new charm has definitely worn off. It is like once you open a Christmas gift and are only interested in it for a few minutes. After that time has passed it gets shoved to the side to be forgotten, except it is kind of hard to forget a massive building filled with complete strangers.

As I look at my schedule it causes my stomach to drop knowing I will not have my best friend with me every step of the way. We were supposed to do this together. We are always together. My breathing starts to accelerate, feeling people bump into me, their posture screaming impatience. Feeling the judgment from each one as it hits me in waves. I am sure my pale skin is the color of snow. Is it even possible for me to be that white? I am starting to get worked up, which will lead to a panic attack.

"This is just another response to the trauma", comes clanging through my head as visions of another doctor in a white coat encroaches on my sanity. I place my hands up to my ears trying to drown out the voices that say nothing is wrong inside of my mind That everything is because of the trauma. I am not crazy and I know something magical is behind this.

I attempt to slow my breathing once again and my body fails me. I concentrate on removing the signs of my panic attack one by one, when my shoulder is yanked hard enough to be pulled out of socket. Brina's grip is one of iron on my upper arm as she pushes past students. Muttering half-assed apologies while she pushes me into the bathroom next to our first period class.

Brina stands there waiting until I get a grip on myself. She gives me time and space, but most importantly, patience. These panic attacks use to happen just every once in a while, but the moment we moved to back to Ronan, Montana, they have happened every day. I slowly battle my monster and place it back into its cage at the depths of my soul. I take the angst and turn it into determination as I straighten my shoulders and place my midnight blue curls into an intricate braid. Lying to myself by thinking if I place a little order into my life it might not feel as out of control.

"We are going to be okay, darling." I just cannot help but laugh when she piles on her accent as thick as she just did with the word darling. She knows it makes me giggle at how funny she sounds when she draws out her words. I nod my head ever so slightly. We walk hand in hand to calculus just as the bell is ringing. It is just then I realize we don't have any books. Mental face palm. My palms begin to sweat as dread fills me to my core when I realize

I don't even have my backpack because it is sitting on the floorboard of the jeep.

Brina hands me her designer bag with extra supplies. Yet again, as if noticing what I was feeling. Her empath abilities amaze me every time I see them in action. "Thanks, Brina. What would I do without you?" My voice is barely above a murmur but I know she would have no problem hearing it. She just gives me her dazzling grin and winks. "Like this isn't how we start every first day, honey."

Arm in arm, we walk in and go straight to the teacher's desk. "You know Brina, I try to have my life together." Brina laughs and I cannot help but understand where she is coming from. "Dear, you would lose your head if it wasn't attached to your shoulders."

The moment we break through the door facing into our first classroom, I take everything in. "You know Ads, maybe we should have given him a red apple." Brina's statement causes me to laugh at how often characters in movies put a red apple on the teacher's desk. The space has messy papers. There is a little gold name plate with "Mr. Green" engraved on it. Jars full of pens and pencils and some old books mixed in with textbooks.

As I admire the books on his desk, I cannot help but think that they resemble a grimoire and an ancient one at that. They are bound in old leather and the paper has a yellow, almost translucent tint. I peer over to glance the writing which has a dark brown, handwritten quality. The energy radiating from these books has a dark and powerful aura. They are calling me to just graze a page, one page would suffice to give me all the answers I have been searching for. The moment my hand almost touches the corner of the page, Mr. Green clears his throat and slams the cover shut on the book closest to where we are standing.

Mr. Green stood before the class and hushes the students with a raspy, monotonous voice. "Class we have two bright new pupils. Please stay silent while they introduce themselves and then we will get started." Out of the corner of my eyes, I watch as Mr. Green's pale, slender hand places his books in a locked cabinet below his desk. His thin rimmed glasses falling down his nose. As if he noticed my longing stares and I made him uncomfortable, his mouth forms a tight line and he nods forward toward the other students.

Turning towards the class, I tried to silently take in my surroundings, but before I could really take in each detail, Brina finishes her introduction. I stand before the call and realize it is now my turn to give our well-rehearsed speeches. "Hello, my name is Adalee Ebony Rosewood. We hope to have a good year. Thank you for your time." I managed to fumble out my last few words as we rushed to take our seat.

Once settled, I notice next to us was this absolutely flawless girl with a wild mane of dark red hair that seemed to fit her quick and daring eyes. Eyes that I was noticing were glaring daggers in my direction. The envy spinning at the surface made it seem like I was unaware of this long-standing war between us.

Once she caught me staring, I could smell the salon fumes as she flipped her hair and snickered in my direction. "I'm Veronica Allen. That's right, Principle Allen's daughter. Head bitch in charge and you would do best to remember that." Puzzled I just look at her like she has lost her mind. "Brina, do you think she is okay? I am afraid she is having a seizure. Just look at how her eyes are moving?" Brina's bell-like laugh chimes across the classroom causing it to become deathly silent.

Veronica looks over and sizes her up. Veronica probably has at least seven inches on her due to her platform wedges, but Brina never backs down. "Bless your heart darling, I know your momma taught you manners, right?" In her thick southern draw and we both busted out laughing. Veronica turned a shade of red, about the color of her hair and was about to let Brina have it when Mr. Green started in on the longest lecture of my life. I slump back into my seat, unsure of how we already have an enemy, and it has only been an hour. I wonder what could possibly be her problem.

Once we are out in the hallway Veronica bumps into us catching us off guard and knocks both of us down. Standing over us she half-heartedly snorts, "I am not the person you want to mess with." We pick ourselves off the ground showing we both don't back down from a challenge. "Brina, do you think mom has bleach at home? I would hate to ruin my white bells." She seems to ponder my question. "You know Adalee, I don't think she is worth ruined pants, especially pants that make you look that good." As nonchalantly as I can, I twirl on my heels. "Yeah, I do look good."

Not used to being challenged, Veronica takes a few hesitant steps backwards. I can feel the anger fuming off of her from being ignored. "You do not want to get on my bad side." I look around and notice kids are starting to line up and down the hallway. Staring at what might happen next. Brina walks up to her graciously and leans in super close. I can feel the vibrations rolling off her back as she growls out a "Try us."

The halls become hushed, and I did not think that was possible. You could hear a pen drop. I grin as Brina turns and sashays back to throw her arm around my shoulders. Winking at a group of younger classmen who are unsure of what to do so they throw a whistle in our direction. Their high pitched sounds drift up and down the quiet hall. When they are done, Brina stares at Veronica who was not expecting that reaction. Surprise is soon replaced with fury. Her jaw becomes clenched as she crosses her arms. The tapping of her foot echoing in the motionless hall. I watch as the throbbing vein in her neck picks up pace. I would bet you could almost witness smoke flowing from her ears.

Brina bows at her audience and sweetly says, "Please excuse us shortcake, we have a class to get too and I don't like to be late." We brush past Veronica and I lean in to where she can hear me give her the icing on the cake. "Especially for a small excuse like yourself." The insult rolls off my lips with such a satisfaction my heart leaps. This display of blatant disrespect makes Veronica seethe as she storms off. "I guess she expected us to bend over, huh doll?" Brina asks me mockingly.

"You know I was hoping to stay under the radar this year." Brina stops walking and looks at me with her hand crossed over her chest. "Who do you think I am, Adalee? I wouldn't know how to stay under the radar if I was in Antarctica." I just shake my head and start taking off down the hall of students whose mouths are still on the floor. "Come on Miss, I don't like to be late."

Chapter 3

My hands itch at the steel handles in front of me. They itch with

anticipation. The Rosewood library feels almost like home when

walking through the double glass doors. A much-needed change.

The sight is breathtaking. It has an open concept floor plan with the

ceiling reaching three stories up. The light reflects off of beautiful

large metal mobiles hanging from the ceiling. The artwork does a

magnificent job in filling the void, but not crowding the space.

There are sky lights that cover the entire ceiling above,

letting in a generous amount of natural light. Rows and rows of

books fill almost every inch of the first two floors. I slowly pace

myself viewing a few of the novels that call this place home. My fingers graze along the spines of the more worn out hardcovers taking in how they feel. How the smell of the pages fills the air.

In the middle of the room on the first floor is a rounded desk. The space is neatly kept with small stacks of papers in different directions. Small figurines placed strategically so your eyes dance around the desk, taking in each detail.

I set the intricate metal witch I was holding back down when I get a whiff of pine trees and cinnamon. Such a delightful smell. I smile at myself and inhale deeply in an attempt to fill my lungs, yet the smell becomes faint. It seems to be slowly fading. I subconsciously start to make my way toward the smell and find myself on the second floor. I start to look around when I am stopped mid stride by an older woman.

Her golden-brown hair in a tight bun and thick rimmed glasses framing her rounded face tell me she is the librarian. She has a twinkle to her blue eyes that looks like trouble and a safe place mixed together. "Hello, Adalee. I have been waiting on our encounter. If you need anything let me know what I can help you with." I stand looking at her kind of funny. I was trying to figure out how she knew my name. She watches me, chuckles, and walks off to help another student on the other side of the library.

I gather my thoughts and make my way to the history section. What better way to use up my study hall period? Determination meets my every cell as I hope to learn about my past and looking into my lineage is a good start. Books about dreams might be another route to check, although I am unsure if such a book even exists. Maybe I can find some answers. Any answers could help at this point. Deep down I pray this might jog some of my memory.

I make my way through the maze. I start studying for one to catch my eye as I casually skim over the spines of each novel. Waiting for one to call to me. I tune into my witchy sense letting the books guide me. Feeling their energy push and pull against me.

I graze up and down the stack of books, row by row, and finally a hunter green book that is decently worn, stands out. Unfortunately, this book is about two rows higher than I can physically reach. I start attempting to jump for the book and after several unsuccessful moments I get fed up and throw my backpack behind me without looking. A loud thud comes from behind me followed by a low growl. The sound causes my feet to become as heavy as lead. My hands stuck in the awkward position as I wonder if I should turn around.

After a few split seconds, I force myself to calm down. Slowly turning around already trying to spit out an apology before I even see who I have hit with my backpack. I stop midsentence when I come face to face with a slender muscled frame that towers over me. I can feel the heat of breath bouncing back off of his chest onto my face due to his proximity.

Rage, annoyance, and then possibly confusion crosses his features. His eyebrows move up and down, finally settling to almost touching in the middle. As I sit, still lost for words, this guy's face turns into an expression of stone. His cheeks could cut diamonds and the thin line his lips are pressed into make me curious if they could be glued shut. "You should watch where you decide to throw things." The irritation in his voice caused me to stagger back just enough to where I was not straining my neck to look up at him.

My body aches the moment we have space between us. I just stand there lost, thinking about what his grey t-shirt would like on me as I slept. Pine and cinnamon obscuring my innermost thoughts making me worse than scrambled eggs. His vitality pulling me towards him like we are tethered together. Where he goes, I'll follow, but I don't even know this guy.

His eyes are a heavenly deep blue, speckled with gold. They are as serene as the morning dew and rimmed with thick long lashes. His eyebrows almost touch together in the middle due to how deeply they are furrowed. I want to reach out and smooth them. He should not have such a defeated gaze. His hair is tasseled in a way that looks like he runs his hands through it. He is breathtakingly beautiful and most woeful.

He clears his throat, and it snaps me back to the harsh reality around me. I notice he is holding a book in his right hand and I look down for split second to notice there are two more books on the floor. My manners seeming to come back. "I'm sorry for the mess." My apology quick and short. I scramble to give him the books. Watching as our hands graze. A gasp escapes his lips causing the books to hit the floor with a thud that seems to echo off of the bookshelves. Did he feel that too? "Who are you?" My voice trembles slightly at the end and I still try to get my thoughts straight.

He starts to speak, but I watch how his shoulders slump with defeat and he bows his head. "No one you need to concern yourself with." The air turns thick with mistrust and hostility and I clear my throat in an attempt to say go to hell, but he beats me to it. "I don't care who you are, so you have no right to who I am." He looks at me once more then spits out, "Next time, watch where you are going." His words dripping with indifference. The deep timber in his voice causing a shiver to snake its way down my body.

He turns promptly on his heels and before he could get out of view, words fly from my mouth before I could close it. "Wait, answer just one question for me. Please." He stops, mid stride, about five steps away but does not face me. "What makes you think you have the right to demand something from me?" He stands in the same spot, never moving. After a few moments, I take his silence and hesitation as a signal to go ahead and speak. "Is this how a normal conversation usually goes for you?" My question being more directed at his demeanor than how our actual exchange is going. I feel prideful as I place more power behind my inquiry. Now that my senses were coming around, I was not going to let him walk all over me.

Slowly I begin walking towards him. My body acting on instinct. I start to place my hand on his shoulder without even thinking about what I was doing. It was as if my body was drawn to touch him. I notice how his shoulder shifts backwards as if my hand were pulling him in. His body heat blazing against my fingertips. The black fabric of his t-shirt almost against my skin. Before our skin could touch, he quickly barked, "Haven't you ever heard of personal space? I asked for you to leave me alone."

The initial sting of the rejection hits me like a tsunami. How can this boy be causing me to inhale so deep I am unsure I'll be able to exhale? Coldness creeps into my bones. Unsure of what could account for his cruelty.

Scratching the side of my neck I attempt to change the topic of conversation with a shaky voice and nervous giggle. "So, do you watch sports?" He whips his head around as if he was making sure I was still behind him. His left eyebrow seems to arch up a little higher and his eyes squint as he processes my question. Deep down I want to ask him a thousand questions, but I know it's not enough to get him to stay.

Each step he takes away makes me feel hollow. His pace starts out slow and timid until it becomes fast and purposeful. His mind finally made. Embarrassment and the utter most regret are what I feel as I walk down the halls. The vivid picture of whoever he is walking away pains my already fragile ego.

Once class is over, I can feel the students who brush past me in the halls avoiding my eye contact. Like they all know. So, I straighten my shoulders back and hold my chin up and out. I swore off of guys and I am not faltering now. My feelings may act like a rollercoaster, but my will has always been made of iron.

Chapter 4

Our next couple of classes go without any miss steps and as the bell dismisses us from yearbook, I cannot help but feel giddy. Lunch is my absolute favorite time in school. Who does not love food? We meet a few friendly faces and the day, despite the rough start, seemed to be looking better.

Walking into the cafeteria I notice it is a pretty standard set up. Round tables with your normal stereotypical groups of students. The popular kids which had Veronica and her two followers. We learned about them in yearbook while our fellow students dished out the gossip to fill us in on the student body. Next you had loaners, jocks, and a few other odd and end students at their respected tables on one side of the room.

The other side of the room had more groups of tables with students around them that seemed to match more in how they looked physically than what they seemed like in personalities. You could almost place a line down the center to determine who was supernatural and who was human.

You had a group of students that were all extremely pale and beautiful in their own way. Vampires almost always draw you in to watching them. "It's almost unnerving." Brina's comment made me turn towards her and I was thankful for the distraction. "What are you talking about? The vampires?" She just nods her head and I notice she shivers slightly. I get the feeling. "They reminded me of Mr. Green from calculus. Wonder if they are in the same clan?" I quickly change to subject by not answering her question.

"What do you think of the girls to your right Brina?" There was of girls who dressed all similar just of darker shades. Each one picking things from the middle of this huge pile of food. "They seem very close to one another, just like they were all sisters. Must be the witches your mom was talking about." Most supernatural creatures can pick up on one another, but witches can be hard seeing as we are the closest to normal humans. "They smell like fire." Watching

Brina's nose crinkle I begin to chuckle. "Mother said this area was home to the Hearthstone Coven who's main power stems from the fire element."

Brina and I continue to go back and forth about different tables and what we thought. The last table we came to discuss stood out among the group of students. They had this wild air about them with their banter that is louder than life itself. They all seemed closer than even the group of witches, as they teased each other mercifully.

"Do you see them throwing food, Adalee? They give wolves a bad name." There was a large group of students, but three seemed to stand out above the rest. My thoughts became consumed with observing them. Two of the wolves seemed like a couple as they sat in a sweet embrace. Then you had another guy just to their left who resonated with authority, the same guy who just walked away from me in the library. A feeling of hatred started to snake its way up to my heart, but I do not know this guy. I do not know his story.

The sure power of influence in the air swirled and clouded around them with such a thickness you could almost physically touch it. "They must be important, huh Brina?" I should have waited for her response, but something about their carefree ways drew me to them. I started to walk in that direction, but I had to stop myself when I noticed the girl was staring at me with a soft smile. Let me pick up my pace. One foot in front of the other. "Geez, I need to get a grip."

"What did you just say, Adalee?" My attention now drawn back to my name. "Oh, you weren't supposed to hear that Brina." We went through the line and grabbed an array of food. We sat down at an empty table across the cafeteria as far away from the wolves as possible.

Brina was steadily going on about how the amount of homework that the teachers had already assigned was outrageous. She went on about what she thought of the teachers and other nonsense until she notices I am only halfway paying attention, and then she states rather loudly, "ADALEE EBONY, are you going to pay attention to me?"

My eyes pick up on the subtle adjustments that this guy who is in a black t-shirt and washed jeans across the room is trying to hide. The same guy who just showed his true colors in the library. "Yeah Brina, promise…" My voice trailing off as I process what I think I see. The way he almost turns in his seat but stops himself and plays it off as a readjustment makes me wonder why he reacted. "He can't be doing that because he heard my name. No way." How the muscles in his back flex with restraint as I toss my hair out of my face. Unable to manage my rambling. I can see how the girl, still in her warm embrace, never takes her eyes off of me as her whole face lit up.

"Adalee, what did you just say? What guy are you talking about?" I can hear Brina turning in her seat and I still can't seem to break my stare. Even as I feel the redness spread across my cheeks and to my ears. My skin becomes clammy and my breathing struggles to keep a calm and collected pace.

My interest becomes drawn back to the girl, regardless of how I fight it. "Do you think they are related Brina?" Catching her off guard I see in my peripheral how her head turns sideways like a puppy. Wolves are so cliché. "Adalee, you have totally lost me." The girl is still sitting on the lap of her partner when he leans into her ear and whispers something that makes her laugh. A laugh made of pure gold which seems out of sort in the low buzz from the cafeteria. Her fangs flash and almost sparkle in the light.

The guy who is still attempting to keep his back towards me slams his hand down and I can see the table is drooped and it appears to be cracked. "No way they can be related Brina. No way." Great. I watch as the guy with shaggy brown hair and a bad attitude seems to slump at his shoulders while he glares sideways at whoever this girl is.

"Gah honey, what am I going to do with you?" Brina pulls me back while laughing at my sheepish look. I'm sure it appeared like I got caught doing something I wasn't supposed to be doing. As I start to push the trio out of my mind he turns in his seat. His bemused and vivid expression showing he wasn't expecting to get caught as my eyes lock with deep pools of blue, giving me a feeling of calmness. An emotion I was not expecting, but needed. It feels as if my world fell apart and then came back together completely upside down. I need to figure out who this guy is.

Chapter 5

A tray slams into our table and I welcome the distraction. Two girls by the name of Laura and Elizabeth sat down and asked if we wanted some company. Their matching loose, slender wavy, brown ponytails lashing against each other as they turn to talk to Brina. I give them a passive nod to acknowledge them, but nothing more because my mind is racing with the question of who this mystery guy may be.

Just as the guy with shaggy, sandy blonde hair was about to turn back towards the guy across from him, Laura nudges me and shakes her head. "Do you want all the details?" she calmly says is a super low voice. I stare back blankly when I notice how all the girls are look at me. Brina is giving me this all knowing smile and then waggles her eyebrows in my direction. "Do I have food across my face or are you all just that happy to see me?" I question. Reveling in my complete and utter ignorance to my surroundings.

"His name is Axel Anderson." Elizabeth states in a matter-of-fact tone. Causing my body to almost become defensive as if she thinks I would care. "Why do I care?" I spit out words laced with spite and realize these girls don't deserve that. My eyes darting to the look of understanding coming from Axel. "Sorry, I just have a lot on my mind. I didn't mean to sound so snappy." Hanging my head, a little bit trying to hope they feel my remorse through my actions. Laura's throaty laugh comes out in a cackling fashion and makes me chuckle along with her. Breathlessly Laura explains her reaction.

"Girl, everyone stares at him that way. Just know that is as far as it usually gets." My laugh becomes louder when I realize how ridiculous she sounds. "Don't worry, Adalee swore off boys a few years ago. Regardless of how hot they are." I watch as Brina's eyes light up with mischief. I am in for it now. "So why is he on a look, but don't touch status?" Her question holding an underlining tone of naughtiness. I try to peak around her, but I am afraid he is listening to every word and that would mean total embarrassment.

"Veronica Allen. That's why." Elizabeth acts like if just saying Veronica's name put a bad taste in her mouth. As if on cue Veronica glides over to the Axel. She sits herself on the top of the table and starts laughing and chit chatting. As if she can feel my eyes on her, she looks up at the same time she runs her fingers through his hair. A feeling of jealousy hits the base of my stomach. I push down my unknown feelings and put a look of boredom across my features. Twirling the spaghetti around my plate.

We go for a few more moments on our stare down and just as she leans in and whispers in Axel's ear, I lose my appetite. What is wrong with me? I look away and go back to the conversation at hand. Hoping that the sadness that clouded Axel's features and the muscle in his jaw that twitches wasn't because of me.

The girls are discussing the bonfire that is happening in a few weeks. "You both have to come, it is a major tradition that everyone attends." Elizabeth's flatness causing me to doubt if she even wanted to go. Julia's cheery voice seems to bring the mood up as she explains the details which I seem to get lost in, until the end. "...after the bonfire there is usually a huge party at someone's house. This year it is supposed to be at the Anderson's house." Usually, I keep to myself in such events unless Brina drags me along, but with the after party being at the Anderson's, I cannot help but have my interest peaked at the thought of getting under Veronica's skin.

"You know that sounds like an amazing time." Making sure I place a great deal of excitement in my words. Clasping my hands together to bring home my point of interest. Brina's mouth falls open so far it might hit the table.

I casually lean over and push it back in place and laugh. "So, who is the girl next to Axel? She seems super sweet." Elizabeth who has a mouth full of food basically spits it everywhere as she explains the girl that is still staring in my direction, is Julia Anderson. Twin sister to Axel.

I look around and Brina catches my eye as I watch her joke and cut up with the two new friends we have made on our first day. I feel the air of change deep down and even though I may struggle with allowing it, I cannot help but find myself smiling. I think to myself that it is not every day that you go against your gut and everything it is screaming. I determine in this moment, this very small moment, that I will become a new Adalee Ebony Rosewood this world has yet to see.

After lunch I hug Brina at my locker and I cannot help but feel like my day is going to go downhill. Just like normal, she seems to sense my hesitation. She smiles at me and gives me the biggest hug while stating she will text me throughout the next couple of classes.

As I make my way to the east side of the building, I cannot help but feel this sense of dread. As I look up, I see Veronica grab Axel's hand from behind. I feel a slight raise of hatred come up from the bottom of my heart. I easily push away the feeling and file it under the major growing dislike I have growing for Veronica.

Just as I am about to walk outside to the greenhouses, which is where botany class is held, I notice that Axel turns towards Veronica and pulls his hand away. She seems a little hurt and then she starts to turn her head in my direction as I walk out the door. The last thing I want is to be caught staring. I already feel somewhat like a creep.

I walk towards the greenhouses and notice a small classroom off to the side. I make my way to find a seat and notice that Laura is sitting up towards the front room and I let my lungs deflate. Letting go of the breath, which I did not know I was holding. She frantically waves over at me and I gladly take a seat beside her.

I keep my gaze forward and notice written in very pretty handwriting and underlined on the white board is the message, "I am Mrs. Evanora or call me Eva." Before I could question Laura about who our teacher is, a short, white haired lady walks in. She has a long-sleeved white shirt paired with a flowing floor length shirt. The dirt across her smock and cheek gives off a sense of peace. My witch radar goes into overdrive and I can feel the positive energy and power coming off of her in waves.

She gives us a tour of the greenhouses, I cannot help but look at how stunning and massive they are. There are three greenhouses that each have a very whimsical atmosphere with bookshelves full of botany books and handwritten journals. There is a very cute table and chairs that remind me of the patio sets that you would see at bistros. On the shelves are an array of beautiful pots that add splashes of color.

Each greenhouse carries a different variety of plants, herbs, and vegetables. I can honestly see how this may become one of my favorite classes. After our tour, we go to the first greenhouse and sit at the table and chairs in the corner. "Hello class." Mrs. Eva's voice beams with pride as she throws her hands out to her side demanding attention.

"I want to welcome you to the best class on campus. I want each one of you to call me Eva. Now, let's all get ready for a fantastic year full of surprises." I am not sure what it is about this woman that makes me feel so comfortable. I feel like I have known her all my life. As if we have some sort of deep connection.

As I am concentrating on replanting a few different herbs, I can hear Mrs. Eva calling students by their name. Hearing the ooh's and ah's as she guesses each name correctly while finding what interest they have in taking botany. I giggle a little knowing her secret to guessing each of their names and realize how neat of a party trick that makes. She wanders on over to where I was sitting and before she can say my name I start with my rehearsed response.

"I have always had this sense of peace with…" and before I could finish, she grabs me in a huge, bone crushing hug. "My. My. My. How could I not notice, you favor her so much." Her voice trails off to a whisper towards the end causing me to almost miss it. I clear my throat and try to pull back without seeming rude and she looks down and chuckles. "Excuse me, like who?"

I know my stance became almost immediately defensive. Hands across my chest and hip cocked out a little bit in an attempt to make me seem serious. My eyebrows furrowing together as I give her a questioning look once I have calmed down slightly. "I guess you don't remember me, do you?" My soul becomes anxious with the possibility of answers, while her question physically feels as if a thousand bricks just hit my chest. I stumble back and my hand reaches out towards the table to steady my balance.

My look of confusion slowly turns into one of bemusement. She giggles even more and grabs the side of my face in a very caring gesture. She then continues to give me some of the most shocking news of the day. "Adalee, I was best friends with Nora, your grandmother." I just look at her flabbergasted. Torn somewhere between a growing sense of betrayal and resolve.

I sit in silence as I struggle with these churning emotions going on internally. I can't seem to get out the words and she takes full notice as uneasiness and what looks like regret flashes in the depths of her eyes. "Your grandmother Nora was the sweetest woman I have ever known." Another knock to my chest. My mind struggling to form a single memory and coming up blank. "She had the best green thumb around. Was a true woman of nature." Mrs. Eva picks up my hands and looks deep into my eyes as if she is trying to uncover the answers I am looking for myself.

"I had no idea your mother was moving you girls back home." She abruptly turns her back on me and starts to fidget with a wilted leave on a plant next to her. I watch as her hand glides from the stem to the tip, causing the wilted leaf to become green again. Even though I have been practicing magic for some time, I still become amazed at the sight of it being performed. Like a child who just caught Santa delivering presents. The wonder and mystery causing me to forget my soul's dilemma for just a moment.

"What has it been eight or nine years now?" Stunned, I looked at her and after a moment or two all I could do was answer with a short reply. "Ten. Ten years ago we moved". She turns around hastily and gives me a sympathetic look that doesn't quite reach all of her features and reads my mind. I can feel her intricate magic tracing through my heart and soul. Her own attempts at finding out answers. "You don't remember, do you?"

She questions quietly. I just shake my head with a feeling of slight shame as I think about how broken I feel. "You know dear, water was made to quench thirst and inquiry to concur the truth." After her words of wisdom, she just walks off, leaving me in shambles.

Chapter 6

The rest of the day goes off in a blur. I fight back silent tears for the remainder of the day. Feelings of fury and treachery course through me every time I hear my phone ding. Brina lied to me. Her words threatening my sanity, "Adalee, are you not excited that we're going on a new adventure? I have always heard Montana was beautiful." How could she do this to me? She knew where we were, and she never bothered to tell me this was part of our past. Part of the past I have been searching for, for answers.

As I am walking to class, I can feel the wind start to pick up. The sky turns from a white clouded sky to one of desolate grey. The pressure becoming intense and the smell of rain comes flooding through my nostrils. I am all but lost as I find myself standing outside the main building on campus out of sight. Trying to fight with the demons that threaten the surface. My hatred building and like a balloon, I feel it will pop. My curls flying out of my braid with a ferocity I try to control. Tring to remember something, anything that happened before the accident. The power in my veins building.

I reach a mindless blank area that fills me with nothing but regret and longing. The more I push to remember, the more it pushes back like a rubber band. Stinging my essence. Desire to remember this place slams into me and it is all I can do to stand upright. Yearning to remember my dad sends me sideways. Wishing to not feel like a freak who can't seem to remember her childhood. What is wrong with me? I feel broken and pathetic and all that does is piss me off even more.

I can feel the rain start to come down as my tears break over the dam. The storm becoming rampantly out of control. I close my eyes and sink down the brick allowing myself to faulter. Allowing myself to feel the emotions I keep buried deep down. With my head leaned back against the wall, the fragrance of pine trees and cinnamon break through the smell of fresh rain. Before I can open my eyes fully, a hand touches my shoulder scaring me near to death.

"What the hell?" comes flying out of my mouth before I can stop it. My hands fly up to keep any other lines of profanity from rushing out when I notice who startled me.

Axel's eyes searching over me. Something about the soft boy-like expression has my body naturally wanting to caress his cheek. "Are you okay?" His deep, velvet voice causes my insides to melt. I continue to blink. The expression void across my face. "Adalee, are you hurt?" His hands run over me as he assesses to see if I am injured.

I think about his smile and it makes my heart flutter to its own unique beat. He leans in and I notice he is trying to say something, but I can't seem to focus on what he could want. I feel the strength in his hands, and he shakes my shoulders. When I still can't seem to pull it together, he wraps his arms around me and pulls me close.

I become extremely aware of my surroundings when the chill from his completely soaked clothes cause my teeth to chatter. Humiliation hits me like a mac truck. I push up and away from him which causes me to almost fall into the wall. I turn around, noticing how close that causes me to become to Axel. I am basically back in his arms causing an intense heat to hit my cheeks. My heart creating an unsteady beat loud enough that it drowns out the thunder and lightning.

"I think you need to breathe. It was supposed to be sunny today." The way his breath hits my ear causes me to shutter. Being this close to Axel causes the storm raging inside to slow. The power begins to retreat, and the down pour turns into a drizzle I feel utterly confused and lost. "I don't know what you are talking about." Getting my wits to me, I try to run the other way. His arms wrapping around my waist as he pulls me closer and turns me to face him. It is as if he knows what I want to do, regardless of how much I fight against my urges. His hand comes up to graze my cheek and before I can let things escalate, I whisper out, "You're getting me wet, Axel."

It is as if saying his name made him realize what he was doing. He dropped his hands and stepped back. Guilt swimming in his eyes. I took this opportunity to bolt. Forcing past him and bursting through the double doors into the school. Never looking back, regardless of how badly I felt I needed too.

As I walk into the library the smell of old books mixes with the pine trees, rain water, and cinnamon still clinging to my clothes.

A huge smile came across my features. A library, any library, has always been a sanctuary of mine. As I look into the ginormous open, three-story room, I cannot help but notice the name above the librarian's desk. In big black letters the words Rosewood Library stood out.

It is like getting hit in the gut by a softball. I start to get dizzy; my breathing quickens all while I feel like I am being sucked into darkness. I need to sit down. I go to a secluded area away from the crowd of people and take a seat. As my bottom hits the chair beneath me my mind goes into another world. Reality bends and morphs until it becomes unrecognizable.

I look around and notice I am standing in the same cabin we just moved into last week. I walk around realizing not much has changed. I hear familiar singing and follow the voice into the kitchen. Moving as if I have lived here all my life. My mother comes into view with her back to me. Long, vibrant, midnight curls bouncing and swirling around her waist while she dances. The elegant air surrounding her makes her silk shorts and white t-shirt seem out of place. The words I feel like need to be said get caught at the back of my throat. My palms become sweaty with nerves.

Suddenly, I hear a voice that feels familiar, but I cannot seem place it. "Oh Adalee, sweetie, what are you doing up?" The unfamiliar voice seems to carry large amounts of concern. I feel drawn to whoever owns it, but my legs feel like jelly. Unable to move, I become stuck in the same place.

"Did you have a bad dream?" Just as he finishes, I notice my mother turns around and scoops me up as I run through the kitchen. She walks out of my peripheral and I hear her speaking in the other room. "Scott, why don't take sweet Ads to bed." My world seems to stops, and I try with all my might to see his face, but in this memory, I am not in control.

I fight with my inner self to turn around and the moment I turn to look at him, my mind snaps back to the present. Despair hits me when I realize where my father's face should be, familiar bookshelves come into view. I silently curse knowing that I missed my chance. I sit stunned.

It is an odd feeling to have a memory. This is the first memory I have had in ten years that was before the accident. I cannot get the masculine voice that would be my father's out of my mind. I look at my watch and I realize as the bell sounds that the school day is over. I gather my things and make my way to my locker. I am in autopilot. Why is this happening now? How, after all of this time does a memory happen now? My mind racing to find a solution for it to happen again.

Chapter 7

Brina is sitting in the jeep when I make my way to the parking lot, slowly and hesitantly. She knows something is up. I am sure she caught on with my red rimmed eyes and tear streaked face. I slowly sit in the passenger side of the jeep never glancing in her direction. She starts to attempt to talk to me and each time I turn my head further from her view. Finally getting the hint, she drives home. Silence is all I want right now.

The tension in the air is so thick I feel like I am choking. Once we get home I jump out of the car and run upstairs as fast as I can thinking she will attempt to stop me. I just do not have it in me to face her. Betrayal still fresh on my soul. This has turned out to be the worst first day of school yet. She deceived me in a way that I cannot fathom. She cut me deep. I go immediately to my room and lock the door. I jump on my bed and bury my face in my pillows. I hear a light knock and ignore it. I do not want to see either of the other two people that reside in this house.

Finally, after getting the hint Brina lightly says, "When you are ready to talk, I will be in my bedroom. Waiting." I feel tears start to form again and they threaten to spill over and run down my already red lined cheeks. We don't fight. This is not who we are. We may argue over who drives, what to eat, or what song to play on the radio, but never something so serious. I know Brina can tell something is really wrong, but I just do not have the strength to talk to her just yet.

How do I not remember any of this house? It feels so foreign. I shudder at the coldness that runs through my body. I hear my mother making dinner downstairs and decide to start with the source of my frustration. After, I'll address my best friend and get to the bottom of what is going on.

My mother is standing in the kitchen with her back to me, wearing a raggedy old white t-shirt and silk shorts much like she was the night from my dream. The big difference is her hair. Instead of the dark midnight black and blue curls we share, she has streaks full of silver and light blue from age. Her swaying is a little slower and not so pronounced. Her voice has a tired, stressed edge to it where that night in my memories she sounded free. She sounded completely happy all of those years ago.

I clear my throat and she continue to look forward, refusing to give me the attention I desperately need during this time of doubt. I am questioning everything about my life. This nagging in the back of my head and pain in my heart that makes me firmly believe that my life is about to be thrown to the wolves. Why, after ten years does the past think it needs to resurface about the time I was ready to live a little.

My mother's voice breaks my internal thoughts that are circling like a hurricane. "My sweet Adalee, what has caused your comfort to sway faulty?" She hums at me while she continues to cook. How can she believe my solace was ever solid? How do you place reassurance in your life when vital years are missing for your timeline?

With all the courage I had left in me for the day, I boldly stated "I had a memory today." I inserted a long dramatic pause.

Hoping she would comment on what I had just said. Nothing. So, I continue. "A memory for the first time in ten years that had my daddy's voice." My voice struggling to remain stable. The scraping sound skipping a few beats as her stirring faulters when I say the word daddy.

"Why are you telling me this?" Her tone being one of complete defensiveness. My heart picks up its pace as I take in her words. "Mom, you don't think that's odd?" Nothing. She gives me no hint as to how she is feeling. "I had a nice talk with Mrs. Evanora today." Bringing my demeanor back to one for passive conversation. Trying to have her give me any indication she feels bad for lying. "Oh really? I had no idea she was still in this area." I watch as her shoulders become tense, causing her stirring to quicken.

"Are you serious? That's all you have to say after you lied?" I watch as my mother calmly takes her spoon and lays it down on the counter. She begins humming and putting spices into the boiling water. My anger starts to rise. Threatening to blind me. "Damn it, mother! Talk to me!" The wind starts whipping my curls. The power of fury threatening to pull me under. "Adalee Ebony watch your tone. I am still your mother and I will demand respect."

I become utterly speechless wondering how she can remain calm. Deflecting doesn't suit her personality. "Mother just answer me. I know the truth." I try to hold it together, but my body has different plans and I slowly feel a tear fall. I am tired of crying today. Pain and concern flash slightly across my mother's eyes. I also notice that possible regret and frustration are buried deep in her gaze and that confuses me.

Why or how could she possibly feel frustration and regret? I'm her child. I change my direction of thinking as fast as the first negative thought forms. It would be preposterous for her to feel that way. She takes hesitant steps in my direction almost like you would towards a wounded animal. Acting as if she thinks I'll get spooked and run.

I continued to look into her iridescent eyes, never moving from the spot my feet seemed to be rooted to. Focusing on anything other than my rage. Her silver irises are mixed with small flecks of pale blue and green. A trademark from her side of the family that is passed down through the females. Mother says my father's eyes were the color of the sun as it was setting. A beautiful color of gold that seemed to have streaks of deep rustic brown and red.

As my thoughts fight back and forth from rational to emotional, I can't help but feel like I'm looking into the future. Besides being about thirty years apart in age and our height differences, we are identical in our features. I quickly think to myself that if I become half as graceful as my mother, then I will be perfectly okay with my adult years.

"Sweetie, I want you to know that your father and I loved you to the best of our abilities." Her warm arms snake their way around me. My body subconsciously pulls away when it registers how forced her words seem. "You may not understand Adalee. One day you will. We are only guaranteed so much safety." As my mother continues giving what feels like a forced comforting and reassuring speech, I slowly take a few steps backwards.

I cannot help but seem to look at her with a thousand questions. "What do you mean we are only guaranteed so much safety? How is that the case when nothing has been done?" She seems to pick up that that I don't believe her. There is more to this than she is letting on about. "All you had to do was tell me before Mrs. Evanora did and I wouldn't be this hurt." My shoulders hang in defeat as I go back to my conversation with Mrs. Eva. I give up after a while of staring at my mother's back. I know all too well this is the end of the conversation.

Before I could make it up the stairs "Maybe Mrs. Eva should have kept her mouth shut about family matters. She knows better." Comes as nothing more than a whisper out of my mother's mouth. I never even consider turning around because I realize that wasn't supposed to be heard. Why would Mrs. Eva be telling me if this is a bad thing? My mother has always said the truth may hurt for a short time but lies will haunt you forever.

Each step I take to my room drops my heart closer to my stomach. Knowing that once I reach the top, I will have to face Brina. I continue to take slow deep breaths to keep myself calm. Feeling the weight of the world pressing down on my shoulders as the two people who are supposed to have my back let me down. I crawl into bed wishing to avoid life so when I wake up it is back to normal. Maybe I can sleep myself back into oblivion.

I've decided that I had over filled my emotional tank for the day, easily. I pulled the covers completely over me and let my body hide in the shelter my covers offer. While I am surrounded by comfort, I begin to hear Brina pacing outside my door. Her worry hitting me like electrical surges. Each step reverberating off the walls as her feet makes contact with the hardwood floor. Normally, I would be okay with confrontation, but I am beyond the point of exhaustion. Facing her will have to wait for another day.

Her footsteps grow silent. She got the message I was not moving from my spot and left my room. I heard her gently close the door and took that as my cue that it was safe to come out from under the covers. I laid and glared out the window for what seemed like hours until my eyes closed, and I was met with a pair of eyes that seemed to only haunt me in my dreams.

Chapter 8

These ice blue eyes seemed to float into the darkness. They surrounded me at every turn in my dream. They reminded me of a glacier in a way. You see what they want you to see on the top of the surface, but underneath they seem to be full of mystery. These eyes seem to watch me with emotions so vast that they could swallow the universe whole. After a while, those piercing eyes seem to fade away with my deep slumber. Each time I see them reminds me just how quickly my life is changing.

Next thing I know my alarm is jolting me awake. I lay in bed for what seems like forever in an attempt to recover from yesterday's drama. I decide while I was staring at the ceiling that a run this morning wasn't worth it. I drag myself out of bed and do a small set of stretches. I grab my clothes and quickly hop into the shower. I let the water warm up until the tiny bathroom is full of steam. When I finally drag myself to get into the shower, I stand under the warm water and let it wash away my thoughts. Hoping the water will give me a sense of clarity.

While getting out of the shower, I hear my mother downstairs and I pick up my pace. Getting dressed and running downstairs just in time to catch mother getting in her car. "Can you give me a ride to the library?" I yell out the door. I turn around to leave Brina a note on the counter. Just because we are not seeing eye to eye does not mean I want her worrying. If the roles were reversed, I would hope for the same.

"Adalee. Hurry up." My mother states very flat from the driver side window. All of my life my mother has been a woman of few words and even fewer emotions. I would like to think that before my father's accident she was full of life. I only know my mother as the woman she is now. In the car she gives me a quick look full of unease. Causing me to question my own decision as my hand falters to open the door.

The ride to school is one of insufferable silence. I am unsure of how to act normal when the pain of disloyalty still haunts my emotions. I think back to how I will act when I see Brina. How will I respond? I should take the high road, it's the way I was raised. "Hold your head up and always let the good shine." My mother's voice bouncing around the inside of my head causing my thoughts to scramble. Thankfully, the Academy's gates come into view as if they offer the perfect rescue.

When I make it to my locker, the sight of Brina brings forth even more thoughts I have tried to bury. Feelings I locked away in a vault, encased in concrete, and tossed into the depths of the ocean. She looks at me with puppy dog eyes and has a chocolate glazed donut in her hand. "You are not getting off that easily." Putting all emphasis on the fact that she isn't forgiven. Something like this type of betrayal does not get swept under the rug. It will always be there, at the back of my mind.

I look at the bag she is actively shaking "Come on Adalee. I'm sorry." The crinkling of her opening the white paper sack drowns out the whining in her voice. The warm chocolate fragrance wafting to my nose makes my mouth water. She knows that those are my weakness and after this morning, I need one. "It won't happen again. Please, Adalee" Her eyelashes bat up and down causing me to turn back to my locker.

I look at her sideways as I hear her voice crack over my name. "Ads, I know I messed up. I'm officially the worst best friend ever." The sigh that comes from my lips allow my shoulders to slump. The weight of what to do causing my head to split. I go through mental scenarios of how this could play out. Each one seeming to get worse as they progress. "You hurt me, Brina. Do you understand that?" The injury she caused coming out in each word. I make sure to keep my back towards her as I slowly pull things out of my locker.

"Adalee, please. I will spend the rest of our lives trying to make up for that mistake." I know I cannot stay mad forever, but it is still hard to look at her and think she kept such a big part of the truth I have been searching for from me. "I just don't understand. You know I have been searching for a piece of the truth. You promised to help me, yet kept a secret this large from me." Tears threaten to fall from my eyes as I try to make sense of why she would do this.

"Adalee. No apology will make this better. I understand that. I only want to say I really thought I was doing what I felt was best." I go to throw my hands up to tell her she has no right when she cuts me off. "I know. I have no clue what is best for you and I should have been honest. I have no excuse for what I have done." I watch as guilt fills Brina's features. "Does this have anything to do with my mother telling me we are only granted so much safety? What does that even mean?"

As I start in with more questions Brina shushes me and brings me in close for a hug. "Adalee, I promise I will tell you everything. Just know, not everyone here is our friend." The ominous way she whispered this made my curiosity peak even more. "What do you mean by that? Brina, I need answers."

I notice a few students were suddenly standing close to our locker. Students who weren't there moments ago. Brina just pulls me in for a long hug and basically bursts my ear drum when she squeals. "I knew you wouldn't be mad for long."

I catch onto her game, still unsure of what kind of danger we could be in. Are we in any kind of danger? "I guess I can forgive you, but you owe me donuts for a year." Her laughter raises above the roaring hall as her arms wrap around my shoulders. "You are also doing all the dishes for forever. Got it?" I can feel my ribs on the verge of breaking. "Don't worry Adalee, I will explain everything later." For once in my life, I am thankful for my super hearing.

Not that I am fully letting go everything that has happened, but I have missed my best friend, even if it was just last night and this morning. I also want to tell her about what went on in the library. Maybe she can offer some advice. After eating our donuts in the hall, we walk arm in arm to our first period. Mr. Green is sitting at his desk and eyes us coming in right at the bell and motions for us to take our seat. He really does give off quite an eerie vibe to be a math teacher. I half expect blood to be running down his fangs.

We get started in lecture and I am trying to pay attention and write down notes. Having examples has always made homework so much easier for me. I am trying to work out some equation when all of a sudden, a small piece of paper lands on my notebook. I look around and no one else seems to notice the note, so I open it.

Noticing the elegant cursive scrawled across the thick stationary. A faint scent of lavender and oranges float up from the page. I look around when I realize all that it states is a time and place. Impresso Expresso. 6 o'clock sharp. The hairs on the back of my neck stand up and a chill creeps down my spine.

I look over my shoulder and a pair of dark, indigo blue eyes that twinkle with kindness are staring back at me. Her lips pull up at the corners giving me a warm and reassuring smile. Knots hit my stomach when I realize it's Julia Anderson. Sweat starts to form at my brow as mortification slithers into my insides. She knows. She has to know what happened with her brother.

Chapter 9

I flash Julia a hesitant smile back and turn in my seat. Wincing as the chair scrapes across the hardwood floors causing the students in front of me to turn around and glare. I lower my head in an attempt to not entertain their blatant staring. Whispering a, "what the hell" under my breath.

As Mr. Green continues explaining how to find the instantaneous change or derivative of various functions it hits me, I bet this is all about her brother. I mean they are twins and she probably knows that I asked him to lunch. I did not even mean it the way it came out. At least I did not think I meant it that way. I just wanted to offer him an apology and my mother always said food solves everything.

We finish lecture and then get up and head to our next class. I show Brina the note and fill her in on some of what happened during the encounter in the library. She seems a little suspicious of Julia's note, but then reassures me she will be at the coffee shop. We breeze through our next few classes and before I even realize it, it is already lunch. My stomach turns in knots thinking about seeing Axel and how embarrassing it will be to face him in the cafeteria.

We get our lunch and pick a table in the corner of the room. Before we can make it across the room, I notice that Julia is motioning us to come over. Waving her arms back and forth. I try to ignore her by turning the other direction, but then Brina takes the lead and starts to walk over with a confidence I wish I could master. She looks at Julia and sizes her up as we get closer. Watching Brina puts me at ease. Wolves are always so territorial and defensive, and predictable.

Julia doesn't seem to notice Brina's glaring as she comes up and quickly steers us near two empty chairs. Her sandy brown waves bouncing around her waist. Her well-built, athletic frame carrying her with such poise and grace. Before we can make it, a guy named Cameron introduces himself and his easy-going personality stands out from most of the table who seems to have grown quiet at our approach.

I quickly take in each of the students around us one by one. Watching as they shuffle uncomfortably at the awkward silence that seemed to follow us. Axel comes into my view last and truthfully, I spend a little too long staring. If he notices, he does not care enough to give me the satisfaction of looking into my eyes. Slowly, he shuffles his food back and forth. My mind tells me to look away, he does nothing. My heart yearns to have him pay attention to me, even if it's just a glance.

A low growl reverberates over the chatter that seemed to pick back up around us. I notice Cameron all of a sudden takes two steps away from me and moves towards Axel. He only breaks his intense gaze off of his food to watch Cameron sit down next to him. I look between the two boys and curiosity crosses my features. Axel quickly averts his eyes and begins eating his food. His body language is a little hard to read, but if I am not mistaken, I notice he seems jealous.

Julia clears her throat, gaining the attention of everyone but Axel himself. I silently thank her for the distraction. "Will you girls join us for lunch? We would love to have you." I am not sure if that is a great idea, but no one objects the offer. You can almost physically feel the animosity coming off of Axel. His face twisting in a look of annoyance.

A smile cross Brina's face and I can tell she has made up her mind. She sits down without even glancing in my direction to notice that I was slightly shaking my head to warn her that this was a hard pass from me. Discomfort appearing all over my features. I look at the table, the only seat available is in front of Axel. Whispers of Brina and Cameron's conversation float into my ears and I can tell they hit it off instantly. Not that I should feel this way, but I cannot help but feel a little tinge of jealously about how easy it is for her to fit in.

After the first few awkward moments of conversation are over, the flow slowly starts to become more like old friends. Burns and laughter flying around. Throughout the course of lunch, I catch myself watching Axel underneath my lashes. Noticing he never once said a word during lunch, but instead kept his gaze fixed on those around me.

I can physically see the analysis of each situation churning in his eyes like he would attack at any minute and needed to be ready. His stare is so intense it gives me butterflies and goose bumps at the same time. I shudder in my seat from just one look of those blue eyes. I wish I would focus on anything else but him. Each second I am in his presence he becomes closer to completely consuming my every thought.

My internal monolog becomes disrupted when I can practically feel the pain from Veronica who is staring daggers at the back of my head. The heat off of her gaze growing as she makes her way over. The pure hatred making it hard for me to breath. The darkness wanting to swallow me whole and drag me down the rabbit hole.

It is not much longer until she shows up next to the table and basically sits herself in Axel's lap. He becomes like a statue. Only shifting his eyes to look in my direction. She notices and tries harder to catch his attention. Her murmuring in his ear sounding like nails on a chalk board. He finally breaks his eye contact and gives her some attention. Passive nodding at whatever she says as his eyes casually drift back towards my direction. The flash of ice blue in his eyes startle me and a feeling of need hits me in my core. I have to blink to make sure I didn't imagine the color change.

I get this massive feeling of anger that hit me unexpectedly. Veronica's jealous energy snaking its way around me, causing my emotions to become clouded. My thoughts scrambled. I stand up and my chair goes flying behind me making a loud thump and causing the whole cafeteria to go silent. Axel's gaze locks with mine, unknown emotions swimming at the surface. The smell of cinnamon and pine tickles my nostrils.

I get up and stomp my way to the trash to dump my tray. Knowing I need to clear my mind. I leave out of the doors with the cafeteria still deathly quiet. The last thing I hear before the door closes is Veronica's laugh echoing through the halls.

I find myself running. I am not sure where I am going until my legs take me to the library. I fly through the doors and make my way to a corner on the second floor where I hope no one will bother me. I am not sure what came over me, why did I feel this way towards Axel and Veronica? Why did it bother me so much? I spend several minutes pacing at the back of the library and before long I notice it is almost time for class to start. I want to blame Veronica and her toxic dynamism for why I acted the way I did, but I know deep down there is another reason.

I gather my bag off of the floor and head to the greenhouses. I walk through the hallways keeping my head down hoping to avoid the stares of curiosity from my peers. Lunch was a tad bit embarrassing on my part. Out of nowhere I am spun around and thrown face first into the lockers by my hair. Pain shooting up my nose and making my eyes water. My scalp burning where my hair might have been ripped out.

I pick myself up off the floor, grabbing the back of my head. "What the hell was that for?" I yell before I have a chance to turn around. I am shoved back into the lockers when I feel nails digging into my skin. "I would advise you to stay in your lane, mutt. Keep your eyes and hands off of Axel." Her words are dripping with venom and it pisses me off.

I push back and turn around to come face to face with Veronica Allen. "Truthfully, that was pretty low, even for you." I turn to brush past her and then stop when we are shoulder to shoulder. Wind begins to whip through the closed hallway. The faint crackling of static from the magic I begin to feel flowing through my veins keeps her from speaking. I take the opportunity to drive my point home. "Veronica, don't you dare lay another hand on me or you will be sorry."

I glance at her sideways and notice her mouth is almost hitting the floor. I reach over and use my index finger to push her jaw up. Rage consuming her features. Behind her, Axel comes out of a doorway and stops mid-step. As I continue to hold his gaze, I make sure they both know. "You can have him." Punctuating each word with a harshness that was very unnecessary.

I pick up my pace and walk away, never turning back around. Regardless of how bad I wanted to see Axel. Our bodies grazing as I rushed past him. Feeling almost an unknown force wanting to drive me back towards him. I fight with every instinct I have to apologize. Focusing on each step to pull me out of the depths of my sentiments.

When I finally make my way into the second greenhouse Mrs. Eva has her back to me, tending to a section of rosemary. She speaks to me without ever turning around. "You sure have caused quite the disturbance in young Axel's mind my dear Adalee. Why do you think that is?" Confused, I simply stand looking at her back and notice she is humming. I listen closer to the soft sound coming from her lips and try to place where I have heard the melody.

It is a beautiful melody and after a few moments I realize where I came across it. "You know Mrs. Eva, that is the same melody my mother still hums around the house." She answers like I should already know the answer, "My dear who do you think taught her that melody? I watched your mother grow up as if she were my own."

I look at her puzzled. Mom never mentioned that she was close to Mrs. Eva. Is this why mother thought she should know better than to tell me I was back home? As if she knows what I am thinking, she slowly turns around and gives a small smile, "Your mother just wants what is best for her little pup." I roll my eyes and she wants to make sure you are safe. Now back to the questions, what have you done to poor Axel?" Her response triggers something in me. Peculiar thing to call a child a pup, but I take it Mrs. Eva is a little funny in everything she does. It's the witch in her.

I look at her and tell her what has happened from beginning to end and huff out a sarcastic response. "I don't see how it is me who has done anything to Axel." She gives me a warm-hearted laugh and I look at her sideways. I normally wouldn't dare to disrespect a teacher nor an elder witch in that way, but she feels more like family. She has from the beginning.

She never responds to my sarcasm and so I start throwing out a few more questions. "How do you know anything has happened between us?" All she does is continue to trim some basil. "Mrs. Eva, why do you assume Axel is having a difficult time?" She laughs once more and then states in a matter of fact tone, "When you are as old as I am, you pick up on things". Before I could get any more questions answered the rest of class barges in and we get started.

I sit down and speculate if she is picking up on something I'm not? I think back to our encounters and attempt to see them from a different angle. Axel has really only been nice when he caught me outside of the main entrance when I felt my world was trying to swallow me whole. I brush off what Mrs. Eva has mentioned because I know that there is no way there could be anything between us. I know for sure there is no way he is having any issue; he has no right if he is having a difficult time.

Chapter 10

As we drive towards the coffee shop, Brina and I start talking about everything that has happened today. I should say that as our usual, Brina does most of the talking with me just sort of answering half-heartedly and throwing occasional questions at her to keep her going. Most of the time we would be on full gossip mode, but I am just not feeling it. I close my eyes and allow the wind to shake my braid down, causing a waterfall of dark curls to flow free behind me.

After some time, we pull up the coffee shop. It's in a quaint little building with an antique vibe. Truthfully, most of the town follows suit with vintage brick buildings lining both sides of the street. I look back and imagine the stories that these building could tell. This whole town gives off an atmosphere of being rich in antiquity. Rich in history that could be connected to me.

As soon as we park, I get a text from an unknown number. Brina excitement distracts me from opening it as she practically drags me along beside her. "Alright Adalee, let's hurry up. I want to see Cameron". I look at her puzzled and she shrugs her shoulders.

"Brina, I don't want to disappoint, but it's supposed to be just Julia." Brina talks to fast I almost don't catch her reply. "I can tell he is here. He smells heavenly. Like driftwood and salt water. Reminds me of the ocean". I look at her like she has lost her mind. What does she mean she can smell him from the parking lot? "Excuse me? You can smell that he is here?" was all I could squeak out. Brina look turns from an award-winning smile to one like she got caught in a mistake. "I didn't realize your sense of smell was that strong. Geez."

The coffee shop is set up to resemble an old book shop. I can't help but feel cozy as Brina and I go to order drinks and a few snacks. The rows of leather-bound books make this place seem so inviting, like you could spend hours getting lost in the tales each one holds. We finally get our goodies and then head to the back and make our way to where Julia and Cameron are sitting. I stop short of the table and my nerves get the best of me for a split second. I push them down and force a smile on my face. I guess this is it, time to figure out what they want.

We sit down and you can tell Brina and I are on guard. Most people don't befriend us, their natural instincts tell them something is not quite right. That we are dangerous, but we aren't in a regular school, so I guess the normal rules don't apply.

Moments after, as if she is reading our mind, Julia puts on a breath-taking smile and shrugs her petite shoulders. She broke the tension first, and I was extremely grateful for that. "So, I am so glad you both came. Cameron and I figured we could all be really good friends after lunch today." With that being said the whole mood changed. "You and Cameron, huh?" was all Brina muttered and then broke into a massive smile.

Once the pressure was broken, we all got along really well. We talked and told stories for what seemed like hours. Julia was so easy going and talkative that it was like we had been friends for ages. "Julia. Have you heard this one?" Cameron was definitely a clown. "What do you call a sad cup of coffee?" The suspense of the punch line causing all of us to move toward the edge of our seat. "A depresso!" The roar of Cameron's laugh rumbling through the café. Tears threaten to come pouring out as I clutch my lower abdomen attempting to slow my own laughter.

I sat back and watched Julia and Cameron. Their playful banter causing my thoughts to drift to Axel. I attempt to push back against the invading visions of his blue eyes. Trying to refuse my curiosity of what it would be like to run my hands through his sandy blonde hair. "So, what's your brother up too Julia?"

Trying to process my own question causes me to almost look around, not believing that it really came from my mouth. "Not that it's any of my business." I quickly and quietly add while making it seem like something under my fingernail was twice as important as the answer to my own question. Holding my hand out and looking at the polish that is starting to become chipped on my thumb.

From under my eyelashes, I notice Julia has a look of confusion, concern, and what I think was sadness contorted her features simultaneously. She let out a low long sigh and her brows furrowed. "Axel is out of town with my father on a business trip." The answer peaks my curiosity and I ignore the awkward tension stirring around the table. "I wouldn't of pegged him to know a thing about how a business is run."

The moment my comment settles around us I regretted how sarcastic it sounded. Wishing I could fold in on myself and disappear. I notice Brina almost chokes on her muffin and sends imaginary daggers my way. "Let's just say that my father keeps him on a tight leash." The seconds after Julia spoke should have been one of heavy emotional magnitude, but thanks to Cameron trying to cover up his laughing the air held more of an awkward flavor swirled with humor.

It was a little hard to swallow Julia's statement. The bitterness in her words cause me to consider what it would be like to have my father back. Would we get along? My mind starts to drift and the last thing that registers is another joke from Cameron. "What do you call a dog that doesn't bark?"

Soon, I am slipping into a time from the past right before the punch line was given. The cool wind blows around me as I watch my feet almost touch the sky. Nothing but clouds in front of me. The smell of fresh cut grass tickles my nose causing me to sneeze. My stomach starts to do flips as the swing starts to fall backwards, causing my vison to shift. In the blink of an eye I am staring at the ground that seems miles away. Only the worn dirt beneath me. My mother and father are sitting on a bench and I can hear them laughing. I try to look over and catch a glimpse of my father, but as I do, I can feel myself slipping from the seat.

When I realize what is fully happening, it is too late. My hands slip from the cool, metal chains. I don't scream, instead I allow myself to welcome the rush that follows losing my grip. Closing my eyes tightly as years seems to pass while I wait for the ground to make an impact against my back. It never comes, instead a surge comes over my body, jerking it around like clothes in a washer. Static and fuzz drown my ears and my hands reach up to cover them instinctively.

"Adalee, my sunshine. You are okay." The deep tone of the voice all around me causing me to feel at ease. Feeling safe and comfortable in that moment, but it doesn't seem to last long. My feet finally touch the ground and when I try to move, my body stumbles forward. Unable to catch myself, I call out for my daddy. Knowing he was right near me just moments ago. Hoping he will catch me. The youth in my voice catching me by surprise.

As my hands hit down against a cool metal table. Pins and needles travel up my arms. I look down and become slightly disorientated when I think of the ground that should be under my fingers, not the metal. Scraping my nails against the steel surface just to be certain. The sound of glass hitting the floor causes my head to shoot up and that's when I notice Brina is shaking my shoulders. I can see her mouth moving, but the noise of the room drowns her out. It is as if the sounds around me should be in the dictionary as the definition of chaos.

As I come back to the present I notice there are the books off the shelves and laying in clusters. People rushing out of the way as salt and pepper shakers fly off of vibrating tables. Bags of coffee spilling from the counter and landing in mounds on the floors.

Someone begins pulling my shirt back and my senses become heightened. I feel a sudden boost of energy as my breathing increases. I turn around with both of my hands up in attack mode to come face to face with Julia. "Oh my, Julia I am so sorry." I see her wolf at the surface as her demeanor has become much more demanding and full of authority. "We have no time to talk. I need you to move now."

Once we are outside Julia rushes us to her car and hauls out of the parking lot. "What the hell was all of that Adalee?" Julia's voice full of worry. The power almost completely dissipated from her. "My dad is going to kill me once he finds out what happened." She hangs her head against the steering wheel. "Julia, I don't know what happened. Honest." She looks over her shoulder at me and her face softens. "It's okay. Really"

"Hey, Adalee and I can work to pay off any damages we caused." Brina always knows how to make things better. "Oh, Alpha Anderson doesn't care about damage." I look over at Cameron and for the first time since I have met him, his tone is one of complete seriousness. "What do you mean he doesn't care about damages? I feel like you aren't telling us something."

I wait for him to answer my question, but it never comes. Instead Julia starts talking, slowly at first, but as her story progressed it picked up speed. "My father is a strong leader. He leads with an iron fist and his rules are incased in concrete." Brina and I exchange looks of hesitation. Should we reply with yes's or just allow her to continue?

"My father believes in the old way of our world. That supernatural species should stay separate." As Julia drives around town, I wonder what it used to be like hundreds of years ago. When the supernatural were hiding in the shadows, afraid of being hunted, only to come out at night. "If your father doesn't believe we should be hanging out, why don't you tell him we ran into you both and all of this was an accident?"

I watch as Julia processes my words. You can practically see the gears turning in her head. Her knuckles white against the steering wheel due to the pressure of her grip. Like it is all she has left. "Oh Adalee, I wish it were that easy." I get slightly confused by her reluctance to see that it really is that easy. "Why wouldn't it be? That is basically the truth."

Julia pulls back around to the coffee shop and stops near our vehicle. "I really wish my father would believe it was an accident. I am afraid his distrustful nature will get the best of him." I want to ask her more about her father, but as I look up, I see what looks to be Alpha Anderson staring at us from the doorway of the coffee shop. Blind and unmeasurable acrimony clouding his vision. I know then, now is not the time for answers.

Chapter 11

The next several days at school go smoothly as I try to forget about the coffee shop. I work on getting a routine down to occupy my mind. My mind which is running out of space for everything that has happened so far. At one corner you have Axel. Questions of who he is and why he seems to show up at every turn swirl in a circle. In another corner you have my dreams. Still unchanging, it is a consistent in my life I have grown to be thankful for. The issues of why it continues and who those ice blue eyes could belong too seem to stay hazy like smoke trapped in a box.

Another small area wonders about Alpha Anderson. What will come of the coffee shop incident? So far Julia has said that he was fine after an hour or so, but the way she brushes off any other inquiries has me believing there is more to that story. The majority of my mind is blank. With the need to reveal the truth clinging to the blank area as if to provide some comfort. When I think about the section of my subconscious, I have a feeling of determination that usually courses through me, but right now all I feel is despair. Will I ever know the truth?

The topic of unresolved questions has me curious if Brina is still holding back information. The sting of betrayal still fresh on my heart. I take my headphones and place them in my ears as I walk towards our car. Hoping to let the melody drown out the raising doubt. Doubt that I have for my best friend.

I look up once I reach the passenger door and notice Brina's lips are moving. She doesn't notice I can't hear her. "What did you say?" I yell back. "Huh, say that again." Watching as her face becomes confused. "Say that one more time. Geez, Brina." I slip up as I start to chuckle noticing how her features morph into annoyance. The scowl between her brows growing and her lips setting into a thin, tight line.

"Okay Brina. My music is off. Tell me one more time what you were trying to say?" Getting into the car I turn my full attention towards her so she can see I really mean what I say. "I was going to tell you that Julia invited us to dinner, but I have too much homework to do for chemistry." The blank stare across my face must give away how lost I am on where she is going with this conversation. "Adalee, I was trying to ask if you wanted to eat with Julia. We only have sandwich stuff at the house."

As if on cue, my stomach growls loud enough to alert the whole parking lot of its demands. "I think that would be a yes, don't you?" I look down and squish my belly button as if it could answer me back. "Ads, do you want me to drop you off and then you can have Julia bring you back home?" I turn over her suggestion for a few moments and even though I would be a little more comfortable with Brina coming to pick me up, I am sure Julia bringing me home would be the easiest. "Yeah, I am sure that would work. I can text Julia really quick to see if it's okay."

What seemed like mere moments later, we show up to a cute little Italian restaurant. I get out and before I can even wave goodbye to Brina, Julia comes out of nowhere and grabs my hand, taking off in a full-blown sprint inside. Full of giggles she breathlessly squeaks out what might pass as a formal sentence. "Come on, we are already running late. They are waiting on us."

Great, here we go is all I could think about as the inside of the restaurant passed in a blur. Julia stopped and I went crashing into her back just about the time a waiter rounded the corner. My ears rang as the clashing and clanking of dishes breaking riveted around the suddenly silent room. I felt my cheeks heat up and my arms instantly went up in front of me as I held myself. Hoping to provide some protection from such judgmental stares.

I could feel Julia start to shake and at first, I thought it was from embarrassment until she turned to face me. Her face screamed pissed. "I cannot believe he just rounded the corner without even looking." Her voice was deathly cold and for the first time in the short week I have known Julia, I can see that her wolf has a temper. Truly, most do. "It's okay Julia. I am sure it was just an accident. It seems really busy in here." I bent down to start picking up the broken dishes and I felt as if someone was watching me. The moment I lifted my gaze I met Axel's blue eyes. They were burning with an intensity that would put the sun to shame. I could feel the heat all the way from across the room causing a dish to slip out of my hands and go crashing back to the floor.

My thoughts became mush as they drifted to his physical characteristics. He was a good-looking guy and had such a mysterious air about him that it was hard to not be intrigued. Every time I thought about him, however, Veronica made her way in my thoughts as well. I hated it.

I will admit he did have a way of making me feel uncomfortable with the way he looked at me. It felt as if I was the only one in the room, and not in a good way. I truly believe I wouldn't get so worked up if I knew he was at least okay with being my acquaintance. One minute he seems to want to be too close for comfort and the next he seems to not want to touch me with a ten-foot stick. The question I need to ask myself is if I would be okay with his answer. I honestly have no idea. Could I stand to not be in his life, better yet, to not have him in mine?

I force myself to focus on the task at hand. Mentally telling myself to grab a plate. Then, place a plate on the tray. Next comes grabbing another plate. Wishing I could just use a spell to clean this all up, but I am unsure how many regular humans could be watching.

"Adalee, I hope you don't mind that the guys join us."

Silently becoming thankful for Julia's voice. Welcoming the

distraction and buffer from the growing awkwardness that seems to

come with how silent the room still remains. "Sure, no problem." I

contemplate trying to form a decent come back to make it sound like

I was anything but okay with having the guys join us, but I knew

deep down, I wanted nothing more.

I should tell her that I would have rather had just us two

eating dinner. That Axel's presence made me confused and

irrational. I wanted to scream at anyone who could hear me that

regardless of how confused he made me, I didn't want to be

anywhere else. Yet, "I think that will be okay" was all that came out

in a whisper. "Huh, who knew my brother pulled off a suit so well."

Julia elbows me in the side and I really have to concentrate to remain

upright. Looking at the way Axel's suit hugs him make my knees

weak.

"I love when Carter wears his black dress pants and maroon

dress shirt." Watching Julia look at Carter made my cheeks slightly

red. "Julia, I think you need to be careful or you might have drool

running out of your mouth." She looks at me and for a moment mortification flickers in her eyes, but it doesn't last long before she becomes full of mischief as she grabs my hands to haul me forward.

Before she could whisk me away I looked at Julia and then over at myself. "Julia, I think we should have changed." Our cut off shorts and tank tops looked out of place and under dressed when compared to the guys. I felt Axel's gaze going up and down my body, so I looked down in shame. I knew he had to be judging me. Who shows up to such a nice restaurant in cut off denim shorts? "Adalee, calm down. My father owns the restaurant. We are fine." Geez, what does Alpha Anderson not own in this town?

Julia and Carter get wrapped in a warm embrace the moment we get close. I continue to sneak peeks at Axel from under my eyelashes while I awkwardly shuffle my feet from side to side. Just looking at him made my breathing come out funny and my heart do flips. I felt knots forming at my stomach and I am afraid something might come up if I don't sit down soon.

I mentally tell myself to get a grip. Wondering what happened to the Adalee that swore off of boys and who had no issue sticking to that notion. I start to sit down, but before my hand can grab the back of the chair, I feel tingles dance along my skin. I look down and notice that Axel has a hold of my wrist. "Don't worry. I've got it for you." He begins to pull out my chair. The sharp sound of the metal legs scraping along the floor causes me to jump at the unpleasant sound. Unsure of what to do with such a sweet jester, I just nod in his direction and take my seat.

A few moments later an attractive waitress with dark brown hair comes to take our order. You can tell this girl has no boundaries as she openly flirts with Axel. When Axel does not give her the time of the day, she turns her attention to Carter. If looks could kill, this girl would be dead. "He would love a cherry coke and I would like a sparkling water. That would be all." Julia is staring daggers at this girl and I can't blame her.

Axel is looking between me and his menu like he wants to say something but is unsure about how to start. We give our drink orders and this girl is not taking a hint. She is making this whole dinner even more awkward than it should be. It is not long before she says some cheesy pick up line and runs her hand down Carter's chest. Julia snaps. You can feel the anger rising off of her and she seems to visibly be shaking in her seat.

Not a second later, a sound I did not think was possible comes from Julia. Before I could blink, she had this girl's arm behind her back and her head pressed against the table. I can see Julia whispering in this girl's ear, but I was unable to focus on what she is telling her. In a flash Carter is behind Julia and attempting to calm her down. "Julia, stop it!" I scream without really thinking about it and Axel is at my side unsure of what to do. His hands moving as if they want to touch me, then pull back as if he is second guessing if he should.

It really looked like she was about to break this girl's arm. Carter casually stands behind Julia, gripping her waste, and murmurs a few things in her ear. I can physically see her body calming in response to Carter and I was thankful he was here, but it wasn't enough. I start to hum a low calming melody. Allowing my magic to surface, which is something I don't do often, to help calm the tension in the air around us. Hoping to allow Julia to become centered once again.

I feel the crackle and popping in my veins as I allow the melody to get a little louder. Watching as the particles in the air begin to buzz with charm. Willing the haze to surround Julia. Slowly feeling her give way to the pull. Noticing how she sways back and forth in Carter's arms. The waitress, unsure of what is going on, remains still and silent. Julia finally steps away from the girl and out of Carter's arms. Worry flashes in her eyes. She looks between the two of us, narrowing in on me, and walks off.

Axel slowly leads me to my seat and then sits down next to me and grabs my hand. I think he was unsure of what to say or do in that moment. His touch helps calm my nerves, and I am internally thankful he remained silent.

Using magic always makes me a little on edge. Mother's words of caution come to my mind when I think about the open display I used. Her warning, "When a witch is using magic it is when she is the most vulnerable" and that is something I have trained myself not to be. Here's to hoping the rest of the night goes smoothly.

Chapter 12

"You weren't supposed to see that side of me." I cannot really figure out how to respond. Julia did seem genuinely upset as she just stared at empty plates in front of her. "A true friend accepts every side of someone, Julia." Hoping to move past the issue with the waitress and on to the food, which still isn't in front of us.

The rest of dinner goes smoothly. Small chit chat and a few jokes later the tension seems to ease. As we get ready to leave, I start pulling out my wallet and Axel lowly growls in my direction. "I have it." I was taken back from the harshness he displayed, and I can tell he didn't realize what he sounded like until I pulled back away from him. It felt unnatural to step out of his proximity, but I do not take kindly to someone being unkind for any reason. "I can handle paying for my own meal, Axel." I made sure to keep my reply as short as I could to bring home the point.

"What kind of gentleman would I be if I let you pay for your own meal?" His voice was as smooth as silk. The amount of kindness that radiated from his voice made me do a double take. I tried not to allow myself to feel anything, but a large smile crept across my face. "Also, Adalee, I would like to drive you home if you would allow me?" I almost had to do a double take. I waved my hand in front of him. "Just checking to make sure this wasn't a hologram or my imagination."

Julia and Carter busted out laughing at my little display of sarcasm. I could feel my ears heating up with humiliation as I didn't realize they were paying attention to us. "I think Julia and Carter need some alone time." The sound in his voice was more like the Axel I had come to know. "There he is. I was worried you were replaced with a stunt double." I take my hand and act like I am wiping sweat off my forehead. Bringing home the point of how rude he seems to be.

I study his features. How his muscles in his shoulders become tense. How a slow, shaky smile comes across his face as he spreads his fingers and places his hand across his chest. "Whew, just checking to make sure it really is me." I cock my head to the side as a small, soft laugh comes whispering out from deep in my chest. "Who knew you had a sense of humor, Axel Anderson."

I thought about it for a moment, he was being nice in this moment, but what would he do once we were alone. Would it all go away? I believed it could be okay, but I kept getting a slight feeling of fear mixed with all of the other emotions I normally felt around Axel. I could call Brina, but I did not want to drag her all the way out here when Axel was offering me a ride.

"Okay. Julia, are you okay with this?" Julia looks at me and then gives me the biggest smile and winks. "Sure. You go ahead Adalee, I will see you guys at lunch tomorrow." I looked at her features and I felt a little better. I grab my things and follow Axel to his truck. He continued to be the proper gentleman and opened my door for me.

Once I was into his truck I reached for the seatbelt and gasped when my hand hit Axel's. I froze. Unsure of what to do. My breath caught in the back of my throat as I felt Axel's hand brush against my curls. I became like a statue as he reached across my lap to buckle me in. The smell of pine trees and cinnamon pleasing my nose. Turning to face Axel and getting eye level with his beautiful bluebird, blue eyes. I studied them like they would be the last thing I would ever see.

The way his dark and dense eyelashes lined his heavy eyelids. I watched as they slowly came down and back up again. I wanted to take my hand and trace his compressed eyebrows, starting with how they came together and furrowed in the middle. I found myself leaning in and wanting to know everything these eyes had seen. I wanted to push his shaggy hair out away from his face.

Noticing how it would almost fall to his nose if it wasn't pushed back and held in place with gel. Only a few stragglers seemed to be out of order. Fighting for attention as they danced in his line of vision. Without realizing what I was doing, I pushed them back. Feeling as if the air he sucked in came directly from me.

As soon as my hand was back in my lap Axel pulled away and slammed the door shut. I watched from the review mirror as he made his was around the truck. He stops at the tailgate and looks up and sighs, running his hand through his hair causing even more pieces to become loose from the rest.

He gets in a few minutes later and takes off towards my house. "You know, your hair might stay in place if you didn't run your hand through it all the time. It looks good pushed back." Radio silence. The cab of the truck filling with tension. After about ten minutes I could not take the silence another second. "Thank you for paying for dinner and bringing me home. I really appreciate the gesture." He looks over at me, goes to speak, but decides against it.

Great, I broke him. My shoulder slumped forward as I let out a sigh and stare out the window. Watching my breath fog up the glass. "Adalee, I have a question." Oh no. My heart sinks to the bottom of my chest with the way he worded that sentence. It's like when someone states they need to talk. What in the hell kind of question could he possibly want to ask me?

I dip my head forward while my hands get all clammy and wait another few minute on the edge of my seat before he finally responds again. "Do you believe we are in charge of our own destiny?" He looks over at me and I am sure he sees my expression turn from one of complete dread to misunderstanding. What kind of question is that?

I chuckle a little and look at him. I take in every feature in front of my vision as his features slightly change. I have a hard time reading the emotions he is displaying as they pass in a blur. Hurt shows in the way he loosely holds the stirring wheel as if it is taking all the strength he has. Frustration in the way he lets out a long-exaggerated sigh. Anger in the way his muscles in his back are tighter than Veronica's shorts.

Could it be a little of all three? "Are you serious?" It was meant to be as clear as water when I asked if he was serious. Did he want to get into such a deep conversation? He stops the car and I realize he understood my questions about as well as if I said it in Latin. He slams his hands on his steering wheel. I continue to stare in his direction, never moving my gaze. "What is your problem? Axel you asked a question and I answered it honestly."

"I didn't think you would understand. I should have never asked." I figured he did not like me laughing at his question, I guess it hurt his pride. What he did next took me by surprise, he leaned over in his seat and became incredibly close to my face. Our lips mere centimeters away from one another. His eyes are the prettiest eyes I have ever seen. I take in a massive deep breath and my nose smells cinnamon and pine. It hits me full force and causes me to close my eyes with how intoxicating the smell was. He reached up slowly to tuck a strand of lose hair behind my ear and the moment that he does, I am warped into darkness.

I hear the familiar laugh of my mother in the distance and soon my vision clears. I look around and I am transported into an unfamiliar house. I can hear little girls laughing. It takes me a moment to realize I am in another memory. It is a small quaint cottage-like house that is decorated very minimally in neutral colors. I hear my mother talking and then hear a voice that I can only assume is my fathers. "Jack, I think Allen might really come around to this idea." It sounded close to the one from my last memory, yet it sounded like a weight had been lifted off his shoulders. He sounded as if he could be free to say what he wanted in this house

"I don't think it will be that simple, Richard. I think you should head with caution." Soon, two other adults join in and I was unsure of who they could be. I noticed the other man was the one disagreeing with my father. "I promise you, we will stand beside you. I am worried that Allen won't. Having him as an enemy wouldn't be a good thing." I think about if I know who they are talking about, but the only Allen I know is our principle. No way it could be the same guy. What kind of danger could they possibly be in?

Two little girls catch my attention as they come running through the house. I can tell who they are immediately. Brina and I look to be about three if not four. "Tag you're it Adwalee" the innocence in our voice showing me just how young we really are. I notice that we seem to be running a little faster than we need to, and I end up tripping over my feet and land fist down into the glass coffee table trying to catch myself.

Younger me starts to cry as my nose wrinkles from the metallic scent lingering in the air. Brina comes to my rescue and helps me up just as my parents are running around the corner. My parents rush to me and the other two adults start scolding Brina for allowing this to happen.

I recognize now that these other people were her parents. I think to myself that it is a little odd that she is being scolded like it was her fault. I look back to my smaller self and notice that I am chanting. Within a few minutes the wounds on my hands are not bleeding and seem to be smaller in size. "You see, Richard. You will not be able to hide her abilities. You just won't."

My father refused to answer him as he focuses all of his attention on my hand. I analyzed how Brina's parents seemed to carry themselves in such a stoic way. I sense that had Brina been able to grow up with her parents, she would stick out like a sore thumb with her high energy self. I try turning back to the little girl to catch a glimpse of her hands and notice she had no cuts on her palms. "Don't worry, pumpkin. Daddy will keep you safe." I try to walk closer to catch the rest of what my father says and before I know it, the surrounding started changing around me. I am coming out of my lost memory.

I notice Axel is looking at me. Both hands on the side of my face in a concerning way. He looks down and quickly pulls away. The cold courses through me as he opens the door and goes outside into the night. I sit in silence for a few moments wondering what I should do. I decide to go follow him and ask what the problem is. By the time I go outside I cannot find him. He is not standing at the front of the truck like he was just a few minutes ago.

"Axel." I call out to my surroundings hoping he is within hearing distance. "Where are you? Let's talk about this." Frustrated after a few minutes of hearing nothing but the truck engine, I turn around to go back and wait on him. As I am about to reach the door I am spun around by my waist. I gasp at the sudden motion and before I know it, Axel is in front of me and his hands are placed firmly on my hips. My back push up against the truck. "Adalee Ebony, what am I going to do with you?"

Do with me? Panic takes over my features. "How do you know my full name?" His head turns sideways, and he lets out a small snicker. "I don't think you realize how loud your friend Brina can be." I turn my head to the left hoping to catch a breath of fresh air. One that doesn't contain Axel's toxic scent. "Tell me what to do Adalee, when my Father wants one thing, but my heart wants another?"

I know nothing about Mr. Anderson—I've never even met the guy? Before I had the chance to ask what he meant his lips were against mine. He was hesitant and slow at first like he was worried I would disappear. Then he began kissing me with a hunger that had my body wanting more. Sparks take over my body and it feels like I am becoming alive with jolts of electricity.

A small moan escapes my lips and that is all the conformation he needs before he is pulling me in even deeper. He kisses me with a passion that could put Aphrodite to shame. I cannot seem to push away from him. I think that I should before I regret something, but my body betrays what my mind is asking. My hands find his hair and I cannot help but run them through his shaggy mess. His hands snake around my waist. I feel his chest vibrate and hear what sounds almost like a low growl come from him. I did not know two people could be so close. After a few minutes, he pulls back. We are both panting and cannot seem to catch our breath. I look up and see a look of pure shock on his face. It tells me that this moment was completely unplanned.

Sadness and then anger crosses his features. He drops his hands from my body and walks back to his side of the truck leaving me there, still trying to catch my breath, just staring into the night. Was that a mistake? Unsure of how I feel, I get back in the truck. The rest of the time is spent in silence. I am on the verge of tears.

How can he sit next to me and not acknowledge what just happened? He is the one who kissed me first. Did he feel the sparks that I felt?

We pull up to my house and before I could get out, he is around the truck opening the door. I hop down and look into those deep blue eyes and sigh a painful sigh. He stands in my way not moving. Fed up with how he is acting I push past him, but he grabs my arm. Turning around to face him once again. I want to lower my head in embarrassment, but the anger I feel towards him covers up all my other swirling emotions.

He tries to place his hand on my cheek, and I turn my head. He then grabs my chin and turns me to stare into his eyes once more. After a moment he moves a stray curl out my face with the other. "Ads, I am sorry. I should not have done what I did. There is so much I want to tell you, but it's out of my control." He drops his hands and turns away coldly from me without giving me the chance to respond.

Feeling fed up I yell back at him. He needs to hear me. He needs to know how serious I am. "That's not good enough, Axel. You need to figure out what ever this is." He walks away and doesn't look back. I walk to my house and turn around once I get to the door. I see his taillight pull away as I feel stuck watching him

pull away. What did he mean he it's out of his control?

Chapter 13

I sit on the porch staring at the blackness in front of me. I hear this gut-wrenching howl that sends a shiver down my spine. It seems that the animal is either hurt or sad. Is that even a thing? Hurt for sure, but can an animal show sadness? I think about a wolf in the woods thinking of what might have made it howl. Maybe its dinner got loose? Who knows, I sit for a few more minutes then finally gather myself and head to my room.

I lay down praying for a peaceful slumber. Really not sure that will happen as Axel will not leave my thoughts alone and if it isn't Axel, it's what Brina said at school the other day. Haunting every second of my memories. I hope that I can sleep at all. It seems the moment my body goes to sleep Brina's alarm is going off across the hall. It felt like all I did was close my eyes for a few moments. A pair of ice blue eyes haunted me in my dreams all night last night.

We go for our morning run and I am praying that after this run, I will feel better. I tell Brina everything that happened last night while we were warming up and she in typical Brina fashion is oohing and ahh-ing. She does not press me with a bunch of questions because she knows it will only make me upset and flustered not being able to answer them. How can I even begin to answer them when Axel has been hot and cold since the moment we met?

"Brina, are you going to tell me about why you were so hush hush at school?" Brina stops in midstride. "Adalee. I think this is a conversation we should have with your mother." Shaking my head, I throw my hands up at her because she has clearly lost her mind. "You know damn well that my mother won't admit to anything. She had the opportunity to tell me the truth. In reality, they both had the chance to tell me the truth and they did not. The stinging in my heart from deception causes me to inhale deeply. Will I ever feel okay deep down with how Brina lied?

"Adalee. This information is sensitive. I think your mother could explain everything better." I can feel my powers wanting to surface. My magic wanting to explode in order to get answers. "I just told you she had the chance like you have the chance now to tell me the truth. Are you going to lie to me again?" Hurt swirls in her eyes. Her hand goes up to her heart and I don't even think she was aware her body reacted that way.

"Okay. I'll tell you." The guilt trip actually worked. I figured I would need to lay it on a little thicker. She starts discussing the council as we find a nice, shady spot to sit. "You remember the congress, right? They are the top leaders for each supernatural race." I lay back and look up at the clouds trying to process what I know. "The congress is who governs us, correct?"

"Yeah, Ads. You are correct. Between your father's accidents and their rules to keep each supernatural race in its own lane, questions were brought up that your mother told me she couldn't answer." I watch as a bird soars above us. Letting myself feel gratitude so profoundly my core could burst. Letting my emotions become overrun with sorrow that my bones ache. Gratitude to finally know the answers and sorrow for everything else entirely.

As I continue to piece together what Brina is telling me I feel her start pacing beside me. "Brina. I just don't understand. You are being too vague. What kind of questions could she not answer?" I can practically see the gears turning in her head with how she cocks it to the side and runs her hands through her hair. Before long she starts walking away. Rather quickly. "Hey. Are you just going to avoid the question?"

When she stops, I almost run into the back of her. "Adalee, I don't know the answer to your questions. I don't know what kind of questions your mother couldn't answer." Her voice comes out shaky as she stands there continuing to face away. "Trust me. I wish I knew the answers. I only know that your mother left because we were in danger. I am just not sure what kind of danger." I see she is speaking the truth, even though I don't want to accept it. I don't want to admit that is all she may know.

I consider every scenario as we take our time walking back to the cabin. I go over and over ideas only to realize how far-fetched they seemed. Were my parents hit men in a mob? Did my father launder money? Did my mother kidnap me? I know it seems absurd. No way could my parents be criminals. My mother doesn't even drive over the speed limit and refuses to eat the grapes out of the bag at the groceries because that's considered stealing.

I decide to file these questions back with the ever-growing pile of things I have no clue about. I have to remind myself there is only so much I am in control over. My mental health will only take so much at a time before it can't be put back together. In this moment, I really should be focusing on school and the potential drama I may find myself in.

Chapter 14

Veronica may be avoiding me, but I avoid Axel at every possible turn. The bell sounds for lunch and instant dread happens at the base of my stomach. Brina and I get our food and we go to sit down. I relax after a few moments when everything seems to be okay. The intertwining of Brina and Cameron's laughter fills the cafeteria and causes my heart to be put at ease. I am silently thanking them both. It makes it easier to be sitting across from Axel and his steady unsure smolder.

Veronica goes over to Axel and places a kiss on his cheek. "You know, baby. I was just telling the girls how excited I was for your party in a few weeks. Think you can save me the first and last dance?" Her voice comes out like screeching tires. The attempt to place a genuine tone caused her voice to become about three octaves too high.

He just continuous to stare in my direction. "Sure. I can do that Veronica." I notice he is not giving her his typical attention, but he is not pushing her completely away either. It's like being at a stale mate in a game of chess. As I grow bored of the food on my plate I bid my goodbyes and walk out of the cafeteria. Never looking back in his direction. I hate the way my body reacts to him as I walk away. The emptiness twinges in my bones.

Before I can take a fresh breath of air I am pulled back and then pushed against the building. All I can think to do is throw a right hook. I warned Veronica what would happen if she tried to do this again. When my knuckles feel the skin, I hear a gut-wrenching sound fill the air. I look up to see Axel. "What in the actual hell, Adalee?"

His voice is muffled from holding his left cheek. I want to act sorry, but he's lucky I didn't send him flying across the lawn. "Maybe you'll think twice before you sneak up on someone." I try to act like my hand isn't already swelling. I mumble a small healing chant under my breath and can feel the pain slowly leaving. Thankfully magic can fix a possible broken bone easily.

"What do you want, Axel?" I can tell he is in a rare mood. He leans back against the brick wall. His navy shirt lifting above his worn-out jeans as he places his hands above his head like runners do. My eyes rake up and down him automatically. "Like the view?" He catches me off guard with his playful tone. "No, just shocked you don't have a tracking device from Veronica. I could see her going for the ankle type."

The anger from getting caught staring is clearly radiating off me. He makes it one hundred times worse when he has the audacity to laugh in my face. I am about tired of trying to determine what he is doing. "Come on Rosewood. Lighten up." When he pushes away from the wall, I can see every vein in his arm pumping blood. I can make out the crease from his biceps. "Not sure why you have to make me the bad guy."

Pissed, I shove him with all my might and he actually stumbles backwards. Impressed with myself, I let my hair flip back and walk off. He catches up and is still slightly chuckling. "If I did not know any better, I would think you were jealous, Adalee. I mean I can tell you she thinks she is my girlfriend, but that is not the case."

"You think this is because of her? I couldn't care less about her, but bravo for thinking either one of you matters enough to make me this way." He hit the nail on the head, but I won't let him know that. Confusion morphs his features reminding me of a puppy. I find myself wanting to take my thumb and smooth out the middle of his eyebrows.

"Would you like to go on a date with me?" I push past him and then turn around a hit him square in the chest. "Don't. You. Even. Start. Axel. I am not some plaything you can try to use whenever you feel like it." I can feel the steam shooting from my ears. "Come on, Ads. I'm done playing by someone else's rules. Humor me and let me take you to get a burger."

"I don't even understand what that means." He is basically making me feel like an idiot. The emotions churning inside of me cause me to think irrationally. I feel unable to even form a coherent sentence. "Just please leave me alone. I seriously want nothing to do with you until you figure out whatever this is." I can see how my words hurt him. How his head hangs down slightly with the weight of guilt. "Not even for a milkshake?"

"I just need figure out for myself what we are Axel." I realized I was basically yelling at him, so I brought it way down. I need him to understand. "I started senior year with questions I needed to answer for myself. I told myself nothing would stand in my way and then I ran into you at the library and you threw me off track." I realized the moment he lifted his head back up how close we were. How in this position he stands a good head taller than me. How perfect I would fit into his arms. "See. This right here is distracting me and I can't have that happen."

"Adalee, I don't want..." A bombing, raspy voice thunders behind me causing me to jump and Axel to stop mid-sentence. My heart leaped out of my chest and I almost felt the need to bend down and search for it. "Axel. What is the meaning of this?" When neither one of us answered he continued on with his questions. "What are you doing here with her?" I look up and Axel's face was whiter than a sheet.

"I'm sorry, do I know who you are?" I meant to sound surer of my question, but the influence I felt from this man caused it to barely come above a shaky whisper. Axel steps past me and reaches for the hand of the man who scared me half to death. It's easy to tell it was a simple way to place himself between us.

I look over Axel's shoulder and see a larger, taller, older version of himself standing in front of me with a clear look of disapproval. "Hello, father. I was just escorting a fellow student to class. I am sure you would want me to make sure that she got there safely." Axel's father looks over at him and with a smirk walks a little closer.

I know he can see me tremble, the amount of authority that is coming off of him is making me squirm where I stand. I can tell his is an Alpha. "Okay, son. Do what you must, but do not think that for one minute I am stupid." I watch as he turns on his heels and the stops. "Oh, and Miss Rosewood, do tell your mother I say hello. I was disappointed to hear she was back in town and didn't make time to stop in." I quickly got the feeling I knew why mother didn't go near him when I heard the sinister tone of his voice.

"Also, Axel you will do best to remember your place." I watch as all that Axel does is bow slightly. "We don't mingle with her kind. You know what people like her did to our family."

Waiting to raise up once his father was completely out of sight. He looks at me and for a brief moment. I see regret swirling where the mischief once swirled. I look down and I can feel him reach for my face, but he stops himself. Like father, like son is the only thing that crosses my mind as I watch him walk away. My mind racing over what Alpha Anderson just said. My kind? As in witches? What could have possibly happened in the past to cause such ill will towards someone he doesn't even know?

Chapter 15

I stand Lost outside the greenhouse when a sweet voice pulls me back to reality. "Adalee, why don't you come help me for just a minute since you happen to be here a little early. I will let you tell me what has your mind all jumbled." I turn to see Mrs. Eva standing at the door. I try to smile at her, but I am completely unsuccessful.

While we get the stuff ready to replant some flowers I just stand there going through the motions in silence. Mrs. Eva never presses me on the issue. Once my mind is somewhat together, I become more aware of what I am doing. It always makes me feel better to have my hands in the dirt. I think it's a witch thing.

"I just don't understand any of it Mrs. Eva. I truly do not understand." My confusion turns into irritation. It's on the rise, and I can feel myself getting extremely irritated. I stop what I am doing and start pacing back and forth. I usually cry when I am angry, and I hate myself for it. I feel like it shows weakness and that is the last thing I want.

"Adalee, I want you to take some deep breaths. Everything will come together in time. I think soon you'll see a whole new light will be shed on the situation." Mrs. Eva's attempts at redirection does no good. I have this burning resentment for Alpha Anderson in the pit of my stomach, and I need to let it out. Just as I finally hit my breaking point, the first tear starts to fall, I scream out loud in an attempt to let out all of my frustration.

The scream gets drowned out by the sudden loud boom of thunder and a crash of lightning inside the greenhouse. The boom is so loud that is causes the glass on the shelves to fall and crash against the floor. It is as if Mother Nature knows to succumb to my mercy. I can hear a steady down pour coming from the sky. The magic within me keeping my focus occupied.

"Adalee! Listen to me child. I know it seems bad. Being at your stage in life is hard. It will get better." The small grip I had on reality gets loose from my fingertips and goes flying like the books from the bookshelves. "I just want my life to go back to how it was. Is that too much to ask?" I throw my hands left and right picking up one plant after another. Never flinching as they shatter against the side of the greenhouse.

Mrs. Eva allows me to throw my tantrum for a few minutes and then the throws her hands out to the side and everything slows to a crawl. She calmly walks over and tells me firmly, "That is enough child. Now, let's get you some tea, you need it." The instant she turns and walks away everything that was suspended drops.

Mrs. Eva cautiously grabs my arm and leads me to her main desk. She starts pulling out a bunch of herbs and mixes me a tea concoction. I am a little hesitant on how it will taste, but I feel my body almost needing to drink it. I feel drained. "Mrs. Eva, why do I feel like I am missing something? Like there is something I don't know and if I did, would it make my life easier?" She chuckles a little at me and pushes the tea to my lips.

"Well, Adalee. No one can go down our journey for us. That is something we must do ourselves. You may be at a disadvantage here, but I am on your side". As she speaks, I notice her words begin to slow down and my body getting heavy. My eyelids drift and it is taking everything in me to keep them open. I remember Mrs. Eva grabbing my hands before I lost the battle and was surrounded into the dark. Unable to stop myself from falling into a deep sleep.

I feel myself falling in a dream that wasn't really vivid. I just knew soon I would hit the ground. It had to come at some point. No one falls for forever. I try to flail my arms back and forth to put me upright, at least what feels upright, but I don't move. I force my eyes to close tighter than the button on my jeans. Feeling the pressure in my head as I continue to try to make my eyes become glued shut.

Suddenly everything stops. I no longer feel the cool, crisp air across my cheeks as I twirl like a carnival ride. I reach my fingers out to find myself brushing up against wet leaves, then cool soil and small rocks. When I open my eyes, I am staring back at a massive wolf. A wolf who's fur puts the midnight sky to shame.

Time seems to crawl by as I take in this magnificent creature. In awe to finally see who owns those icy blue eyes that seem to haunt me at every turn. "So, I finally find out who's been hiding in the shadows." I scramble to my feet and mimic the wolf as he circles around me refusing to allow him at my back.

Unexpectedly the wolf in front of me starts snarling. Low at first, I thought I imagined it until he started stalking towards me. I scrambled backwards too fast and cursing under my breath when my bottom made contact with the ground. My teeth snapping shut hard enough to feel like I shattered them. My palms became super sweaty and my body rocked back and forth as I attempted to take a deep breath.

The animal in front of me never faltered. He continued to stalk forward until he was a paw away from crushing my abdomen. I shut my eyes begging to wake up. Slapping myself a few times to only be granted the sting across my cheeks instead of my eyelids opening to reality.

The wolf never ceases his snarling. It just became louder and louder until I am sure it was rattling trees. I watched, frozen, as the wolf placed both front paws at each side of my head. I could feel his velvet fur with the skin of my shoulders. The ground vibrated as he sunk down in a fighting stance.

I noticed those icy blue eyes seemed to be fixed on the darkness behind me. It was as if the trees became so close together, they disappeared into the black. Shifting my weight, I rolled over slowly onto my belly. Pushing against the damp earth with my forearms trying to understand what was putting this massive wolf on edge. What could cause such a powerful creature to become defensive.

When I am satisfied with my view, I instantly regret my curiosity. From the darkness a shadowy figure emerges. The temperature drops cold enough where I can feel the pain that comes when it freezes my joints in place. I become stiff and unable to do anything but focus on the steam my breathing creates.

The figure in front of us starts walking slowly. I can feel the hostility of the wolf above me as his growling becomes deathly. I use the distraction between the two and slowly crawl away enough to stand up. Bracing my hands for an attack. As I walk around the wolf a twig snaps and catches us both off guard.

A sickening laughter echoes around us and the moment my eyes meet the shadowy figure it comes flying in my direction. I throw up my hands and shout a blasting spell, but nothing happens. My body is absent of magic in this dream. My scream becomes drowned out by the whooshing sound of the wind as I am engulfed in blackness. My feet start to scramble as they become lifted off of the ground. My arms and legs begin to be pulled in different directions causing me to be contorted and twisted in unnatural ways.

I feel as if I will lose myself completely until I hear my name. "ADALEE." One simple word being yelling with an underlining sense of urgency. The deep timber of the voice sounding familiar, sounding like home. That one word was enough to break me free.

"Adalee. Adalee Ebony." Still feeling as if I was dreaming, I throw myself into a standing position, using everything I can to break free of whoever has me. Ease creeping into my soul as I no longer feel hands at my shoulders. I frantically look around when I hear the crash. "Are you serious, Adalee? It's me." I come face to face with my best friend picking herself up off the floor from across the room.

I still feel dazed and unsure what is real. "Adalee. Put your hands down. I can only heal so fast with your magic." It sounds like Brina, but what happened? I slowly sit down on the bed. My eyes moving in a thousand directions trying to assess for any threat. Finally finding my voice once again, it sounds brittle. "Brina. I think I am in danger."

The moments those words leave my lips I find myself even more exhausted than when I started. I lay down and close my eyes. Begging to only sleep because I know that some say your dreams depict your future and I want no part of what I just witnessed.

Chapter 16

When I opened my eyes, I looked around in almost a panic. I was in my bed and trying to remember how I got to my house when the last thing I remember is Mrs. Eva. The greenhouse. My body feels like it has had the life sucked out of it. I feel super sluggish. Geez, she can brew a cup of tea. I raise slowly. I sit up and stop, then I dangle my feet above the floor for a while.

Dizziness is hitting me in waves. Once the dizziness passes, I try to stand. I take my sweet time because trying to fight the spinning room in front of me is almost a losing battle. I proceed to place one foot in front of the other. I make my way down the hall and look at the steps below my feet. I groan at the thought of having walk down the steps. As I am figuring out how not to roll headfirst into the living room, I hear voices being carried up the staircase.

"You need to tell her. It is time. She has no idea what is going on and it is only causing her mayhem." I notice that the first voice belongs to Mrs. Eva. Why is she at my house? Oh right, she gave me tea that made me pass out. She probably brought me home. How embarrassing it must have been to have me fall asleep right in front of her. "Eva, I can't do that. She is not strong enough. I have to think of her safety." My mother's voice floats up the stairs barely above a whisper. "I do not think you are making the right choice, Rebecca, but I will go along with what you think is best." What is she talking about?

I want to get a little closer so I can listen to them better. "She is close to piecing it altogether isn't she?" My mother seems to be distressed with the thought of me actually finding out real answers. "I don't think she realizes how much she actually knows." Mrs. Eva sounds like this is an everyday conversation they are having.

I start to take a step when I hear Brina squeal and run towards me. "Adalee Ebony, you should have come and told me you were up. Gosh, I was so worried about you! Are you okay?" I look back and mentally curse my best friend for ruining my chance at being able to hear more. I turn my attention back to the stairs and see my mother and Mrs. Eva at the bottom. I make my way down the bottom of the stairs and slowly walk to the table.

My mother has dinner laid out. "Well, that smells amazing mom. I'm starving". Brina chuckles and my mother gives her a quick glance to shut her up. My mother hesitantly begins to talk, "Well, Ads. Have you not been sleeping?" Never one for small talk. She pauses and then looks around as if I would admit to her about anything that has happened. It would not do any good seeing as she would just ignore it. "No. I have been sleeping fine."

She acts as if she wants to say more. Instead, she gets up and starts to fix several plates of spaghetti. "Mrs. Eva, will you be staying for dinner?" I finally ask since everyone just keeps staring at me like a broken toy no one knows how to fix. "Oh no child, I need to get ready for the new week of school. It is Sunday evening." What? "You do mean Saturday, right?" I look around and every one of their faces read guilt in their own way. Brina's face screams she wants to tell me, but my mother keeps a glare fixed in her direction. Mrs. Eva seems to avoid looking at me altogether.

"That calming tea really did a number on you. You will be fine, just come to school tomorrow and things will be better. I know it" Mrs. Eva pulls me into a hug and then says her goodbyes. "Remind me not to ask you for any kind of drink again."

I stare at my plate of spaghetti. I eat my dinner in silence. Unsure of what to say. I listen to Brina chat about what has gone on at school, but my mind continues to play back everything that has happened this last week. It plays back to everything that happened in my dream. "I appreciate dinner mom, but I think I am going to go back and lay down." I go to my room after some time with mom and Brina and try to go back to bed but sleep never comes.

I hear Brina's alarm go off next door. "You know nothing like getting back into our routine to make things seem better!" She yells through the house. I know she can hear me fidgeting in bed. "Why do you insist on getting up at five-thirty?" My response is nothing but a whisper, but I know she can hear it. "Just meet me downstairs in ten, Ads."

After we finish our run I jump into a much-needed shower. Brina and I get ready for school and to start a new week. I do feel a little better moving my muscles after I slept for almost 48 hours.

"You know Axel is out of town this week, right?" I think Brina is trying to give me some good news, but I just have this feeling of emptiness knowing he won't be at school. I am still unsure of what is going on with him. Maybe I will be able to figure out a few things.

We walk into class and Mr. Green looks me up and down and if I am not mistaken, slightly sniffs at the air. "You seem a little different, Adalee." Slightly creeped out, I walk to my seat. "Brina, there really is something off about that guy even for a vampire." I catch her side eyeing me. Am I the only one who sees it? I start pulling out my notebook when Veronica looks at me and her eyes narrow. Great, what I have done now?

Halfway through the class, Mr. Green has to leave to grab a few things from the principle and the moment he leaves the entire class breaks out into chaos. I attempt to focus on my work, but I keep getting bits of Veronica's conversation with the girl who is sitting in front of her. "I know our fathers are in a business deal." The first sentence I catch hardly has my attention, it's the next few pieces that I hear that makes my blood boil.

"I cannot stand Julia. She acts like she is so much better than the rest of us." I listen to them rag on Julia and before I can defend her, she turns in her seat and shuts up before Mr. Green walks back in the door. She knew I could hear her, but that was the whole point.

I was concentrating so hard on my work that when my phone buzzes in my pocket, it makes me almost jump out of my seat.

Adalee, I want you to know I am sorry for how I left. I will be gone for almost two weeks and when I get back, we need to talk.- Axel.

Great what do I say to that? Well, I decided to not respond and told myself I would allow some time to figure out what to say. I will ask Brina about it tomorrow during our run and she can help me figure out an answer.

As I am in study hall, I cannot help but wonder around the library and look at all the intricate woodwork used. From the railings to the bookshelves and tables. It looks so warm and friendly whereas the rest of the school gives off a cold vibe due to the stonework.

I catch myself going back to the second floor and making my way to the history section. Once I am near the rows of books I sit down and play back the memory of meeting Axel. He was so cold and annoyed that day, I still am curious as to why he acted in such a manner to only turn around and kiss me outside his truck.

I pick myself up after a few minutes and decide to walk around the third floor to clear my mind a little. The third floor is mainly study classrooms and tables for student to use for schoolwork. They also have resource books and an entire section worth of computers.

I walk around a bit and decide to make my way to a study room off in the corner of the third floor to get away from everyone. Some quiet might be nice. I walk right in seeing as the lights are off and find Veronica lip locked with some guy from the football team. I stand there unsure of what to do.

I mentally face palm myself for realizing I keep digging myself deeper into this love drama. So much for avoiding it. I look down and try to leave as quickly as possible when someone grabs me by my shirt and slams me against the wall. "You sure do have a habit of putting your nose where it doesn't belong, trash. I am going to tell you this once." Veronica leans super close to my ear and I hear the guy behind her laugh out loud. She hisses in his direction and he shuts up immediately. "You will stay out of my way. Do you understand? Axel is mine. I will not have some scrawny, half breed taking what is mine. Am I clear"?

She pushed me back and then precedes to stare me down. I am normally not confrontational, but she has stepped on my toes for the last time. How dare she think she can talk to me that way when I have not done a damn thing wrong. "I know you may be use to throwing some threats around and people listening but I do not care for you or what you have to say." I take a few steps closer to her and look her square in the eye. "I can promise you, I want nothing to do with whatever this is, but if you want to keep Axel, you better start acting like you have him in the first place." The click of my heels sounds so much louder than they should as I walk away from whatever the hell she is doing.

The bell finally rings and I meet Brina at the Jeep. We get in and decide to blare music on the way to the coffee shop. Some girl time is just what I need to take me away from all the drama with Veronica. I let the wind blow through my hair and try to clear my mind of worry.

I am not even sure how the drama started, honestly. Just hope it ends soon. We pull and I notice that Julia is the only one here. We make our way to the back figuring that would be where Julia is seated. When we all get settled in, I come right out in the open and tell her everything that happened in math. "Julia, I am not sure what is going on with Veronica, but is it always like this?" I watch as she slowly takes a sip of her coffee pondering how to answer my questions.

"Veronica is somewhat of an acquired taste. One that I am unfortunately stuck with." I take this time alone with just Julia and Brina to get some answers I desperately need. "Does that have to do with the business arrangement?" I try to casually act as if it does not interest me. Guess I was not very successful seeing the smirks that are across Julia and Brina's face. "Was that not public knowledge?" I quickly add hoping to not have crossed a boundary.

"No, it is not really a secret just not something that Axel likes people to know about. The deal involves both Axel and Veronica taking over the family business." I mean it makes sense for Axel to inherit the business, but what does Veronica have to do about it?

"Veronica's dad is the principle of the school, but you may not know that he is also an Alpha." Brina chokes on her tea causing drops to fly across the table. "Ew, gross. Put your hand over your mouth when you do that."

"Sorry my dying was an inconvenience, Adalee. I am so touched that you cared that I could not breathe." I pick up the muffin in front of me and act as if I need to dissect its contents. I look at the oats, chocolate, and sugar coating the top. I twist it back and forth trying to process what Julia could be saying.

"I personally don't agree with the arrangement. I don't think we need to combine both areas of land." I hold up my hand to stop her for just a moment. "May I ask a few questions before you continue?" She nods her head and I go ahead with what I wanted to ask. I needed a better picture of everything to not be so lost in what she was trying to explain. "So how much territory does your father own? How much does Allen own?" She chuckles nervously as if biding time to make sure she does not give too much information away.

"In our territory we have a little over eight thousand acres. Most of it starts here and goes up into Canada." Was not expecting that answer. "Axel and my father are actually securing another two thousand this week. Veronica's father has a little over ten thousand acres that stretched towards the south west." So, I can see why most people follow what Veronica says. If she comes from Alpha blood, then she is in line to be the next alpha. One thing about wolves is that they are loyal to their leader.

"Our fathers are using the business as a power move. My father is obsessed with power and he refuses to let anyone come in the way of that goal, unfortunately." I sit back in my chair and try to process what I am hearing. "So, let me get this straight, your father wants power. To achieve that, he needs Allen's pack? Am I following this right?"

Julia looks over and you can see the internal struggle come across her features for a few moments. The way she drags her hand slowly to pick at the edge of the coaster. How she slumps back in her seat and lets out a long sigh. "Yes. I don't agree. I hate it for Axel and the fact that he will be stuck having to deal with that bitch. He deserves happiness, he deserves his mate."

I start to try and process the information shared. It makes me wonder if that is why Axel has been harsh most of the time I see him. "Julia, can I ask when they decided to make this business arrangement?" She looks at me as if wondering why I cared to know. "Um, I think they signed the contract a few days before school started. Why do you ask?" The feeling my gut gets is one that is heavy with sadness at the thought of Axel having to manage all of that.

"Oh, no reason. Just curiosity I guess." She gives me a look like she wants to question but decides to not press me much further. I sit back thinking that maybe that was what was wrong with Axel the day I met him. Maybe he felt backed into a corner. I still do not understand how that can be done; how can a father do that to a son? How can a father place that kind of stress on their child? I guess I will never know seeing as I am not in his shoes.

I wish I could leave it alone. I need to hear out loud the thoughts racing through my head. "So, when you say they are going to merge the packs, that means Axel will be with Veronica. Not just as business partners, but married?" My palms become sweaty as I watch the clock in my peripherals waiting on Julia to answer. "Unfortunately, in Wolf law if one chooses to not find his destined mate, you can have a chosen mate. Most packs look down on this for the very reason my father is pursuing it. It is a move for control and power and nothing more." I just slowly nod my head back and forth as I process that information.

"Is there anyway Axel can get out of it?" Brina again chokes on her tea. "Brina, I think you need to watch how fast you drink that or you might not be here tomorrow." She sticks her tongue out at me and that causes Julia to light up some with a small chuckle. "Once the contract is signed, Axel has a hundred days to find his mate. That is the only thing that would cause the contract to become void if he wants." This time I spit my coffee all over the table. Geez Louise.

"Why would he not want to break the contract?" Unknown anger seething in my voice. "You know Adalee, I thought I knew my brother. The hopeless romantic who has talked about finding his mate for years. Yet, I am not sure he would go against our father." Defeat. Defeat is all I hear coming from her. What could Axel's father hold over him that would make him go along with such a ridiculous notion?

Chapter 17

We finish our coffee in silence, hug Julia, and head back to the house. Brina goes for her nightly run and I decided to go up to my room. I sit on my bed and decided to attempt to close my eyes hoping sleep finds me soon. I still felt a little out of it from Mrs. Eva's tea. It was not long before I gave into the darkness.

Welcoming it to overcome my senses. I fall into a slumber with a smile across my face. As much as I wished to have a peaceful night's sleep, my mind thought otherwise. Over the last week I have almost become familiar with the forest and ice blue eyes that watch me as I dream. I slowly start to panic as I feel a growing need to see the forest. Unsure of what danger or peace could be waiting for me.

It gives me a feeling of belonging, even though I am surrounded by endless trees in my dream. This time, my mind takes on a different route. I am in a clearing and not in the forest like normal. Sadness creeps into my soul and I try to fight back the urge to wake myself up. Fear rearing its ugly head deep in my soul.

As I look around at my surroundings, I notice the clearing holds a small pond. I think back to the area a few miles from my house that Brina and I run to sometimes. This clearing, although it is similar, has subtle differences. The main one being how I feel completely at ease. I walk towards the huge pond in the center and out onto the dock. Something in me is trusting to walk the rickety planks hoping I do not fall through. I know it is just a dream, but sometimes I feel like if I get a scrape during my dream, I can feel it once I wake up. I was unsure of what it would feel like to have my foot go through one of those boards.

I sit down at the end of the dock and dangle my legs in the water. I am not a huge fan of water. How can you enjoy something when you cannot see what is under the surface? Looking up into the sky I notice the moon is large and seems to shine with a brightness that is unique in itself. I hear a rustling in the leaves behind me and I do not even need to turn around.

My body has grown accustom to this part of my dream. My heart no longer races when I hear those sounds. I know what is coming. If I were to look back at the edge of the tree line behind me, I would see a pair of ice blue eyes. Eyes that look like winter. Usually, the smell of cinnamon and pine seems to linger. I think it is because those are the smells I associate with calmness. That smell in particular is what draws me into Axel, regardless of how much I want to run in the other direction.

Winter is my happy place. I used to dream of nothing but winter nights when we moved. It has always been my constant. I would dream about ice skating and Christmas trees. I would have visions of drinking hot chocolate with whipped cream and cinnamon on top while I sat by a fire. I would dream of Brina and I making snowmen and having snowball fights. I would dream of warm coats and soft scarfs. Winter has always held a special place in my heart.

If I concentrate hard enough I can small the fresh snow. Feel the wool from my scarf and gloves. The sting present in my lungs as I inhale the cold night's air. I can feel the way a snowflake melts on my nose. If I think hard enough, I can almost make that place come to life.

Brina loved when we moved to states that did not have a winter. I always felt like I was missing a part of me when someone would say winter for them was the sun shining and sixty degrees out. Texas was a great example of how on Christmas Day, we were outside in short sleeved shirts and sandals. I want the large coats and thick fleece hats. I want to see my breath in the cold night air as I sit on the front porch wrapped in fifteen blankets. I wanted winter. I wanted the smell of cinnamon and pine.

As my thoughts turn back to what is in front of me, I cannot help but wonder why this person or animal comes to see me. I like to think they are guarding me after my last dream, but I am not sure what they really want. I normally do not speak to the eyes that seem to watch my every move. Maybe I should? Would that make me crazy? Something about tonight seems different though. It feels different. I have a serenity that has washed over me, and it feels nice to be able to forget about what is going on outside of my own little world.

"I don't know who you are, but I appreciate you. More than you will know." Nothing comes back to me as a reply. I am not sure why I expected to hear anything back. "You know, I am not sure why you are here, but you give me peace regardless of your reasonings." I shift to sit on the dock. Feeling the raw and exposed wood scratch at the back of my legs.

"My life outside of here is becoming more complicated than what I would like it to be and I thank you for not making this the same way. Maybe one night you will allow me to get close enough to see who my saving grace is in the chaotic storm of a life I live outside." I hear nothing and go back to letting my legs dangle in the water. Silently patting my back for putting myself out there.

I lay down on the dock with my back against the warped wood and look into the night sky. My mind starts to wander and race around like a train off its tracks. "Do you ever watch the stars?" Still silence. I notice the clouds start to shift and I feel myself missing my father. I feel myself really urning for him and not just the idea of him. It feels different than before.

I roll over to my side and pull my knees up to my chest. My back is turned away from the water and away from the ice blue eyes.

I feel myself trying to cry. Anger rises up at myself for not being able to picture my father. I want to invasion his face. Thunder booms and lightning strikes are heard miles away.

I let the tears fall after trying to fight with them, giving up all together. Who will see me cry in my own dream? I begin to feel totally at peace with the way I am ugly crying at the moment. I am lost in my tears and staring at the water when I hear shuffling. I do not care at this point. I just continue to allow the water to come down with steady streams across my cheeks.

After several minutes I hear the creak of the boards on the dock. "You can come closer. Although I have no desire to see you at this point in time." I hear a soft whimper from behind me. I am a little taken back that the creature seems to understand me. I wait for a few moments and hear another whimper, this one sounding closer than the last.

It was a soft almost puppy-like whimper and I feel my heart drop out of my chest. The amount of sadness it held brought my tears to fall even faster. Why do I have to be so emotional right now? I'm not sure why, but thinking of some poor little puppy made my heart break even more.

I continue to lay in this position even though every ounce of my being wanted to turn around once I heard the wolf behind me whine. Every bit of me who just moments ago that couldn't care less is now fighting to keep my word of not turning around and throw my arms around the neck of the beast behind me.

The creature continues to come closer and finally I can feel its breath on the back of my neck. The moment I feel the hot rush of air my body breaks out in shivers and goosebumps. I do not dare turn around with him being so close. My heart rate picks up, not from fear but from anticipation. My breath catches in the back of my throat and the eagerness I feel has me almost squirming.

"Okay, I am not going to turn around, but I am going to put my hand up. I don't want to startle you." I sure am hoping this creature can understand me. I place my right hand up with the palm facing my back and just wait. After what seems like an eternity, I feel the softest fur I have ever felt in my entire life. It feels what I imagine a cloud would feel like if you could lay on one. After several minutes of allowing the creature to nuzzle my palm I place my hand back down and shift my position. The creature lets out a low warning growl as if they think I am going to turn around and catch them.

I roll my eyes at this, "Don't get all worked up. I am just shifting my hip off of the board a little." I notice the boards shift and suddenly feel him lay down beside me and it lets out what seems like a sigh of content. Do animals have all of these emotions? Not sure if they do in real life, but in my dream, I guess they do. I feel tiny curled up next to this wolf. A massive wolf. I feel at home. I feel okay with the world.

After what felt like hours laying on the pier and having one sided conversation the next thing I know is I close my eyes and open them to see a figure jumping on my bed. My body reacted as I turn over and land a kick to the mystery person's side. I hear a thud and look down to see Brina clutching her side. "Well good morning to you too, Ads. What was that for?" I look down at her and just bust out laughing. I could not help it.

"When will you learn to not startle me awake?" The sight of her looked hilarious as she gets to her feet, "That's an extra mile, just so you know. We'll be doing six miles this morning". She is such a party pooper. We get up and do our normal routine. I did not bother to ask her about what I should say to Axel. I personally decided that I would not worry with it until he got back in from his business trip. Now to just get through the next two weeks of school.

During school nothing exciting happens, thankfully. Veronica leaves me alone to an extent. School consists of going to class and then Brina and I meeting Julia after school for the next two weeks. We all seem to become super close as we continue to make preparations for the afterparty that is happening at the Anderson's.

As Julia and Brina discuss the details, I find myself thinking back to my dreams. Is it possible to have your dreams and nightmares intertwine? I have a feeling that everything is about to change and not for the best. Well, they always say your eighteenth birthday is a big one. Let's hope tomorrow brings new beginnings.

Chapter 18

Brina and I spend the day like we normally do for our birthday celebration. We get takeout and spend the day laying around watching our favorite movies. Brina has a soft spot for the early 2000's chick flicks. I prefer action movies, so we usually rotate which genera we decide to watch for the day. After about five movies, we finally decide to get ready. I text Julia and let her know we are getting ready and will be headed to the bonfire around seven. I sigh as my palms start to sweat, and the knots are back in my stomach. I guess the night will happen regardless.

I am normally not a very social person, but I promised Brina that I would try this year. I somewhat regret allowing her to talk me into going to this bonfire to begin with. I am slightly curious on what it will be like in regard to finally getting to have some fun. It is our birthday after all, which is not something I usually celebrate in a big manor since my father's death. I appreciate just chilling at the house and vegging out while Brina and I have a movie marathon.

"You need to clean your mirror. How do I know if I look good if I can't see myself?" In typical Brina fashion, she breaks my inner dialog. "OMG girl. You look prettier than a cactus flower. You look better than a tall drink of water." She gushes in her overly thick southern accent which makes me respond with a huge eye roll.

"I look pretty great, huh?" I was really feeling myself and she just grabs my arm and hauls me down the stairs. Brina has the largest smile on her face and it warms my heart that we are back to being close and the feeling of secrets is gone. We stop before we head out and look for mom, who is usually in the kitchen at this time either cooking or at the table doing work of some sort.

"Momma dear, we want to show you how amazing your daughters look before we go to the bonfire!" Brina yells out sweetly. I could not help but double over in laughter. Brina gives me side eyes and I can just hear the bless your heart she is saying in her head.

Mom makes her way out from the study that is off of the living room. When she rounds the corner, she looks us up and down and almost stops in her tracks with a look of pure surprise. The kind that her eyes might pop out of her head. She hugs us both quietly telling me, "I know today is a special day for you. Enjoy your night. I love you, my sweetheart."

I pull back, catching how she drew out our hug, but before I could ask why she pulls me in again. "Remember that whatever comes your way to take it head on and you will always succeed." She looks me up and down and then turns away, but before we can go out the door, she throws us one more piece of advice. "Brina, makes sure you take care of her. Also, Adalee the silver body suit really looks good on you." I pull out my phone and text Julia, Elizabeth, and Laura that we are on our way as we go running through the door.

When we pull up to the school, the sun is just starting to set. The night has a crispness to the air and I can smell the smoke from the parking lot. The bonfire is set up at the back of the school in an open area. The fire is huge. It stands almost to the second story. I can feel the heat as the flames come into view. I look around and take in the crowd of people. Most of the school seemed to show up in attendance. There was music blaring and people dancing with drinks in hand, chatting in large groups.

As we are walking towards the bonfire, I call Julia and she does not answer. We decide to just walk through the crowd, we will find her at some point. There are so many people that after some time, I accidently get separated from Brina. No big deal, I will continue to walk the same way I was going and occasionally call her name. But I still cannot seem to spot her.

I start to feel claustrophobic as I try to navigate through the sea of people. Pushing through becomes harder and harder causing me to start panicking. I start to slowly push air in front of me with each step I take, hoping to help separate the crowd some. It seems to do the trick and I finally make it to an open space. My lungs thank me as I bend over placing my hands on my knees.

I will attempt to call Brina. What does she do? Not answer my call. I start to call Julia. No answer from Julia either. I text both of them just in case. These girls are working my nerves. I walk a little further away from the crowd so that way when they answer, they can hear me.

I go to start dialing Laura's number when I am shoved from behind. I stumble a little bit but catch myself before I fall face first into the dirt. I turn around to see who the hell just shoved me. I am met with a jock type guy who I have never seen before. He stands at about six feet four inches, has a thick muscular build and skin so pale it is almost translucent. His eyes are so dark they look almost black and he has dark circles underneath them. He is pretty good looking, but I would not tell him that with the way he just shoved into me.

As I look at him, speechless, a super creepy grin comes across his face. "I am sorry. Don't know what came over me. Where are my manners? Must have tripped. Any who... where is that cute little blonde you normally hang out with?" He casually asks. I am hesitant to answer, but he did apologize for bumping into me just a second ago. "I think you are talking about Brina. Do I know you?"

"No, you don't. Your loss really." I start to step back to get a little bit of space between us. I'm not too fond of a vampire being so close, they tend to lose their cool. Maybe some distraction. "I just stepped out here to make a phone call. I didn't catch your name?" He does not respond, but instead keeps taking slow steps in my direction until my back is up against the tree.

He puts his arms on either side of me and leans super close into my ear. His voice comes out barely above a hiss. "So, you're telling me a beautiful girl like you came over here without any friends nearby?" You know I might have taken the compliment and run with it if he wasn't so offensive. "Excuse me. I can handle myself."

"Did not they teach you anything about what goes bump in the night? I would think a poor, helpless girl like yourself would take more caution." His grin widens and I cannot help but stare into his eyes. Almost feeling hypnotized by the obsidian that seemed to swirl like a lake. He lets out a deathly laugh and grabs ahold of my arm where I feel a pinch and starts dragging me towards the forest.

"What the hell was that?" I let out the loudest scream I can. "Let go of me." Useless with how loud the crowd and music have become. I know my friends had to have noticed I was missing by now. I swear it has been thirty minutes. I look around and start trying to get out of the grip of whoever this guy is. I start to chant hoping to melt his face off. He has an iron hold on my arm, and I am pretty sure there will be a massive bruise in the shape of his hand tomorrow.

Nothing is happening with my chanting. I start to try and manipulate the weather. Zero movement. He continues dragging me along, letting out a chuckle here and there. "You know, Adalee, I like my prey to be feisty. Your magic won't save you this time." My blood runs cold. How does he know my name and what does he mean prey?

All of a sudden, I hear a low growl coming from the trees directly in front of where I am being dragged. I take the distraction and kick my body away using his abdomen as my push off point. He never flinches and all I do is hurt my arm even more. I look towards the darkness and shudder.

The mystery guy stops walking, pulls me close to him, and wraps his arm around my waist, pinning my arms to my side. I can taste the bile at the back of my throat. The guy leans in and gives my forehead a kiss while holding me uncomfortably close. The hairs on my neck stand tall and I feel a flutter in my heart. This is it. I am going to die, and if it is not from the guy who still has a hold on me, it will be because my heart gives out.

"Why don't you come out and join the party? I was just about to have a little fun Anderson." Hearing that Axel is in front of me gives me a newfound courage. I take my mouth and bit down on his arm. Rock hard. Pretty sure I now have messed up my teeth. "That does no good sweetie." The way he whispers into my ear makes me want to hurl.

"I have heard you like to have fun sometimes too. At least that is what Veronica says. Who knows how true that really is?" The mystery guy who is still clenching onto my arm yells into the darkness. After what seems like an eternity of silence and anticipation, a figure starts to emerge from the blackness and my heart sinks when I can make out who it is that stands before me. It is none other than Axel Anderson, dressed in dark washed jeans and a black t-shirt. A cold air sweeps over me and he looks as good as the devil himself.

He looks me up and down and I notice that his eyes seem to glow. I lose my breath. They are so hauntingly beautiful. I continue to stare and plead into them as if my life depends on it. In reality my life rests in his hands.

I hear this small voice in the far depths of my mind telling me calmly, to trust him. Shaking my head, I quickly shove those thoughts out and focus on what he is going to say to the mystery guy. "So, Anderson, are you just going to stand there or are you going to get out of my way?" I wait for a reply. He can't really be contemplating him taking me, can he?

"I think you need to let my friend go before you end up dead." I can see him visibly shaking. "You think you can stop me, Anderson? Why don't you go ahead and try?" Before the guy holding me could get out a full laugh, I was being dropped and Axel has this guy by his throat up against a tree. His feet were lifted off of the ground and flailing around as he attempted to make contact with Axel.

I notice the more he struggled, the harder it was for him to breathe. He draws blood while clawing at Axel in an attempt to break his hold. Axel looks over at me and then back to the guy and I cannot help but melt under the intensity of his quick gaze. I feel like putty.

I get to my feet and I slowly make my way to Axel, cautiously placing my hand on his shoulder. His body relaxes to my touch and I feel a small streak of sparks under my skin. I remove my hand in shock, but my body wants more. It feels cold without the sparks. I quickly shake away the feeling and manage to squeak out a response to Axel.

"Axel. It is okay. Just let him go. Look, you do not need to get in trouble over me. You do not even like me. I appreciate you helping me, but I think this guy learned his lesson." He looks over his shoulder at me and his expression softened. He looks like someone who lost their best friend. The sadness makes my heart break. "Adalee, are you okay? Did he hurt you in any way?" He turns back to the guy still in his death grip. "I will kill him if he hurt you, I do not care who he is related to."

The fury in his voice making me back away slightly. Would Axel be capable of such a horrendous act of violence? The questions shocked me to an extent. I am speechless. How do I answer that question when all I can see is Axel killing the guy in front of us and walking off?

Axel starts to look me up and down and that is when he notices I am holding my arm in the same spot the guy had his grip. Axel whips his head so fast that I almost didn't notice it turn back around and lets out a deep growly sound saying, "If you ever think to touch or even look at what is mine, I will kill you Demetri. Do you understand me? I will not lose her. I do not care who you are related too." His tone screamed danger.

Did he just say mine? "Axel just let him go. I am fine. I do not want you in trouble over me. Please." I say one more time with all the pleading I could manage. I find the strength to get close to him and try placing my hand back on his shoulder. He drops Demetri and when he looks back at me it is nothing but rage.

I turn around to run back to the crowd. He terrified me with the look in his eye. I feel myself stumble over a large stick and know I am about to land on my face. I close my eyes, waiting for the impact but instead of hitting the dirt I land in warm arms. The smell of cinnamon and pine trees hit my nose and it makes me feel warm and cozy like being by the fire in the winter with my mom's special hot chocolate. "Adalee. Please stop. He won't hurt you."

I open my eyes and see Axel's bright, icy blue eyes shining even brighter than before. They are mesmerizing and remind me of the way light shines through icicles. He looks at me with nothing but a look of pure vulnerability running deep. "I wasn't running from Demetri, I was running from you."

I reach to place my hand on his cheek and before I can reach, his expression hardens. He sets me down on the ground and then quickly takes off walking. I practically have to run in order to catch up. I grab him by the arm and pull to stop him. "Look, I appreciate what you did for me. I do, but the Axel I just saw is not one I ever want to see again." When he turns around and I notice his eyes are back to their normal shade of blue.

"Explain to me what you meant to not touch what is yours?" I want him to say it. I need him to say it again. "Adalee. It was nothing. The adrenaline must have had you hearing things." It shatters. My heart slowly breaks into a thousand pieces as I listen to him once again pulling me in and the pushing me away.

As I turn around and walk off, he grabs my wrist. "Last time I checked you had a girlfriend named Veronica. Keep the mind games to yourself. I will not be played with like some doll, Axel." Before I could finish my rant, he snakes his arm around my waist and pulls me into a hug. He buries his nose in my neck and sighs.

"Did you know you smell like roses and rainwater? Reminds me of spring. Such warmth to such coldness."

I jump out of his arms and when I do it is like he realized that what he just did was a mistake, and it pisses me off even more. "Don't you dare give me that look like you did something that was wrong, like I have something wrong with me." I think back to every time we get close and he shuts down.

"I am tired of this. You wanted to talk. Let us have it out, right here, right now because if you choose to walk away from me this will be the last time." He looks at me and his demeanor turns to mirroring his father. "How dare you question me? You should be doing nothing but thanking me for saving your ass."

"You don't think I have the right to question being treated the way I have? I don't know who you think you are talking to Axel, but I am not some girl who will just jump because you ask me too." I can see how my words affect him. How they make him clench his fist. How when he takes a few steps towards me, he stomps his feet.

"You do not get it. Forget everything that I have done. You are the whole problem with Veronica and me. You don't even get it and I can't make you get it." The coldness in his voice makes my blood turn to ice. The hate he is spewing is enough to make tears start to form but I won't let them. This will be the last time he ever considers speaking to me this way.

As I walk away, Axel grabs my arm causing me to flinch from the pain Demetri caused. I look at him over my shoulder, but before I could say anything I get pulled into a massive hug. Julia pulls back and looks between me and her brother. "Come on Julia. Let's just get out of here."

"Axel, what in the world is wrong with you? Why do you have to fight everything to the point that it comes crumbling around you?" She looks her brother up and down and all he can respond with is, "How do I chose between what is meant to be and what needs to be?" You can see his body shaking like he is struggling with something internally. He then turns and walks away never looking back.

Brina lets me go and Julia looks me over and demands I tell her what happened. I go into detail about everything, even telling Julia about how her brother acted. When I was describing what happened, her look was almost like she had sympathy for Axel. It is like he is fighting against his nature and I do not understand that at all. He has not even given me a second of his time and then he comes in like prince charming and expects me to just go with his rollercoaster of emotions? What is up with all of that?

Just as I was about to ask Julia if I could talk with her, Carter comes up and says that he pulled the car around. Julia looks directly at me but addresses the group of people who slowly started to gather around. "I figured if you guys wouldn't mind coming to the house a little early and helping me set up for the party, I sure would appreciate it".

Brina and I make our way to the Jeep and once we were out of ear shot from the others, Brina pulls me in for another big hug. "Adalee, I am so sorry about what happened. Take your jacket off and let us see if that ass hat made a mark. I am so sorry we got separated." I took my jacket off expecting there to be a huge bruise when in reality it was just a little red.

"Maybe I was being a little dramatic earlier. I really thought he was going to break my arm." I still feel as if I should have a bigger bruise.

"Brina, why do you think Axel said what he did? About me being his, he has no right to say something like that. All it does is make things confusing." Laying out my confessions to Brina, I expected her to side with me but instead, she gave me a longing look and hopped in the driver's side of the car. I follow suit and hop in the passenger side giving her side eyes the entire time.

"Ads, do you believe in soulmates? Do you think we are destined to have someone that is meant to be ours?" Still not sure where she is going with this, I just nod my head. "I think after tonight you will receive all the answers you have been asking for." Still unsure of why my best friend became very fortune cookie like, but I'll go with it. Maybe this birthday will bring about the air of change.

Chapter 19

After about thirty minutes of us driving and jamming out, we pull up to an iron gate with Anderson written across the middle of it. I call Julia and let her know that we are out front and before I could hang up, the gate automatically opens. Once we pull up to the house, my jaw drops. This place is massive and absolutely gorgeous. We pull up to a circle drive and a guy comes up and states he will park our jeep for us. "Super fancy, Julia never mentioned any of this." I whisper to Brina.

She looks over and just nods her head. The house almost looks out of place in the vast forest that surrounds the area. The house stands three stories tall and the front gives off Victorian mansion vibes with sleek tall columns in all white, while the porch is decorated with multiple sets of patio furniture and porch swings. The front of the house gave off a large modern farmhouse feeling which was odd with most of the house being some kind of woodsy cabin.

We walk up a set of wooden painted steps and arrive at a large set of black doors with huge iron knockers in the middle. "Adalee, do we use these?" I throw my hands up because I have no clue. This place looks like it should be out of a magazine. "Maybe I should call Julia again."

Before Brina could use the knockers, Cameron opens the door like he was waiting on us to arrive. I notice his face instantly lights up when he sees Brina and I cannot help but think maybe he should ask her out. "You sure do look nice in that grey suit, Cam." It would be good for her to do something other than stick by me like glue. I will have to remind myself later to bring the idea up with him once the party starts and Brina is occupied. "Thanks, I am super excited you are here. Let us give you the tour and then we can help Julia with the party, lord knows she needs it." From a faint distance we heard her she spat back. "You jerk. Now hurry up." All Cameron could do was bust out laughing.

We started the tour of the house and in typical Cameron fashion, he made a joke out of everything and told stories about both his family and the Anderson's throughout each new part we came to in the house. "This is where I started a massive food fight." My jaw dropped as I took in each detail of the kitchen which is large enough to cook for hundreds of people.

"Axel and I used to take Julia's mattress and surf down the grand staircase." Watching Cameron talk about his memories made my heart warm. "Julia would kill me for telling this story, but when she started wearing bras, I would hang them on the bannisters from the second and third floors." I laugh knowing that Julia would be stop sign red right now if she knew what we just heard.

He told us about how Carter and Julia got caught by their parents in the theater room on more than one occasion and that his parents like to bring it up at family dinner to embarrass Julia. He told us tons of stories about each person in their group of friends, including Axel, and it made me see each of them in a new light. The way he talked about his parents made me miss my father and wish that I could see mom and dad do the same stunts his parents pull on each of the kids.

The Youngs, which are Cameron's parents, seemed like such a close, laid back couple where the Andersons seems a little more distant and tough. Cameron had a bunch of stories about Axel's mother, but hardly any of his father. It even makes me think Mr. Anderson may be only doing what he feels is right with the whole tough love act.

As he finishes telling us more embarrassing stories, we round the dining hall and come face to face with a wall of large glass windows overlooking the prettiest backyard I have laid eyes on. The wall of windows went all the way from the first floor to the third. Once you walked out of these massive French glass doors, you come to the back porch which was massive itself.

It was a beautiful double deck porch made of] dark rich wood and had trees coming up through the middle in some places with wooden benches that were built in and surrounded the trees. They had beautiful lights strung throughout the backyard with scattered tables. "Do you guys play a lot of sports? That is a nice set of basketball courts by the pool." Brina would notice the courts and not the picturesque flower gardens and arrangement of plants in different sized planters scattered throughout the property. "Yeah, we tend to get really competitive with one another in the pack." Safe to say, it is all absolutely stunning.

"Hey girl, are you going to just stand there or are you going to help me set up all of this food?" Julia's voice brings me back to reality and I notice everyone is kind of just standing their staring at me. "Oh, I am so sorry just trying to figure out why you have never had us over before now!" The smug grin creeping up on Julia's face tells me she does not like to brag. "I like to make sure my friends want to be friends with me before they see where I live and how we live."

I think back to how easy it is to get along with Julia and doubt anyone would not enjoy being in her company. "Now get over here and help me dump all of these chips out." Looking down at hundreds of small bags chips I get to work throwing them into a large metal bucket. "So, where's your brother off too and why is he not helping?" A tinge of anticipation snakes its way into the bottom of my stomach. I question if I am sure I want to know.

"He is up in his office tending to affairs for my father." My mind races thinking about what kind of work he is doing. After chips, we iced all of the drinks and set out all of the other finger foods Julia's chefs prepared. After we were done, I am pretty sure she had ten tables full of food and multiple places with drinks iced down. "Alright, I am going to show the DJ where to set up if you want to grab one more box of cups out of the kitchen."

I make my way through the house attempting to remember where the kitchen is and as I round the corner, I run into Axel. Running into him caught me off guard and I fell backwards. Before I could hit the ground, Axel caught me and held me for just a moment before bringing me to my feet. I am not sure if it was the shock or his arms around me that made me lose my breath.

I look up and all I see is complete sadness in his torn expression. "You should smile. There is a party about to happen after all." I cannot explain it, but I am drawn to be near him. To feel his touch. His touch that feels like fireflies dancing on my skin in a lightning show. I lean in a little closer and he seems to notice. "Why did you have to move back?" Rejection, no matter how many times you face it, never gets easier. He takes a large step backwards and puts some space between us. I understand why, but it does not feel right if I am being truthful.

I take a step closer to him. "You know we really need to talk about things. I don't like how everything went down and I have questions I would like answered." He looks me up and down and then nods his head. He acts like he has to convince himself that this is the right choice. "Adalee. All I seem to do is put you in danger." He seems like he is placed between a rock and hard place. The torn smile he forces looks unnatural on his face.

"I do not understand what you mean by that Axel." I look at him for a few moments. He was still wearing his dark washed jeans and black t-shirt. He looked good in dark colors. His hair was tousled, and it seemed he ran his hands through it periodically. I had so many questions racing through my jumbled mind. "How come every time you play with fire you end up burned?"

His question causes me to cock my head sideways. "What?" The hand of his that seemed to sneak its way up to play with my hair drops to his side. "Axel, you really are not making any sense. Just say whatever it is you need to say and stop speaking in riddles." The color flashes in his eyes while his feet shuffle backwards like they carry the weight of the world.

Chapter 20

I find the massive box of solo cups and carry them outside. When I get done placing the cups where Julia wanted them, I start looking for Brina. I walk around the massive backyard for a little while and finally find her and Cameron talking on a bench by the pool. She looked so happy in that moment and I hated to ruin it for her, so I slowly walked back to where people were starting to gather.

The DJ had started playing music and I decided to get myself a drink. I get my drink from a giant drink dispenser. "You know that's spiked, right?" A tall guy comes out from the shadows on the porch and proceeds to take my glass from me. Once he is finished filling it up, he hands it back to me. The moment my skin made contact with his I got a bad feeling. "Well I guess there is a first time for everything."

"You should really watch who you fall in love with, Adalee." The moment this guy spoke my name I realized I was in trouble. "How do you know my name?" I shiver as his crackled laugh seems to echo in my soul. "The how is not important. It is the why that you should be curious about." I start taking steps backwards realizing just how far everyone seems to be.

Can I turn and shout? Will they get to me in time? Do I blast him with magic and risk exposure? I attempt to keep him talking while I devise a plan to escape. "So, since you know my name, can I know yours?" His contorted smile made me believe that he was not going to answer my question. "Just know the council is watching you, Adalee. Not everyone is your friend." With that sinister sentence he takes his long slender fingers and snaps. He is gone before my eyes.

"What the hell." Is all I can say or think. Who was that guy? After a few moments, Julia shows up beside me. "Enjoying the view of that bush?" My laugh comes out a little breathless and nervous as the last sentence from the mysterious man repeats in my mind. "You know I love to throw a good party, but I don't care to partake in the action. Seems a little backwards right?" I look at her sideways and cannot help but wonder if I should tell her about what just happened.

Julia pulls my attention back to her by grabbing me and hauling me into the house and taking me to her room. On the way up, she fills me in on what we are doing. "Alright Adalee, I want to give you your birthday present. I spent hours trying to pick out the right thing." The way Julia's love is shown makes all worries disappear from my core. "We only have an hour or so until your official birthday starts after all!"

We finally reach her room and she proceed to look through a series of drawers in her dresser. "Gah, Ads give me a second. I know I hid it around here somewhere. My brother tend to snoop." I chuckle a little at her and have a hard time seeing Axel wanting to pry though anything. "You know he comes by it honestly. My father cannot help but meddle in my business." It does not surprise me that Mr. Anderson likes to snoop.

After a few moments and choice curse words from Julia, she finally finds a small silver box. She hands it to me and grins like a little kid on Christmas. "This is always my favorite part of giving gifts. The reaction is always the best, so do not disappoint me okay?" I suddenly feel like I have huge shoes to fill with how I react.

I look at the small silver box and hesitantly pull apart the bow on the top. "You know Adalee, I did the packaging all by myself!" Julia beamed with pride as she spoke about the tiny little silver box. "The wrapping paper is almost to pretty to rip!" She did a beautiful job on the presentation. I pull off the lid and remove the tissue paper from inside. My mouth drops when I pull out a stunning charm bracelet. It is made of a thin silver, making it have a delicate feeling. I hold it up and look at the charms picked out, there are three. There is a rose, a crescent moon, and lastly a wolf in a howling position.

I look at her and tears start to form as she comes over and pulls me into a hug. "Julia, I don't know how to thank you. This is all too much. It really is beautiful." She looks at me and her smile grows exponentially, if that was even possible. "So, I picked the rose because of your last name. I picked the moon because of the silver in your eyes and I picked the wolf because I have made you a member of my own little pack?" She holds up her wrist and reveals a charm bracelet identical to mine, except it only has the wolf charm dangling from the dainty silver. "Brina has one too."

"You truly have become one of my best friends and for that I am forever grateful." I pull her into a hug once more. I notice her clock on the nightstand and realize how late it has gotten. "Hey, do you think you could show me to your brother's office? We were supposed to meet to talk about a few things." Julia looks at me kind of confused at first and then nods her head.

She walks me to the other end of the house and stops about fifteen feet from the closed office door. "It is the door right at the end there. I am not sure if he is in there." I look back at the door and then back at Julia. The wink and smile she gave me made my cheeks burn a deeper red than a rose. I was still shy about my feelings towards Axel and knowing that Julia had picked up on them made me blush badly.

"Julia, are you sure about just walking in?" She looks at me and a slight sadness replaces what was just the playful glint in her eyes. "Undoubtably." Julia then proceeds to push me to the door before she walks back to the party. "Oh, and Adalee, have fun and tell me all about it in the morning." Cue the major blushing once again.

I walk up to the door and stand there for a few moments. Attempting to take my face from maroon to my normal pale, pink tint. Thanks to Julia, I had to work extra hard. Do I knock or just open it? What is the proper thing to do in a situation like this? A situation where I am not sure what is really going to happen.

Axel one moment saves me and seems to show interest in me, then the next, I turn around and he is running in the other direction. I am hoping to get to the bottom of not only my feelings, but his as well. I sit for just a few minutes and attempt to gather up enough courage. I have never had a guy affect me in this manner. I do not really know how to act around him, I tend to turn into a hot melting mess. Brina would say, "You are melting hotter than a popsicle on a hot Texas day. At least popsicles taste even better melted."

Usually, a slow groan escapes my lips when she says things in that way. I go back to my internal struggle of opening the door or knocking. I decided to just go with my gut and turn the handle and let the door swing open. When it stops about halfway, I felt it was a good time to casually state out in the air, "Hey Axel, are you here? Julia said to just come on in."

At first it takes a little bit for my eyes to adjust due to the hallway being so bright and the office being dark. My ears pick up on the shuffling that seems to be happening in the dim lighting, so someone is in here. After feeling like a total creep, I decided I should open the door more to make sure I was not missing him sitting at his desk.

I was expecting to find no one in the office because no one answered when I announced my presence. I figured my ears were playing tricks on me. I take a few steps in and once the door is completely opened, I stand there staring, not being able to move. It feels like my heart got hit by a bullet.

I see Veronica, half-naked on top of Axel's desk with her legs spread to either side while she pulled at his tie with one hand and ran her fingers through his hair with the other. He does not notice me but why would he? This answers all of my questions about how he feels. I sit there stunned for a minute or two just watching them. Anger, hurt, and betrayal hit me in waves. One after another, my emotions rage like a storm, building, and building until I knew they would break the dam.

I held my hand up to knock a little louder on the door and put on my best smirk. He was not going to make me look like a fool. Brina always likes to say, "Hell hath no fury like a woman scorned." Right now, I was over the way Axel seemed to constantly be degrading me. Axel and Veronica were so entangled with each other they still had no clue I was in the room.

I took the opportunity to lean up against a bookshelf waiting just a few seconds to think of what the hell I was going to do next. A thought hit me and the only smooth remark I could think of to say was, "I see where I stand." I muster up all of the confidence and authority I could and was pretty proud of how my voice did not break when my insides were shaking.

The moment I started to speak, Axel jumped and started to shove Veronica back, but he did not try hard enough. She had a death grip on him, "Did you want to see the show?" Veronica slurred at me and I laughed. I gave it the most cynical laugh and replied simply back to Axel more than Veronica. Never taking my eyes off of his. I wanted him to see how serious I was and to see the look of regret flash across his eyes. "Don't worry, all I see is a cheap homemade movie in the making."

I continued to stare and could not bring myself to stop. I am not sure what I really wanted to see from Axel. Part of me wanted to make him mad at the indifference I tried to sell. To see him hurt for being caught doing something that seemed to be very wrong. Part of me wanted him to come after me and say it was all a misunderstanding while he begged for my forgiveness. I wanted him to throw Veronica on the floor and never look back.

Not sure why I thought the last option should be considered. When I really think about it, I was nothing more than someone who happened to be in the wrong place at the wrong time. Axel probably saw me as some damsel in distress. I was just some pathetic girl who needed saving. As I thought about how ridiculous Axel had made me feel over and over and over again when it came to Veronica I shouldn't be surprised.

I really should be apologizing for coming between two people. I know I was not the only one, Axel had done his fair share of leading me on in ways I would not think would be appropriate if he was dating Veronica. Had Axel really led me on? I would like to believe that I had not made up everything that has happened over the last several weeks.

As Axel and I still continued to stare at one another, I was silently begging for some kind of emotion. He was as cold as ice. His expression was hard as stone. This reaction floored me, and I know he could tell. I was fuming with anger and rage. If I had been in a cartoon, steam would have come from my ears. I turn abruptly on my heels and march down the stairs with my head held high.

The further away I got, the more pissed I become at Axel. He made me look like a fool, like he wasn't the one who wanted to talk. Like he wasn't the one who always showed up like I needed him. Once I had gotten out of ear shot from the office, I could not help but suddenly let all of my anger out and I screamed at the top of my lungs. Sparks flew as the lights busted above me and glass shattered. I did not care why or how that happened, all I knew was I needed fresh air. I needed to get away for the toxic energy that I felt consuming me.

Chapter 21

I cannot help but feel like he should be mine. I cannot help but feel like we are one when I look at him. It also hurts me knowing that I know Veronica's secret and he does not have a clue. I make it back to the party and the first thing that catches my eye is that group of guys that I asked Julia about earlier in the night. They are on the other side of the party so I casually make my way over, not sure what I would really do if I approached any of the guys.

They had a different air about them that drew me in a little. Not in the way I was drawn to Axel, but I wanted to know why they seemed different. It also helped that they were incredibly hot, and I wanted a distraction. I continue to make my way over in that direction and I stop halfway through the crowd. This is not me, what am I doing?

I have never once thought about taking out my frustration with some random guy. I was not raised that way. Axel has a way of getting under my skin and I am not sure what to do about it, but I know one thing. This is not the answer. I stand looking around at the people dancing and I suddenly feel super alone. I look up and try to steadily blink back tears. I turn my back towards the house and begin walking, unsure of where my destination was.

I catch myself walking around the backyard and then I turn my attention to the forest that stands in front of me. I start walking a little faster than before and I take off not caring about anything in the moment. I push past some people who were a little way from the party in small groups and get dirty looks. I halfway mutter an apology even though I do not really care.

I feel suffocated and my anxiety starts to spike. A sudden gust of wind comes from behind me that seems to push me faster towards the forest and for once I do not fight it. I let the air help guide me from this house and all of these people. The air pushing me helps me realize maybe I am getting close to my breath of fresh air and away from all the negative. I stop for a moment and all I can hear is the rush of wind. It seems to have picked up and I wonder out loud if we are having a storm roll in the area. I shake the thought out of my head and start to get my feet moving forward. After a few moments I am standing at the edge of the forest and looking back at the party, everyone seems to be enjoying themselves.

I look around a few minutes more when I notice Axel come busting out of the door looking around desperately. He is walking around and talking to different people quickly before moving on to the next group. I do not really understand why he is looking around so frantically, but once I see how his clothes are all crinkled and his hair is a mess my heart leaps out of my chest. I feel stinging in my eyes and I refuse to give him that satisfaction of making me cry. I turn on my heels and I do not give him a chance to see me as I take off in the thick woods before.

I stop once I am a good way inside and the silence I hear is inviting. If I listen closely, I can hear the music depending on which way the wind shifts. I still am not far enough away. I start to take a step forward. Why am I going towards something that looks as if it will swallow me whole? The darkness, as eerie as it seems, pulls me in like the tide of the ocean. Back to safety and into the unknown.

I consider turning around and going back to the party. The wind comes up from behind me. It pushes me forward once again. My movement causes birds to come rushing near me, beckoning me with a warning to not move. Not sure how the wind can push me with such a force. The forest is so thick I can have a hard time pushing through the underbrush. It is like I am compelled to not listen, my feet shifting even though in the back of my mind, I know that it is not a good idea. I feel a sense of déjà vu.

As I make my way deeper into the trees, I notice that I have no idea where I am going. My body seems to work on autopilot. Like it is normal for me to go for a walk through the forest at almost midnight. Yay for me, I am spending my birthday alone in the woods, probably lost. I shrug my shoulders and keep on going. Yet, where am I going? I am not sure. All I know is that I need to put distance between myself and Axel. A feeling of dread with a handful of knots form at the pit of my stomach and I push down the urge to throw up.

Why does he make me feel this way? The hairs on the back of my neck stand tall and goosebumps raise along my arms. Before I know what my own body will do, I take off into a dead sprint. Running. Faster than I thought humanly possible. I do not stop and mentally thank Brina for making me run all of those mornings when she knows I hate it. I push past trees and underbrush, not caring that my clothes were being ripped. My arms and legs feel like they have been torn to shreds. The stinging in my skin begging me to stop, if only for a moment. Do you think I listen? I run for what seems like miles when my body betrays me and stops suddenly. I double over and fling my hands above my head trying to catch my breath.

While I am doubled over, I listen and hear nothing but stillness. I compel my body to take me forward, regardless of how my legs feel and my lungs beg me to stop. I walk for what seems like an hour with my hands above my head. I notice the further I go inward, the thinner the trees become and it makes it a little easier to put distance between me and the Anderson's house.

After what feels like another mile of walking, I come to a clearing. I look around and suck in my breath. It is the clearing from my dream. I rub my eyes and blink a few times knowing this cannot be real. Did I fall asleep at the party and dream all of this up? There is no way that this is what has happened. I would have known I had fallen asleep. I know I did not drink any spiked punch, so that is not it. I pull out my phone to see if I get service, nope, but I notice the time and sure enough it is about ten minutes from my eighteenth birthday. What a way to spend it. It could be worse, I guess.

I walk toward the pond and feel comfort in my surroundings as it creeps into my bones. I look up to the moon, it is not shinning as brightly as it does in my dreams, but it does have a nice glow to it. I make my way to the pier and pray it is sturdy. The pier holds up and I let my feet dangle in the water. The cool black of the water feels almost surreal. I close my eyes and attempt to calm my racing mind, but it does not last long. I feel a familiar presence behind me. "You can come out. I don't bite, although you might." I hear the rustling of brush and the thud of paws on the ground which I expected. What I do not expect is to hear those thuds soften and start sounding like footsteps.

I freeze, who could have followed me out into the woods this far? Did I piss off someone from the pack? Did I mistake the sound of a person for the sound of an animal because in my dreams that is who comes to visit? I swear it sounded like paws, yet it could not be paws. I must have misheard, and I must be wishing I were in my dream. That would be better than any place at this moment. I like to think of it as guarding me, as a protector of my dreams. I know it seems a little silly, but a girl can make her dream anything she wants.

I turn my attention back to whoever is behind me and walking towards my direction. I should be scared, but I am more pissed that someone has come to ruin my birthday. I attempt to push down the anger, yet I cannot seem to do that at this moment. I hear thunder and a flash of lightning dances across the sky. I welcome mother nature in all her glory as I can feel the air changing.

As if the person behind me notices I stiffen, they stop walking. The only sound is of my breath catching in my throat. I hear another few steps and then I almost jump out of my skin when I hear him speak. "Adalee. Are you okay? You worried me when I could not find you at the party." How dare he come looking for me. "I had to track you here and you didn't make it easy." Who gave him that right to come near me after what he did to me?

I do not answer. I refuse to give him that satisfaction. Flames dance along my skin as I feel Axel's hands grip the sides my waist. I am being picked up and turned around to face him. I scream and attempt to push myself backwards. "If I let you go Adalee, you would fall backwards into this pond and I don't think you want that."

The heat that courses through my body as his eyes rake up and down it makes me want to go closer. The inch we are apart seems too far. "Your outfit looks too good for all of that." I look at him stunned at the audacity this man has and cross my arms over my chest. He has a glint of amusement in his eyes and I see nothing funny about this situation. "What you have done is wrong, Axel." The frustration builds and I let out a huge sigh. I turn my head away in an attempt to not feel something for him and he is making that hard.

I can feel the vibrations in the way his muscles move as he takes a few steps back from the end of the pier. I can see in my peripheral how a drop of sweat runs down his chest. I hope he gets a cold seeing as the idiot is in nothing but a pair of black jogger pants. He brings his hands up to my chin and turns my face to look at him. He hurt me and to look into his face as it shows nothing but sincerity brings the stabbing pain in my heart back in full force. His eyes search mine for any information they may give. A worried look comes across his face.

"Don't you dare look at me like you care for me at all, Axel. You clearly have other obligations, and I don't want to get involved." He shakes his head and then goes to caress my cheek with his hand, I cannot help but push him back when I think about him and Veronica. I figured he would fight me pushing back again, but instead he let me break free enough to put some space between us without falling into the pond. "Adalee, please let me explain."

I throw my hands up and let out a sound of annoyance. I walk around him and off the pier. Another flash of lightning dances across the sky. The power in my veins building as my emotions get stronger. I get about four or five steps away and turn around expecting him to be in the same spot he was just in. Yet as I turn around, I basically hit him square in the chest with my elbow and almost get knocked off the pier.

He catches me and my resentment for him replaces the need to be in his arms. Thunder bombs in the sky and the wind starts to pick up. With a wave of my hands, I hit him with a gust of wind powerful enough to allow me the room I need to think. "How dare you do that to me! How dare you act like you care for me or are worried about my wellbeing! You do not have to keep saving me, I am capable of that myself Axel."

"Adalee. Like I said earlier. Let me explain." I cut him off. I start steadily walking and he matches me step by step. Not allowing me to get more than several inches away from him. I would like to think he did not affect me but being this close to him made me want to throw my legs around his waist and have him carry me back to his house. I could not allow my needs to betray the rational side of my brain. I turned away and ran. He caught my wrist and a look of hurt crossed his eyes.

"Do you really not want to be near me, Adalee?" I almost wanted to console him and then I had a flash back of Veronica and I hit him square in the chest. The wind picked up some more and caused my hair to whip around my face. "What do you think? Do you think what we are doing is healthy? Is all of this normal to you?" I pulled it back from my eyes just in time to see the look of shock that crossed his face.

"Adalee, what you saw was not what you think." I throw my hands down and lightning strikes the ground. "Let me explain. Please." Why would I need him to explain? What good will that do now? "You saved me, called me yours, and then walked away. I know I have no right to judge. I have no clue how it is to be in your shoes but let me make this simple for you and let me walk away. You act like you care, but really what is all of this?" Lightning and thunder danced in the sky to my heartbeat. Wild and erratic.

I look at him, really look at him, and all I can think about is Veronica. I hate her. I gesture between us with my hands and he catches my wrists and pulls me close, I hate the way my body reacts to his touch. "Adalee, I don't know what it is that draws me to you. I feel like we are almost like thunder and lightning in the sky. We are meant to coexist. Yet our timing is off, and I am not sure it can or will be fixed."

He looks at me with my wrists still in his hands and he brings my palms up to kiss them. I pull away with all my might. The earth shudders with the thunder overhead and the wind makes me stumble. I back away from him while he stands there allowing me to put some space between us. I think he needed space to think rationally, just as much as I did. "I don't care what you say Axel. What you have done is wrong. You should not treat me this way."

I continue backwards until I feel my back against a tree, I stand there and cross my arms over my chest. "I do not deserve what you have put me through emotionally." He walks up to me slowly and I know I should run or stop him, but my body will not allow what my mind knows is right. "I know, Adalee. I am sorry. When it comes to you all of my rational thoughts are thrown out of the window."

He leans down to my ear and softly whispers. I could hardly hear him due to the rushing of the wind. "I just do not know how to explain what you do to me." He pulls back and I look into his blue eyes, I can tell that he really means what he is saying. My heart drops at the sight of him and I hate that my body betrays me once again by feeling something for him. Yelling is all I can think about right now and I let it out.

"Axel how dare you do this to me once again. I caught you lip locked in an inappropriate way with Veronica and this is what I get? Some half-assed apology from you?" I cannot help it, but I slam my fist into his chest. "You think some vague gesture will work to make all of this okay? You have to choose." Thunder goes off again. "You have been the one that has been back and forth Axel."

My fist makes contact once again and lightning hits the ground. "You are the one that thinks you can hurt me and that I will be right here when you need me to be. I am done Axel." Again, I throw my fist. "I don't want you Axel." He stands there and his face falls as I continue to yell. "I don't need you Axel." Tears fall down my face and a gust of wind hits us. He still just stands there.

"I want you gone and out of my life Axel." I hit him, yet a little less than before. My blows become that of a light tap. My heart shattering at the thought of him walking away for good. Lightning strikes and thunder booms. "Axel, do you even know how foolish you make me feel? You shouldn't do that to someone you care for."

I go to pull my fist up once more and he catches my wrist. He never looks up, but just holds onto my wrists and will not let them go. "You shouldn't do anything you have done to someone you care for, Axel. You have done nothing but play with me." This time to tears come full force. "Adalee. Please don't do this. I can tell you nothing in my life will come between us again."

My knees buckle and I would drop to the ground if it were not for Axel still holding my wrists. He has them pressed to his chest and I feel water hit my hands. I look up and there is no rain. I look back at my hands and notice the water that is continuing to hit my hands. I pull my hands back, but he does not resist me and lets them go. I pull his chin up, yet he will not look at me.

I kick myself mentally for being so harsh and then I realize, I should be, the thought of Veronica fills my minds again. I pick his face up even more. I spit out as harshly as I could, "Axel look at me. I deserve that decency. I deserve the decency of a man who knows what he wants." I had all intentions to chew him out again, but the moment I look into his icy blue eyes, it is as if the world stops.

It feels like I was falling and now I finally have something to hold me up. It feels like when you take the first sip of hot chocolate for the season. It is as if I was surrounded in darkness and now, I see light. Everything around me goes blurry except for him. His eyes are such a vibrant blue that they would make the ocean jealous. With my hand still on his chin, I pull him to me and kiss him just once.

A soft, tender kiss on the lips with the intentions of pulling back. I find myself melting into his touch as he kisses me harder with a passion that burns like a wildfire. After a few moments, I pull back gasping for air and I slowly open my eyes again to look into his. As I look at him and pull him closer to me by the waist the words "Mine. Mate." escap my lips before I could stop them.

The moment I spoke those words it felt like my head got hit by lightning and then my world started to spin. I could halfway make out what he was trying to say and the only thing that stuck out in my mind was, "Adalee, stay with me. Please." Then against everything I had, my knees buckled and my head hit the ground with a thud. Darkness took over my vision.

Chapter 22

Floating. Floating is a feeling that most people feel in a freed state of mind. Nothing tying them down. No problems or worries to weigh on their shoulders. I have always felt most people attempt to get a sense of that when they try to suspend in water. I was never one to dive down and suspend myself in the water like Brina used to do when we would swim. She would take a deep breath and stay down as long as she could while the push and pull of the water swayed her body. My mother loves to float above the water with her arms stretched wide to her side and her head barely above the surface. She always reminded me of a bobber in the water just waiting to go and stay under.

I prefer to stay clear of the water. I do not mind being near water, just the thought of swimming for hours was not something I preferred to do as an activity. I usually sat on the edge and dangled my feet. The water has always given me a feeling of dread and suffocation. The idea of drowning scares me to my core. The thought that you could be mere feet away from someone and slip into the water's depths while not being able to scream for help is terrifying. The feeling of your lungs being filled up with water is not something I would wish to experience ever in this lifetime. I do not think I would wish it upon my worst enemy, or maybe I would?

My mind is so fuzzy, it feels like the static on your radio when it does not work quite right, so you flip between stations. It is as if my body is stuck in no man's land on the radio station. One minute a song is playing and then static takes over. Sometimes two different stations are overlapping, but there is still so much static I cannot make out what is happening.

Usually when this happens on the radio, you tune the knob one direction or another until one of the songs becomes clear. How do I do that now? One minute I feel my body is being carried and the next I feel as if my body being pulled in two directions. Like someone is attempting to pull me up from a ledge. I am dangling with my arms being pulled while gravity takes my lower half.

One minute, I hear the sounds of people's muffled talking and the next it is covered with the rustling of wind, almost like I am near the ocean. The roar of wind drowning out an incomprehensible word, but I know someone out there is speaking. One second, I smell the duskiness of a forest and then there is mixes of sunshine and wildflowers. This battle feels as much of a mental level as it does a physical level. My mind feels like it is being bombarded with thoughts and yet completely blank to whatever is causing the commotion. I feel like I am in this state for days, going in and out. Being pushed and pulled.

It seemed like I was sinking to the bottom of a lake. My body felt like it was swaying back and forth. My mind wanted to give up and just accept the fear that plagues my soul. I struggled mentally and physically in this state of push and pull. My body wanted to push while my mind was pulling in the opposite direction. I struggled with this feeling of hopelessness. I felt like I should scream, but my mouth betrayed me and would not allow even a single sound to call out. Drowning, it gave me a feeling of drowning.

I felt that if I could just open my eyes maybe I could figure out how to leave this feeling. I struggled and attempted to fight, but the feeling only got worse.

I struggled and struggled and still nothing happened. I could tell I was lying flat, but I had no clue where I was at this moment in time. I finally gave up and sat in the silence. "Excuse me. Visiting hours are over. You can come back tomorrow morning." I heard nothing that would act as a reply. I could tell it was my mother. Not sure how I know, but when she grabbed my hand I just did. She did not resist, even though I wish she would have just a little. I could hear her gathering her things and I wish I could scream out loud and keep her beside me. I do not want to be alone. I am scared, scared of the unknown and this is all very unknown.

I am not sure why I am like this. I hate that I feel so lost. Almost in what I imagine is a twilight zone. The last thing I remember was Axel finding me in the woods and then everything goes blank. I know we were arguing and I caused a storm to roll in, but why can't I remember anything after that moment? I was just at the woods what seemed to be moments ago.

I wonder what time it is. It must be super late for visiting hours to be over. Where am I that would need visiting hours? I do not want to be left alone. It was almost midnight the last time I looked at a clock. I heard and felt what would seem like the nurse taking vitals and tidying up the room. After she left, I sat and listened to the clock tick away. Wondering what was going on outside my voided state. What was happening to me?

I was so lost inside my own head, I almost did not sense someone had entered the room. I felt this jolt of electricity run through my hand and up my arm. "Oh Adalee, what have I done? I feel like this is solely my fault. I should have stopped this earlier, regardless of what was expected of me." I was shocked that he came to see me in this state. Then I remember Veronica on top of him at his desk, and him making a fool of me. I shudder at the thought. Anger swirling around me like a thick cloud. Threatening to cut off my air supply.

"Adalee, how am I supposed to show you and make you understand. I am weak without my other half. I found her, I found you, unfortunately, I was too late." What does he mean he found me? I feel like there is something I should be remember. "I should have stood my ground, instead I let things get complicated."

I think to what Axel means to me. I honestly don't know him that well. What I do know is how my body reacts to his. That has to count for something. "Adalee, she is beautiful and compliments everything about me to make me a better man. I am complicated and cold where she is simple and warm. It's like winter and spring." I can feel him grab my hand. The raw emotions that he is showing now makes me frantic to reach out to grab him and never let go. "One is always wished away while the other is always welcomed. She is the one made for me. I know she is, yet I messed things up. I messed things up with you"

It made my heart feel like a piece of stained glass, broken into a thousand pieces. The only hope I had was thinking maybe it will be a beautiful masterpiece once I put it back together. "Gosh Adalee, I don't even know why I am here. I wish I had some indication that you could hear me, even though I should not be saying any of this out loud." Just about the time I was ready to push past everything, he had told me he has to go and say something stupid like that.

"I was given hope on your birthday to have it ripped away. You walked in and everything became unclear. I didn't know what to do, things became complicated." Another shot to the heart. I do not know how much more I could handle of this confession. "My father knows none of this. He would be so disappointed if he knew I messed up like I have already."

The thought that I could be a disappointment booms through the darkness. The weight of those words pushing me down, deep into darkness. "I must fix this. I am supposed to be getting ready to travel to yet another pack meeting in about four days. I do not want to go. I do not feel ready to be handling the weight of this responsibility." He sets my hand down and coldness runs through my veins, leaving me feeling numb.

"I am weak without you by my side and now I don't think you will be next to me again." He sighs, and I cannot help but feel the need to wrap him in a hug. The sincerity and complete transparency are another side of Axel that I have not met yet and really want to know more about. It is not my place to know more however, I am not the one he is talking about in this confession. He had made that clear by saying that he messed things up with me. I know it was not just his fault, I put myself in the equation even though I did not plan on anything of the sort.

Axel goes on for what seems like hours. He discusses his father and where their business trip is taking them this time. I listen, because in this state that is all I can do. I can tell when Axel moves my hair or caresses my cheeks due to the sparks that follow. I wonder if he feels those too. Does he feel them for me?

I turn my mind back to what he is saying at the moment. Axel continues to go back and forth from serious confessions to talking about his father. "I just cannot side with father's reason to what he demands. How can he ask me to give you up when it is written in the stars for you to be mine?" I imagine myself stomping around in frustration, not being able to take offense to Axel's previous statement. Why would his father have control over what happens between the two of us?

I sit and think about what could possibly cause Alpha Anderson to have an issue with me. Nothing that I can think of comes to mind. "Whatever this is, I have to try. This is my fault, I know it is, without a doubt." He sighs in what seems to be complete exasperation. Axel eventually gets up to leave after what feels like hours and I am surrounded with silence once more. I cannot help but think about all that he has said regarding what I now know to be the matter of us. My mind drifts to the future. One I am not sure I will get to have.

Chapter 23

Throughout the next three or four days, it is much of the same routine. Truthfully, it gets a little mixed up in my mind. The days seem to run together. My mother comes and cries at my bedside. After my mother leaves, Brina and Cameron come in and talk to me. They have no clue I can hear them, but they act like I am able to answer whatever question they ask. Brina even gives an answer she knows I would more than likely say.

She is about ninety percent accurate with her responses. Cameron and Brina seem to have really hit it off. I am thankful she has him at this point. I ponder my own questions while I picture them in my mind. All cuddled up in the corner and having a one-sided conversation. Waiting for me to just wake up and answer one of them back.

After Brina and Cameron come in and have alone time with me, Julia usually comes in with Carter and all four visit for a while. I have gotten to keep up with the school gossip and their lives as a non-interacting spectator. This is better than not knowing at all, I guess. They usually leave once the nurse shoos them off.

Everything had a pattern it seemed. Day in and day out. I was okay with most of it until Axel's last visit before his work trip. Just like the many days before, I had everyone come visit, and then the nurse kicked them out because visiting hours were over. The next thing I hear is the slam of a door which is odd.

I know it has to be Axel, but he is usually so quiet when he comes to visit me. I keep telling myself it had to be him. He is the only one who visits after hours, but it makes me nervous that it might not be him but someone else. Why would he slam the door like he did?

I wait and wait until I finally hear him toss some things around. He was groaning and it sounded like he was being inconvenienced. I listen intently and can hear him pacing. He was walking so heavily that I can make out the sounds of his shoes as they go tap, tap, tap on the tile.

He sighs and I can feel the disappointment hit me without even needing to see his face. I know for sure that is what he is feeling once I hear his voice. "I just don't know why this is my life. My father thinks he can control my life, why does he get to decide you're not worth it?" I heard what sounded like a fist hitting the wall.

He is basically yelling at this point and I hear what sounds like a chair breaking against the wall or door. "Why is he like this?" I hear a fist go through the wall again. I have never seen this side of Axel and it is scary. Is this his dark secret? That he has raging anger issues? I have seen Julia act out at the Italian restaurant, but this is something entirely different.

"I almost don't care what he has to say, but I do care about the people. What if the rules are wrong? What if the old way is not the best way? Why does the council feel like they have a right to dictate who I love?" Metal crashing and stuffing being scattered on the floors is all I can focus on.

I really hope someone comes and calms him down soon. I do not know what is left of this room. "He wanted me to go through the rejection process. I do not understand The Moon Goddess all of the time, but I do not question mates. I don't question her for fear of her wrath." The word rejection causes a pain to ripple through my body I did not know could exist and yet I still lay here lifeless on the table. I do not know what his father has done in regard to Axel, but if it caused this reaction, I am not sure I would want to see what it was.

Another fist through the wall. If I could have moved, I am not sure I would have wanted to be around Axel at this point. "I do not care about an ancient feud between the wolves and witches. Why does he do this to me?" I think he is past the point of attempting to calm down and if someone confronted him, I am afraid they might get hurt. I have a hard time makes sense of the words as his voice continues to raise.

He sounds almost like he is growling. I also am having a hard time listening fully due to the amount of destruction I hear. The background noise is so loud. I do not think he would ever hurt me, but at the same time, I do not know this Axel. I partially keep waiting to be hit or thrown myself, seeing as I can't move. It almost feels like I am a piece of the furniture waiting for my turn to go flying.

All of a sudden, I feel him grab my hands and internally I shudder at the thought of what he might do to me. Panic starts to consume my thoughts and I can hear the monitors pick up as my heart rate picks up. He keeps randomly shouting things about the rejection and half breeds. "The damn council only wants what is good for their pockets and status. They care nothing about the actual people they rule."

I hear silence and then Axel's heavy breathing next to my left ear. My head swarming with what Axel just said about the council and knowing the power that they hold. The destruction seems to have slowly stopped. "Moon Goddess, please forgive me for what I am about to do. I just seem to make things way more complicated than they have to be but I do not know how to fix it. How do I get where I am supposed to go? How can I love her and continue to act the way I do? I need to let her go; it would be what is best. Yet, I am selfish, and I can't help it."

He places his head against mine and rests there for just a few minutes. "Adalee, forgive me for how selfish I am." As my mind begins to race faster and faster it comes to a sudden stop when I feel the sparks hit my lips. The moment Axle's lips hit mine it is like my world exploded and came back together in a beautiful puzzle with all of its pieces.

All I can hear is the monitors going haywire. I can feel my body starting to attempt to move. I feel the urge to jump off of the table and into Axel's arms but the only thing that happens is my hands start to move. My body feels heavy, heavier than it has in my entire life.

I did not think that my body feeling this way was possible. The way my body felt after all of the miles that Brina has made me run is nothing in comparison to now. I feel Axel grab my hands and he slowly begin to speak. "Ads, Adalee can you hear me? I need you to squeeze my hand if you can hear me. Please, I need you." I hear what he has to say but I am unsure of what I should do in regard to what he asked of me.

Do I squeeze my hands and let him know that I can hear him? Do I sit back and wait for him to leave and then try to get up? Will he be as angry as he was earlier if I get up once he leaves?

Could he hurt me if he became angry enough? Why does he need me?

A sense of braveness fills me, and I decide that enough is enough. As I have been sitting here pondering what I should do I can slowly feel my strength begin to come back to me. The first thing I do is decide to open my eyes. I decide to face the beast head on. Would I normally call Axel a beast?

No. Axel may be wishy washy but before I would have never even thought of calling him a beast. What I have just witnessed in the last hour has me questioning my judge of character. I begin fluttering my eyes in attempt to get them use to the blinding light above. I picked up my hands slowly and place them in front of my face to shield me from the awful light above. I feel Axel hover over me like a mom hovers over a toddler. I can feel the worry radiating off of him. I slowly make my way into a sitting position. I notice Axel attempts to help me and for that I am thankful, I am weaker than I thought I would be. I slowly take in my surroundings and I do not have words for what I see.

The room which should have been in mint condition looked like a tornado had come through and decided to stay a while. The wall had multiple holes in it and the furniture was smashed to pieces. All I could do was gasp at the sight in front of me. I could not believe the fact that Axel could cause all of this and that he had done all of this with his bare hands. Once I had digested what the room had looked like, I turned to Axel and did the only thing I thought would be rational at this moment in time.

I yelled "Nurse. Nurse. Nurse" over and over at the top of my lungs until finally someone came through the door. The look on Axel's face almost made me regret rushing into yelling for someone to come help me. Maybe I should have heard him out. Maybe I should have asked why he caused that kind of destruction, but he already told me. His father caused him to lose his temper like this. I could not imagine what someone had done to him, family or not, that would make him act this way.

Pain and sadness fill his expression at first, but then it turned into nothing but pure anger. It scared me to my core. I was worried he might send his fist through the wall and if not the wall that he might aim a it in my direction. It was mere moments before the nurses rushed in and demanded that Axel leave the room.

They began to get to work right away to make sure I was okay, and I was thankful for the company. They did not press me for information right away. Axel attempted to argue that he needed to stay, but they were not having any of that and demanded that he leave, or they would call his father. He seemed uncertain still, until they mentioned his father, and after a few minutes he left without a word. I thought that I wanted him gone.

As soon as he left, I was wishing someone whom I knew was beside me if only for silent support. The nurses began asking me all kinds of questions. They asked questions regarding what I knew about what happened and if I remembered anything that could help them figure out why I was in a comatose state. I thought it kind of silly because I felt like it should be their job to know why I was the way I was. Then I realized that they were probably asking to try to gather information. The guy at the party's voice coming back to haunt me. How do I know if I am safe?

It was short lived when a doctor came in to assess me from head to toe. I kept trying to find my phone, but it was nowhere to be found. I needed to call my mother. I felt overwhelmed and they were not making it any easier. Finally, the doctor got done and someone else came in and drew multiple vials worth of labs and did tests after tests.

I was becoming more impatient and finally after about two hours of everyone coming in and looking me over like a lab rat, I had had enough. I stood up and started ripping everything off of my body the moment they gave me a break. The machines went haywire and suddenly people started filling into the room. I could not take it anymore. I let out a scream as they started trying to place me on the bed and strap me in tightly. If they would just listen to me none of this would have had to happen. They would not even let me speak.

I continued to fight, and they were not giving up. I heard a doctor give some kind of order for a shot and I lost it. I began screaming and the only person I could think of to scream for was Axel. It was not a minute longer when suddenly, an inhuman sound filled every inch of the tiny room and the doctors and nurses stopped. I began crying and looked over my right shoulder at the door and there he came walking in the room with a look of panic on his face.

He came to save me once again and this time I was not going to fight it. "Axel, please. Please get me out of here. Please. I do not know what is going on. I am scared. I just want to go home. I need to get home. Axel, please." As I continued to beg him to let me out, he looked over me and I thought I had seen him angry before. The look was terrifying on his face and he looked at each one of the doctors and nurses in the eyes and then took a deep breath.

"I don't know what is going on, but you all need to step away from Adalee this instant." He spoke so calmly it made a shiver run down my spine. Everyone bowed, but no one moved. "Do I need to repeat myself? Everyone moves, now." He spoke with such authority that it fascinated me to watch them obey. Here were grown adults listening to what Axel had commanded.

It may have been because of his father, but I think the authoritative tone of his voice also helped. Axel began walking over to me and I sat there with my head down almost in tears. "Are you okay, Ads? Did they hurt you? I was standing in the lobby and I heard you scream my name. I came running as fast as I could." He spoke as soft as I think he could, he acted as if I could break if he were too harsh in his tone. I would laugh at the thought of being so gentle because I can handle my own normally. "No. I just feel like I am in danger. I don't know who to trust."

My body started violently shaking and tears finally fell from my eyes. I was restrained and uncomfortable with the need to be in my own bed. As if he understood, he slowly took off my restraints one by one. "I need bandages and some ointment. Now" He demanded from a nurse who was still in the room. She came back and handed him everything he asked for.

He picked up each of my wrists like they were made of glass and carefully placed ointment where the restraints had left red marks. After that he wrapped each one in bandages. Once he was done, he took a step back and a smile spread across his face like he was very proud of the work he did on my wrist.

I attempted to get up off of the bed and before I could sit all the way up Axel wrapped his arms around my and held me tight. "Trust me, okay Adalee? I know I scared you earlier, and for that I am sorry. Just trust me to take you home safely. I know your mother and Brina are anxiously waiting for you to return." He lifted me up gently and began to walk out of the room. A doctor attempted to stop him, but he just looked in her direction and she backed down instantly. He carried me bridal style, through the hospital and it made me a little embarrassed, so I buried my face in his chest to hide who I was from the curious onlookers.

"Don't worry, Ads. They will not say anything. I am going to carry you to the car and then take you home right away. Are you okay?" I shake my head that is still buried in his chest. He tightens his grip and before long, we are in the car. He lowers me down, but I am hesitant to let him go. I feel safer and I am not sure how that could be seeing as he was the one who scared me so badly back at the hospital. He seems to notice me being hesitant to let go and picks me back up and goes to get in on the driver's side of his truck. He makes it look effortless carrying me and for that I am thankful. He never says a word as he drives me home. He just lets me sit there with my head buried in his chest. When we arrive I look at him, really look at his face and notice he seems content.

"Thank you doing this for me. I am not sure what I would have done had you not been there for me. You always seem to be at the right place at the right time. I hope Veronica is okay with this. I don't want to cause any problems." With the mention of Veronica, I feel Axel stiffen and his expression goes cold. I start to crawl off his lap and he stops me. Butterflies hit my stomach and I look away as pink hits my cheeks. Axel looks me up and down and then helps me

get out of his truck. He carries me to the front door and before he

could set me down, Brina busts through the door and stands there

with her mouth touching the floor.

Chapter 24

Brina sat there in the doorway and then it was not long until my mother joined behind her and was just staring at both of us with a look of content. Why was she not freaking out? Axel stood there rooted in his position like none of this was a big deal. All this staring made me feel uncomfortable and I started squirming in my seat. My mother noticed and as politely as I have ever seen her act calmly states, "Axel, nice to meet you. I appreciate you getting her home safely." Axel looks at her for a moment and then back to me.

He acts like he does not want to set me down. "Adalee stated at the hospital she felt unsafe." His grip tightens and his mouth sets into a straight, tight line. He is not moving. It is like he is afraid something might happen to me. He finally sets me down slowly. When my feet hit the floor, he is cautious to move from my side.

"Axel, do you think you could help me inside? I think Brina and my mother can take over from there." I ask feeling like he wants to make sure I am okay and inside our house before he leaves. I feel like I need him to help me inside. Shock registers on his face and he looks toward my mother, asking a silent question if that would be okay. My mother nods her head and Axel helps me inside and to the couch. I feel super weak, like I am unable to hold my own weight.

As soon as Axel notices I am okay, he bids his goodbye and then leaves out the door. It is about five minutes later that I hear his truck leave and I turn my attention to my mother and Brina. Before I could say anything, a flash of white platinum blonde made its way through the room with such a speed I almost did not notice that it was attached to my best friend.

"Come here. You have no idea the heart attack you gave me sweetheart!" Brina yells as she wraps me in the biggest hug I've ever had in my life. After her squeezing the life out of me for what felt like forever, she calmed down and sat beside me. The only thing I could think of to say was, "So, you and Cameron, huh?" I wish I would have had a camera because I have never seen Brina turn as red as she did at the mention of Cameron's name.

The next couple hours flew by as the house was filled up with nothing but chatter from my mother and Brina as they filled me in with everything that had happened. I found out that I passed out at the party that was hosted at the Anderson's. Axel found me and brought me to the hospital located on their land and I was in a comatose state for about a month. I thought that hearing I had been basically asleep for a month would make me freak out more than it did, but part of me felt like I did not miss much. I could hear everything around me for part of the time. After a while, my mother said it was time for her to head to bed, Brina and I made it up the stairs and proceeded to sit on my bed and talk for hours.

"So, tell me about you and Axel. Huh. Huh. Do I need to sing Adalee and Axel sitting in a tree?" She let out a giggle and nudged me playfully. I know I had to of blushed almost as deep as Brina did when I mentioned Cameron. "I don't know what to talk about, Brina. He was there for me when I needed someone." Brina seemed to ponder everything as I fill her in with everything that I heard at the hospital. I admitted what I was feeling, and it was nice to get it off my chest. "You know sugar, I think you might have to wait this one out to see how it ends. I don't think this is one you can guess the conclusion to, and it become correct." I look at Brina and think about what she said, but the only question in my mind is there even an ending?

We wrap up our conversation and Brina demanded that I go straight to bed once she realized the time. She told me she would bring me a super late supper or an early breakfast depending on how you viewed food at two in the morning. Brina was super hesitant after we ate but finally left me alone long enough to take a shower. It felt nice finally being able to shower and do something that seemed normal. Once I returned to my room and got dressed, Brina immediately came in and started fixing the bed so that we could get some sleep. I automatically assumed that she would want to sleep beside me and I was thankful that I was not wrong.

I know I was not alone while I was at the hospital, but it still sometimes felt that way. I know people were around me all the time, but I could not help but have this deep nagging sense of loneliness. I will never take for granted the ability to get up and communicate with somebody ever again. I know that everybody thinks that I was asleep for a month, but I was not at all. I feel like I was up the entire time. My mother was worried that I would not be able to sleep and had brought up some medication before she fell asleep, but truthfully, I had no problems once I was snuggled in bed next to my best friend. I closed my eyes and drifted off wishing for peaceful sleep.

I was hoping to dream of the forest. To have a sense of normal to me. I was hoping to have my dream wolf beside me. I know if I could just see him in my dream, I would be able to feel truly safe. Luck was not on my side as it hadn't been for the past two months. I fell into a dreamless sleep. I was half expecting that Brina would wake me up to run. I silently cursed under my breath when I finally opened my eyes and the clocks showed 11:00 AM.

I sat up in bed and Brina came out of nowhere and assessed me up and down, probably better than some of the nurses at the hospital. I could not help but laugh at her and the way she seemed to worry so much. "Don't worry, I'm fine. Truly Brina, look at me!" I said as I got up and started doing a dance around my bedroom. I shook my butt to the left and shook my butt to the right and even did a finale twirl just to prove I was okay. My stellar dance moves finally made Brina bust out laughing so hard that she ended up falling back on the bed. She laughed so hard it would have been one of those laughs that shot your drink up your nose. I smiled being able to see her and hear her laugh.

After taking another shower and finally feeling somewhat like my old self, I went back to my room and found Brina sitting on my bed picking out movies. What do you think you are doing? "Duh, you silly little duck, I'm picking out what movies were going to watch today." I shook my head at her and sighed heavily, "No ma'am. That is not happening today. I know the doctor gave me light bed rest and told me not to overdo it, but I'm not going to sit around for the next two weeks when that's all I did for a solid month."

Brina looks at me and just shakes her head, but before she could attempt to keep me locked away in the house I ran out of my room and down the stairs. She caught up to me in a matter of seconds and gave me a what have you done with my best friend look. I laughed and then bolted out the door and into the sunlight. I twirled in circles and for the first time felt so free in the crisp October air.

After some time on the porch and a much-needed gossip session, I decided that I needed to go see Mrs. Eva and Brina told me that she would drive me to the school. When it became about three in the afternoon, we headed out to hopefully catch her during free period. Once we got to the school we headed straight to the greenhouse. I had thoughts to confront Julia about Axel's behavior instead of coming to visit Mrs. Eva, but with the way Julia acted that day at the Italian restaurant gave me a feeling they share anger issues. I walked into the greenhouse and I could not help but smile, besides the library, this had become of my favorite places on the school grounds.

I walked around to the first greenhouse and did not find Mrs. Eva, so I continued until I got to the third greenhouse where she was busy with different vials of herbs. As I opened the door she never turned around when she greeted me, "Adalee Ebony, if I didn't know any better, I would say you have come to me to help solve all of life's problems." She chuckled lightheartedly at her statement and it made me feel at ease. I am really not sure how she always knew when I walked into a room, but I was kind of thankful she did.

Mrs. Eva had become my favorite teacher at Rose Prep Academy. Not sure if it is because she felt like a grandmother or if it is because it felt like we were connected on a different level then most students. "Mrs. Eva, I came to ask you a few questions. Is that okay?" I guess I finally got her attention well enough for her to stop what she was doing. She proceeded to close the lids on several different older looking jars of all different colors and sizes and then turned her attention towards me.

"Sure, what is troubling your mind?" Well, I guess I will just go out and say it. "I need to know what the council has against me." I become a little worried when I watch Mrs. Eva choke on the tea she is drinking. "Adalee. I need you to be very careful how you word your response to what I am about to ask. Why do you feel like the council has something against you?"

Great. I feel like it seems silly now with her nonchalant tone. "Well. I had a tall, slender guy at the party tell me I should watch my back and…" before I could get any more information out, she shushes me. Her surprisingly warm finger pressed against my lips. The mixed scent of rosemary and thyme floating to my nostrils.

"Adalee. I think this is a discussion you need to have with your mother. I need to stay out of it." Her words process through me and ill will surges through my being. "What do you mean you need to stay out of it? You are the one person who I thought could help." My voice goes up a few octaves as I try to remain calm. "There are somethings that cannot be explained right now. You need to have a talk with your mother."

I know I should not have laughed in her face, but that is exactly what I did. "What do you mean talk to my mother? How about I go and talk to the walls in my cabin because they are there consistently where my mother shows her face like once a week." Her tormented frown causes me to remember my place, but only slightly.

"Dear, she is doing the best she can for you. Give her some slack. She is trying to make sure you stay alive." I watch as Mrs. Eva continuously looks over her shoulder as if something could just come and snatch her up in broad daylight. "Listen child. You need to go home and lay low. You are not safe if Hector has his sights set on you." Who's Hector? Before I could ask questions, Mrs. Eva is pushing me out of the greenhouse and muttering really low under her breath.

"You will understand all of this later. Just know you happen to be stuck between two sides of a very long issue. One that might just get you killed if you do not lay low." It is hard to remain unmoved as if what she just said had no effect on me. As if she just did not say I could lose my life. What could possibly be going on? Whatever it is, it is something I need to know the answer to.

Chapter 25

I text Brina and let her know that I am on my way to the Jeep. While I casually walk, I take in the scenery unfolding as school is being let out. I sit down on a bench under a large tree that happened to be a few feet from where Brina and I are meeting up.

I watch students coming out of the school and get lost people watching. Unaware of my surroundings. I jumped out of my seat when the person behind me let out a laugh that was low and throaty. One I knew was no good.

Before I could turn around, nails dug into my shoulders, putting holes in my favorite sweater and only stopping once blood started seeping from my skin. "Oh, you poor, poor girl. Did you not think I would not find out about you and Axel?" Are you serious?

Veronica is the last person I wanted to deal with. "I think you should take any ill will you have up with Axel."

If possible, her nails grow deeper into my skin. My favorite shirt is officially ruined. "Do you know who I am? I have people all over this town who follow me, because they know what happens when you go against me." Her voice sounds almost as annoying as teeth scraping a metal fork. You know it is almost as irritating as hearing her breath.

"You know I am not sure what you are talking about." With every word I say in rebuttal, her nails turn into claws. "Hairy hands are not becoming for a lady to have." I can hear her attempt at a deep growl. "You should watch your mouth half breed. I know what you are now, and you should be ashamed. I cannot believe I did not smell it on you before." I can feel her smelling up and down my neck. Snarling as she takes in a huge whiff.

Before I can push her away, she moves her hands to my throat. "Your mother must have done a good job, or should I say whoever she hired did a good job. I know she wouldn't be strong enough to cover it up, because she is about as pathetic as you are." I flinch only at how she has her hands around my windpipe. The thought of being without air causing my body to swarm with adrenaline. I can feel it coating my insides.

"How dare you think you can talk to me like you know anything about me. Just because you're the daughter of the damn principle does not give you this right." She didn't hesitate as she yanked me from the bench backwards. Spots filling my vision as my head bounced against the ground. The taste of metal filling my mouth.

As I am trying to get my bearings, Veronica glides over and sits on my chest. "I will tell you this once and not ever again mongrel. Stop sticking your nose where it does not belong. You deserve nothing more than to lay in the dirt like you are now." She can piss off now I have had enough. I start to wiggle trying to find a way to get my hands out from underneath her. "I can promise you that you do not stand a chance against me and you never will. Your parents should be ashamed they brought you into this world."

Still trying to get my hands out from under her, I think of the only thing that might distract her and I spit blood in her face. I was not about to let this punk get away with trying to hurt me again. What is the saying, sticks and stones may break my bones, but words will never hurt me? Yeah well, she was not about to lay a hand on me either. She already had a cheap shot coming from behind me, but I will be damned if she had the opportunity for another one.

As she started her down swing, it was like my body took over control and I did not fight my actions. I moved my head and in a swift move flipped her over and pinned her down. I felt like I had a newfound strength and used it to my advantage. "I promise I have dealt with bigger problems in my life than some washed up, want to be barbie that has daddy get her everything in life. Grow up and get over yourself. The world doesn't revolve around you." As I got off of her, you could see Veronica was livid.

Before I could get more than a few feet away, Veronica lets out a sneer that ricocheted through the courtyard. "Way to be discreet." The sounds of her heels make a clickety click sound as she pounded away at the pavement. "He. Is. Mine. That. Title. Is. Mine. You will not take it from me." Her voice held a slight touch of authority, but she should have more being from Alpha blood.

I whipped around just in time to throw my hands up. I sent her flying across the lawn. She lands funny on her feet as I watch one of her heels break. "Those were my favorite!" I can see her body shaking violently and I do the only thing I can think of doing. I snap my fingers and hit her hot-headed ass with a blast of lightning.

Just as I was starting to yell at her and I was about to panic that I severely hurt her on campus, water hit her face. I look up and see Brina standing there with an empty water bottle. The smirk on her face is priceless.

I look down and Veronica starts to open her eyes, slowly at first and then she seems to come to and looks around frantically. As soon as she focuses well enough to see Brina standing over her and me beside her, panic comes across her eyes. "What did you do to me? I want you to stay back. Get away from me." She backs away quickly and as soon as she can stand, she takes off across the school yard.

"Guess she didn't like the lightning?" Brina's high pitched laugh causes me to cover my ears seeing as my head is still pounding from being thrown to the ground. "You know, Adalee, if you would have been more careful, you might not have had your ass beat." I hope the cold shoulder I am giving her lets her know I don't appreciate what she just said. "Hey, do not get your panties in a bunch. All I am saying is you should be careful." I guess she got the point, because like a child I am facing completely away from her and she lets it go. My ego might be hurt just a tad.

As Brina and I made our way back to the house to relax, we both randomly get a message from Julia. She wanted us to come out for a girl's night to the movies at 8. I look at Brina and she just shrugs her shoulders, "What do you want to do sweet cakes? You can't avoid her forever. She is, or was, well still should be one of your best friends. Also, Axel should still be gone right?" I give her side eyes and cannot help but sigh in defeat.

"I just do not want things to be awkward and I feel like they might be." I look down at my hands and then back at my best friend. "We were and are such good friends but how do I explain what I am to her brother when I do not understand it myself? I did not tell you, but Axel came and visited me for hours after everyone was told to leave. He just talked to me and held my hand. He confessed things, things I do not know how to handle." The physical pain Brina shows to not squeal and jump up and down makes the gravity of this situation lighter.

When I know for sure she would remain quiet, I continued. "He showed a side that I hope I will see again. I feel drawn to Axel and I kick myself hourly for how much I think about him. He has obligations and I cannot fathom standing in the way of what he was born to do. Do I ask him to choose his people over the possibility we could be happy?"

As I finish my rant about my feelings for Axel, I look away from Brina in embarrassment. I know she would do nothing but show me support for how I feel. It is just a hard thing to admit these things to her. "You know sugar, what if he was born to love you?" When those words left Brina's mouth, I shot my head up so fast my neck might snap.

I looked at her and really took her in as she was sitting cross legged on the other end of the couch. She had on a sun dress that was flowy and she looked almost like a small child waiting on ice cream. I am not sure how I had not noticed before, but she had a glow to her. She looked positively happy.

Her long pale blonde hair up in a high ponytail and a small smile across her lips. I looked around for a moment and noticed that whatever chick flick was on the TV was getting to the best part. I turned my attention from her for just a moment to watch the part of the movie that is usually at the end. You know the part, we all know the part, when the main characters fall in love after they fight. There is something sweet about the right people ending up together.

"You know, Ads. You cannot avoid your destiny forever. Why don't you consider going to the movies? I know how much you love the buttery popcorn! Oh, and the slushies, red and white mixed always was your favorite."

"How do you always know what to say?" A sheepish grin creeping up at the corner of my lips. "Don't worry sugar pie, it is my specialty. Call it southern hospitality. Always is the best!" When she lays on the accent extra thick, I cannot help but laugh. She knows it gets me every time.

As I sit back and really think about what the harm could be with going to the movies with Julia, my mind slips back to Axel. I know he should still be out of town, yet I cannot help but feel this is not a good idea. "Adalee, just text her and tell her we are going... better yet I will text her and let her know we are going. Go get your butt ready because we are getting out of this house."

Should I tell Brina it feels like a truck full of rocks just hit my stomach? The bile rising in my throat makes me question if I should even consider going. "I think it will help your mood! I am tired of you looking like you might pass out from the amount of strain you are putting yourself through thinking about what to do. It is all over your face with your eyebrows pulled together and nose scrunched. I am making your mind up for you, pumpkin." Before Brina could get in another word, I sighed and flopped back. "Fine, go pick me out an outfit please." I did not even have to look up to know that she had already sprinted off to look through my closet.

All I can think about is how everything seems right, yet something seems off. Like I am living in a horror movie and the anticipation of something going bump in the night is what will kill me. It is hard to explain, the feeling inside that has been a little off kilter since my birthday. Maybe it is because all I can remember is Veronica and Axel and then hearing his confession. His confession about what we are supposed to be, over and over. Regardless of the apologies, I need to see action. I need to know if the things he said are true. I need to see him.

I looked over to the kitchen hoping my mother was there. "Mom is gone in a meeting, she left her card and told me to have some safe fun with you." I laughed as I watched Brina put air quotes around the word safe.

I missed my mother all the time. I feel that most of the time it is like having only Brina here with me. I just wished she were home a little more and when she was, we didn't fight like a tsunami meeting the shore. Two unmovable forces that continue to collide with each other and eventually recede back to coexist from a distance.

We head to the movies and I cannot help but feel a tingle of mixed feelings. Most involving nervousness with a hint of being worried and excited all at the same time. It made me think that I might not keep my popcorn down. We walked in and went to the ticket counter to buy our tickets, looking for Julia in the main lobby but she was nowhere to be seen.

When I ask the sales lady for two tickets to the thriller that Julia wanted to see, she calmly tells us that it is not needed and to head up to the counter and get whatever we would like. She tells us with a smile and wink that any friend of Julia's is a friend to the theater. Kind of confused we walk up and get a few snacks and ask the lady where we were to meet Julia.

Before the poor lady could answer, we were wrapped in a hug and heard Julia squeal in our ears. "Oh my goodness, I was almost afraid you guys would bail on me. I am so excited you are here." After she said that I knew that we were all okay. We were probably all okay before, yet I know she heard about what happened at the hospital. She had to of heard.

I know being twins it must be hard to see each other at their worst. On the bright side, you do have someone beside you for life to always make you see the good. You have someone who is bonded to you in a special way. Twins are said to be special and I do believe they are nothing short of special. Which is why I was not wanting to see Julia until some time had passed between what happened to Axel and me at the hospital. I heard things I do not think I was supposed to hear and witnessed things I wish I had not. It is hard to not feel awkward when I have no idea what Axel told his sister.

I was mindlessly following Julia and Brina through the movie theater while lost in my thoughts. I finally caught up and caught on to part of the conversation. "Yes, so my father owns several different businesses. We own the theater, so I thought it would be fun to have a girl's night and watch a movie. That is why we did not need tickets. We will be in our own private show room. Hope that is okay for you guys. I only want the best for my friends."

Julia is always so polite. I can see how since we are not use to this life it could seem out of place for us, but I was rather enjoying seeing a different side of things.

"You know Julia, I really think this will be amazing and I am glad we could do this." As I addressed her directly for the first time, she turned around and pulled me into a huge hug once again. "You have no idea how happy I am to have you here Adalee." Julia pulled back and grabbed both of mine and Brina's hands and led us through the back, to a small room. Well, it was small compared to a theater room, but still larger than a normal bedroom. It held about twenty individual large theater chairs that leaned all the way back. There was a large snack bar and drink station. It was set up almost like a large living room and was super cozy.

"Well hot damn sugar, this is super fancy." Is all Brina can think to say and I do not blame her. Julia blushes and blows off our comments. We make us some more snacks and settle in for what seems to be a great evening. After watching the movie, we sit back in our comfy chairs and catch up. I am thankful Julia never brings up Axel. I am still not sure how to discuss what needs to be said. I am afraid it would make things awkward. After a while, I look at the time and it is a little past midnight. Brina decides that it is about time we head home.

I agree and we get up to leave when I hear Brina's phone ring. She starts acting all shy and I realize its Cameron on the other end. Brina looks at me and then Julia and back at me. "Brina, why don't you get a ride with Julia, if she is okay with it, and go hang a few hours with Cameron. I am sure he would not mind bringing you home in a few hours, right? Mom is not home and I won't tell a soul you were out this late." I can't help but laugh as she turns as red as a strawberry. This was becoming fun to pick on her about it.

"You sure Ads? I do not want you to feel lonely. You just got back home." I laugh at her and shake my head. "Girl, I am telling you I am fine. Just give me the keys and I will drive home. What is the worst thing that can happen? I will call you if I need you." She looks me over and then says a few things to Cameron over the phone. She looks at Julia and then finally hands me the keys. I burst out laughing as she turns red once more. We make our way to the parking lot and part ways after some quick goodbyes. I plug my phone into the jeep and find some nice tunes to jam out to and start my way home. A bubble bath is calling my name.

Chapter 26

The drive home is about forty-five minutes and I honestly am okay with how long it will take to get home. I have learned to appreciate the time in the car as reflection time. It is a time for me to really think about things and just have some quiet time. Brina usually does most of the talking when we drive. She also does most of the driving.

I really do not know what my life would look like without her in it. I think I would be really lost. I begin to think about my friendship with Brina and how we became friends. I know our mothers were super good friends and that we shared a crib together. The actual first memory I have of us is when we were playing at a playground when some older kids pushed me off of the swing and I fell down and scraped my knee. Brina was on the merry go round and jumped off mid spin to come see if I was okay. Once she realized I was okay, she proceeded to give the two older kids a piece of her mind and by the end of it they came and apologized to me. After that day we became thick as thieves.

As I was reminiscing, I could not help but think about all of the great memories we have had. The day mom took us to learn to drive was a day I will never forget. Brina took to driving with no issue and I hit every traffic cone mom set up in the abandoned parking lot by our house. We were living in Tennessee at the time. I always liked our time spent in that state. They always had some kind of music event going on and Brina and I love to dance. We spent many nights in teenage dance halls learning all the different country moves. I love to spin and twirl and line dances are also a blast. We had a lot of fun in Tennessee.

Texas had to be Brina's favorite state we lived in, aside from home, I guess. She loves that everything was bigger in Texas. The people were so friendly, and the tea was sweeter. We lived on a few hundred acres and loved to ride the ATV for hours. We learned to fish and what good barbeque was really like. Texas likes to have cook-offs every weekend in the summer. It was a time of wonderful memories. I am not sure what my favorite state we have lived in would be. I really liked up towards the north but only for the winter months.

We spent time in New York, and I loved every museum that I stepped foot in. I would drag Brina for hours on Saturdays to see all the different kinds of museums. Brina likes central park, it's about the only green area in the state, I think. California was okay, Brina got into roller blading and we spent a lot of time on the coast watching the surfers crash in the waves. We spent time in Florida, and I preferred the East coast over the West coast just due to how the water seemed warmer. My mother seemed to like Colorado. She still talks about wanting to take a trip to the mountains. I look back and think sometimes how terrible it has been to be a new student as much as Brina and I have had to be, but the memories make it worth it.

Thinking of all the things Brina and I have done makes me wish my father could have seen all of these places. I am not sure how he grew up. Did he get to experience life and go all over the world? The thought of my dad makes my heart heavy with sadness. I stare out at the road and attempt to not think about him anymore. I know that sounds selfish, I have had my fair deal of being sad the last few months, I want some happy memories here. I want to add fun memories to our ever-growing list of states. Each one we visit has at least a couple distinct happy memories.

I turn down the radio and think that the rest of the drive might be better in silence. I only have about fifteen minutes left until I get home and I feel I have done enough reminiscing. I look out ahead of me at the winding road and the tall trees and think about how beautiful it is here. The forest around me is something that I have really grown to love in all aspects of my life. Hell, it haunted me in my dreams at first. I laugh in ward at myself at that one and cannot help but shake my head. Who would have thought that something as simple as a forest would play such an important part to me in this new journey I have been on?

I hear my phone buzz and I pick it up to see who it is. I want to make sure it is not my mother. She gives us a curfew of one in the morning and right now it is about thirty minutes until one. I notice that it is Brina thanking me for allowing her to spend some time with Cameron and I smile from ear to ear.

It is about time she dated someone. All of these years she has not even looked in the direction of another boy. My best friend is gorgeous, it is not because she has not had options, but it is because she has not given them the time of the day. I send her a couple of quick heart emojis back and look up just in time to see a large black bear. At least I think it is a bear crossing the road. Whatever it was, it was massive.

I notice my vision starts to cloud over and I panic thinking about the fact that I am driving. It is like I am on autopilot and I do not know what is happening. I start to become transformed into another lost memory. In this memory we are in a house that is different than the one we are staying in right now. I look to be about six and I run in a large room with a canopy bed in the middle. There are toys scattered around and I notice I am in pajamas. I run to the bed and start jumping up and down yelling, "Daddy. Daddy. Daddy. It is time for my story. Come tell me my favorite story. Please!"

I look around and notice behind me the door swings open and in walks a man who was tall, around 6'4 and lean. He had dark brown hair with a few small grey patches throughout and it was slicked back. His eyes held a softness that was directed towards the little girl and were a beautiful shade of honey brown. He was dressed in business slacks and a white button-down shirt. My heart leaped out of my chest. "Okay. Come here my little Rose."

I know who this man is with all of my soul. It was my father. He walked over and picked me up and twirled me around. My mother popped her head in and casually tells my father to not make it a super long story this time. I have dance practice in the morning and then fencing practice for lunch. My father runs over to my mother with me still in one arm and picks her up with the other. He swings us around and laughter fills the room. Happiness is all I see in this memory. My father proceeds to let my mother down and carry me over to the bed where he starts to tell me a story.

"The story is of a prince in search of his princess." I sat down on the bed and reached out to my family. I know it is a memory, but to be able to hug my father once more would make all of this so much better. "This man was the ruler of a kingdom and he needed his queen. He told of a great moon goddess who had gifted the young prince with powers and told him that he had his soulmate out in the world, but he would have to go on a long journey to find her. He was told this mate would have powers, but not like his own."

The ooh's and ah's from my younger self made me giggle. The way her eyes followed my father's hand as he illustrated this elaborate story.

"She would be different, and that this was not to discourage the young prince. He was to bring her home and make her his queen from another world. This prince was determined and spent years searching while he took care of his kingdom." This went on and on and I felt as if I was becoming lost in the memory and truthfully, I was completely okay with it. "He went to country after country. Attended party after party and meeting after meeting in search for his one true love. He remembered what the great moon goddess had told him, and he grew more impatient as the years passed. The more impatient he grew, the angrier he became. He started to get discouraged and started to lose what the moon goddess had given him as special gifts."

Father told the little girl version of myself that after so long, if a prince does not find his queen, his gifts become weak and he will not become a king. He then becomes vulnerable and other kings notice and attempt to take what is not theirs. This is exactly what happened to the poor young prince. I smile as I listen to my father become engrossed in telling the story.

"The prince had to fight for his kingdom when an evil king thought he needed more power and was determined to take what was not his. This young prince was not completely prepared for war because his mind was still set on finding his queen. That did not stop the other king from coming, however." This story, although made up, seems to hit my heart. The hundreds of times my father told me this story come rushing back.

"On one cold night, the evil king launched an attack on the young prince's land and there was great sacrifice but the young prince seemed to defeat the evil king. After the young prince slayed the evil king, he went to his kingdom to attempt to make peace with his son. The son was reasonable, and a treaty was signed that kept them from going to war once again. Both sides had suffered greatly at the evil king's selfishness."

"After the treaty was signed the prince was invited to stay at the castle until morning, where he would get a fresh start home. On his way home, his carriage fell under attack. When he went to defend his carriage, he noticed a woman in a hooded cloak. Something about her drew him in." It was getting to the best part of the story.

"The woman was part of the group of ladies who was attacking the carriage, but the prince noticed she was hesitant. The prince allowed them to take whatever food they needed and after some time, she rode away with the others. One of the gifts the moon goddess had given the prince was the ability to track anything he wanted." Younger me sat on the edge of her seat with her knees under her, leaning so far forward that she almost fell over.

"He tracked this young lady until he came to a part of his land he never knew was there. It was a small community and he searched for the young woman for hours asking anyone who would give him a chance. My mother came and sat down on the bed and pulled the younger me close. "Shhh Adalee, let your father finish."

"Finally!" My father was winding up for the big finale. His deep timber voice booming throughout the bedroom. "The young prince tracked her down to a different king's land. He had a discussion with the generous king about who he was looking for and the king was unsure of anyone who would attack a royal carriage. The king allowed the prince to stay a few nights and continue his search once the prince explained what the moon goddess had told him."

My father takes the smaller version of me from my mother and swings me around the room. "You see, this generous king was also gifted in different ways than the moon goddess. On the third night at dinner, the generous king's daughter made it home from a trip out of town and the moment the princes eyes met hers, it was love at first sight."

He took me and placed me under the covers. Pulling the dark pink duvet up to my nose. "The generous king was shocked that the young prince mated with his only daughter, not only because they were of different blood, but because she happened to be with the group of women who attacked the young prince's carriage. It had come out that on their travel, a makeshift royal carriage had stolen all of their things and they thought the young prince's carriage was where their belongings were." My father grabbed my mother by her hand and pulled her close.

"Please father. Tell me the rest." The younger version of me had her sentence broken up by a huge yawn. I follow my parents as they shut the door. "You know Scott, one of these days she is going to figure out that your tale is an elaborated version of how we met."

My mother's words hit my soul. The ache in my head causing me to snap back to the reality. I snapped back just in time to come face to face with a tree.

Before I could hear the rest of the story, my vision snapped back to the road and before me stood a large, black animal. Before I could react to hit my breaks, I hit the animal with the front of my jeep and then ended up hitting a tree. My head swarmed and my vision went spotty for just a few moments before I became aware of my surroundings. I could tell the jeep was totaled because the air bags deployed, and the front end was completely smashed. I fumbled with the seatbelt and finally got that off. Now it was time to get the door open. I thought I would struggle because it looked like the frame had shifted, but surprisingly when I pushed against the handle the entire door came off its hinges.

Chapter 27

I have never understood the expression of someone's life flashing before their eyes until this moment. The impact with the tree threw me so hard against my seatbelt that I was afraid it would give. The crunch of my collarbone will forever be etched into my mind. My hands came up just as the air bags filled my cab. White power became suspended in the air and coated my lungs.

My head swarmed and my vision went spotty. Panic set in as pain shot through every fiber of my being. I could not tell which way was up and which was down. I felt as if I had just been placed into a dryer. Tumbled. Rolled. Tossed for all of eternity. My lungs felt heavy as the power from the air bags settled and coated the inside. I felt as if someone had poured pancake batter down my windpipe.

I worked on breathing though the pain. Slowly, I came back to my surroundings. I fumbled with the seatbelt and finally got that off. Now it was time to get the door open. I thought I would struggle because it looked like the frame had shifted, but surprisingly when I pushed against the handle, the entire door came off its hinges.

I stepped out of the mangled jeep and looked around to see what kind of damage I did. I leaned against the jeep to help support my weight. Step by step, I concentrate on making it to the front. I place both hands down on the hood and allow myself to get my bearings beneath me. Once the swarming in my head and the ringing in my ears stop, I feel a little more centered.

I examine the front. My mom's going to kill me. There is nothing more to think about. I feel a panic attack coming, I need to get away. I started walking slowly up from the ditch and once I was almost to the pavement of the road, I hit my knees. I became dizzy and needed to stop for just a few minutes. My left shoulder was killing me, and my head was pounding. I am not sure I should be walking, but what else was I supposed to do? I was at the edge of the road on my hands and knees when I noticed about twenty feet from me was a person.

My heart sank. It hit the bottom of my soul. My gasping became so quick and fast it felt like I was not breathing. My lungs burning while my throat felt like it was closing. I sat on my knees and began clawing at my throat. Feeling my nails digging into my skin, but I do not care. I cannot breathe. My lungs are not working. I feel myself go sideways. My hands that were still clutching my airway unable to stop my momentum.

When my shoulder hit white spots of vision entered as pain from my collarbone. As I rolled on my back, I knew this would be where my family found me. This is where they would place a cross in the ground in the ditch. I can see Brina and my mother packing up and leaving. Leaving me here with a piece of wood for random bystanders to question who I was.

My silent tears soon become sobs. This cannot be all that is left for me in this world. I dug my hands into the dirt, ignoring the blinding pain and centered myself. I felt the power from the earth. My spirit sucking up whatever was available to me. Once I feel myself humming and vibrating with energy, I concentrate on my collarbone first. I envision it being whole again. Calling out to the moon goddess for strength as I slowly repair myself.

Once I am able to move, I quicken my pace and shuffle as fast as I can. In the road was a person completely naked and sprawled out. I called out to them but they did not respond. I started crawling as fast as my body would carry me. I can promise you it probably felt faster than it really was. "Excuse me. Sir. Can you hear me? Are you okay?" I kept calling out to them and still no response. "Hey you! Can you hear me?" I can feel my body wanting to betray me as I start hyperventilating thinking I had just killed someone.

"Come on, Adalee. Stay strong. You are a badass. You can do this." I say this out loud. Over and over again as I get closer to this man in front of me still unconscious. For the first time since having them, I cursed the memory of my father. Had I not had one while driving, I would have noticed the person in the road.

They might be alive right now had I only been able to pay attention. The tears came faster the closer I got to whomever was laying in the road. Their back was to me and I could not make much of any other features. I stopped when I was about five feet away and froze. What if I had just killed someone? What was I going to do? How would I explain what happened?

I would be considered mentally unstable and locked in a psychiatric facility somewhere. They would make me the cover of newspapers everywhere. Crazy girl kills innocent pedestrian after she states she had a vision of dead father while driving. I can see it now. I attempt to calm myself enough to go the last five feet or so praying with the hope that maybe this person will be alive.

"Hey, can you hear me? I need to know if you are okay. Please answer me. At least move or something." I shout in the direction of the person laid out in the middle of the road. Maybe they will be okay. What kind of person is out at this time of night in the middle of the woods anyhow? How can I call someone? I do not even know where my cellphone is located. I bet it is in that mess of a jeep. My mom is going to kill me because of the jeep. I will not have to worry about being locked up when I am buried next to this guy six feet under. Mother is seriously going to murder me. How do I get help? I wonder how close I am to the house.

I look around and it all looks the same. Trees after trees. It was so dark out tonight too. The moon was only a quarter of its size and the clouds covered what little light it might have aided in this situation. The air of the night was silent. I could only make occasional noises from the jeep that I know should not be happening.

I listened closely trying to hear if this guy was breathing and I could not make anything out. Panic hit again. What in the hell was I going to do? I am in no shape to carry them anywhere. This guy looked like he was a foot taller than me. I really wish I knew how close the house was, but if I took off trying to get to the house what do I do with him? Do you know how bad it would hurt to drag someone across asphalt? I do not know and do not want to find out. Could I even make it to the house to use a phone?

I turn myself back to the guy in front of me and I really try to focus. My vision keeps going in and out of focus. It is so dark outside. This is why mother says nothing good happens after midnight. I crawl a little closer and my heart sinks when I notice the sandy brown curls of the person laying in the road.

Pine and cinnamon hit my nostrils and I almost empty my stomach right there in the road. My mouth becomes dry and my knees faulter almost causing me to stumble over as I pick up my pace. I get a newfound strength and I crawl a few more feet. I start shaking, the tears are coming down so fast. I roll the person over and my world shatters. There laying in the road was Axel Anderson. I attempt to shake him, but he still is not moving. I lean down and try to listen, but I am trembling so badly that I cannot make anything out. What have I done?

Chapter 28

The next thing I know, I feel myself being carried. I smell cinnamon and pine and I smile. A deep, show all your teeth beam. This is heaven. I do not know what happened, but I am in heaven. I snuggle in closer to the warmth and hear someone chuckle. I am still halfway out of it when I hear, "glad you think that this is such a nice situation." I snap out of whatever la-la land I was in.

I hit the ground with a loud thud and back away. My back hurts and it causes my head to feel like it is splitting. I look around and notice we are at the steps of my house. I begin rubbing my temples with my hands and then the flash backs hit me. I look at him with a look of pure horror.

"What? How? What are you doing here? How are you walking? Where did your clothes come from? What is happening to me? You were... You were..." I started rambling and before I could spit out what I needed to say, Axel stopped me by his roaring laugh. "Gah Ads, you really hit your head hard. Do you not remember what happened? You called me and said you had a wreck. I came over as soon as I could, and you demanded that I drive you home before you passed out on me. See?" He points behind me and I see his truck parked in the driveway and I start shaking my head. "No, that is not what happened. Axel, I remember. I remember seeing you on the side of the road. I hit a tree. I crawled over to you lying in the middle of the road. I thought you were dead." He looks at me and worry crosses over his face. He is doing the thing again where his eyebrows come together in the middle, almost touching. It causes deep creases across his forehead and I want to hold the side of his face and rub the concern away with my thumbs.

He tries to help me get back up and I push him away. "Answer me, Axel. Answer me. Tell me the truth. I don't understand why you are lying to me." He looks over at me again and steps closer. I can feel the hot air from the sigh out of his nose. "Adalee, I did tell you the truth. You called me and told me you had a wreck. I pulled up and you were passed out in the driver's side of the Jeep. It is totaled. I think you got hit by the air bag too hard." I throw my hands up to stop him abruptly.

"Axel stop lying. Why are you doing this?" I do not understand why he is doing this. "I pulled you out and you came to momentarily and muttered something about your dad and how your mom is going to kill you. You asked that I take you home. I tried to tell you I would take you to the hospital and you begged me not to before you passed out again." I start shaking my head and muttering no, repeatedly. "Axel do not do this to me. I know what I saw. You were in the middle of the road. I thought I killed you."

He comes over and sits beside me. "Adalee, look at me. Not a scratch on me. Don't you think that if you had hit me, I would have some kind of scratch on me? You might have almost hit an animal. That I believe. You probably swerved and hit a tree trying to avoid the animal." I look at him and tears spring to my eyes. Why doesn't he believe me? I know I probably sound like a crazy person, but I swear that is what happened.

"Yeah, I did hit an animal and that animal was you." I look over at him and I notice his expression turns into regret. I do not know why he would look at me that way unless he regretted coming to get me. "Fine, just leave me. I know you do not want to be here. All you do is save me and every time you have a look of regret in your eye. I know you hate having to come save me. I am sure you don't have to save Veronica." I get up and run to the door.

I pump my legs faster than they should go and they ache with every step. I go to open the door and Axel spins me around and pins me against it. "Why do you do that Adalee? Every time. Every time you read my expressions, you guess what it could mean and then throw Veronica in my face." I could feel the anger radiating off of him in waves. The vibrations of his wolf wanting to come out and play.

"What am I supposed to think Axel? You had her and then I came along and got in the middle of everything. I know you only come because that is the person you are. Yet, I know it has to be annoying to constantly come to my rescue." I sigh and notice that Axel's lips are mere inches away from mine and I want nothing more than to kiss him. His head drops and he acts like he wants to tell me more, but he will not allow himself to be that open.

"Spit it out Axel. Am I wrong for thinking these things? Am I wrong for knowing that you keep running back to Veronica when you leave me here wanting nothing more than to be in your arms? You cannot tell me you are so oblivious as to what I want. I feel the sparks and the draw between us, do you not feel those things too Axel?" I was becoming fed up with the back and forth. I push him away and attempt to open the door again. Its locked. I can tell he is right behind me and wants to say something. "Don't you dare say a word, Axel unless it is the truth for once. I know what I saw." I continue to pull against the door handle, but it will not budge. I am becoming frustrated and finally, I scream and pull at the door and the lock brakes. I look at it stunned for just a moment and I stomp inside. Not even caring that I didn't use an ounce of magic.

Axel follows right behind me and that infuriates me even more. "Adalee, how am I supposed to tell you the truth when I am afraid you won't accept it? How do I show you my biggest secret?" I turn so fast on my heels that Axel bumps into me. "How dare you bring that same excuse up! Every time you question whether I can handle it or not. You do not know what I can handle because you won't trust me enough to even try." I look at him and wait. Hoping my pleading expression would show him he has nothing to fear.

Of course, he just stands there like a stone statue. "I do not know what has you so worried, but I am not going to vanish whether you want that to happen or not. I am here to stay. This was originally my home and I do not plan on going anywhere soon. As for you and Veronica, I do not know what your relationship is like. I can tell you that I know she is not faithful. I see that she does not care about you. If you want to stay with someone like that, it is your choice. You have no idea what kind of woman I am because you have not asked." I was so frustrated I tried to turn around again to go up the stairs, but Axel caught my arm and spun me around. He kissed me with all of the passion I think he had, and it made my knees weak.

Before I could pull away, I close my eyes and I feel myself start to become dizzy. All of a sudden, I notice that we are being pulled into what seems like another memory. This one seems different though. This time we are at the Anderson's house. I look over, half expecting to be alone when I notice Axel is beside me with a look of shock on his face. "Adalee, what is going on. What is this?" He asks rather skeptically as he steps in front of me as a way to protect me. I laugh at him when all of a sudden from the side of us a younger looking Axel runs through us. "Okay Adalee, now would be the time to give some answers." I look over at him and I am at a loss for words.

Chapter 29

I look around and notice that even though this memory may be Axel's it feels as if I am supposed to be here. "Well Axel, usually when this happens it is my own memory. I think we might be in one of yours and I honestly have no idea why we are both here." His grip on me gets stronger and instinctively my thumb starts to rub the back of his hand. "This should not be possible. You should not see this." His voice is laced deep with disdain.

"I don't have control over what it shows me, Axel. I first started having my lost memories appear when I moved back. My first one being in the library on the first day of school. I think they are a way to show me things that I need to see." He looks over at me and the back to his surroundings. "So that is what was happening the first day I met you." I look at him curiously and he just shrugs his shoulders. "Adalee, I will admit you caught my attention in the library the first time we met. After that fateful moment, you consumed my every thought. I felt like I needed to protect you and so I kept a watch on you from a distance. Julia noticed and told me we should invite you both to lunch, but I knew Veronica would not like that."

Here in this moment, I can tell Axel is being as open as I have ever seen him. I will not lie it gave me butterflies knowing I caught his interest. "Julia did not care what she thought. Well, on the first day I kept asking Julia questions about you and she started teasing me, so I stopped voicing my curiosity. When I walked into the library during the last period, a smell of roses and rainwater hit my nose. It smelt heavenly, so I followed it and I noticed you were sitting in the corner of the library by yourself. I tried to get your attention, but you were so zoned out I decided it was best if I left you alone. I stayed out of the way, far enough to look out for you and not let you catch me." I am sure my face showed pure shock as Axel, for the first time, admitted something that seemed like the truth. He looks a little sheepish confessing all of this. I turn back to the memory and it starts to change to where Axel looks to be about ten.

I start walking and he never releases the grip on my hand. I think he was afraid of what might happen if he became disconnected from me. His grip giving way to the nerves he must be feeling underneath. "Adalee, what are we doing? Can we walk through my memory like this? Can they see us?" I looked over at him and could see the tension in the vein running down his neck as it pulsated continuously. The muscles in his neck shoulders looked like they carried the weight of the world on them.

"Axel, I can tell you that they cannot see us. We are seeing a memory that you have in a different view. This one looks like you might be eight or so, I am not sure. Do you remember this?" I notice he looks around and we start to walk through the house chasing after his younger self. The house is full of tons of people prepping for a party of some sort it seems like. "Oh no. Why would it pick this memory?" He groans out loud.

I causally answer what I feel is right. Unsure, if it will help him to become at ease. "Like I said earlier, usually when this happens it is because my memory has something it needs to show me, one way or another." I notice he starts pulling me to a different room. "Adalee, I don't think we need to see this memory. Is there not some way for you to change it?" I laugh at his suggestion.

"Axel, you act like I am in control over this. I just go along with it." Before Axel could get anything else out, I hear shouting from the other room. I walk around the corner and Axel follows me with his head down. I can feel his shudder as the vibrations rocket up my arm. "How dare you question me!" I hear his father's voice and I walk into what I assume is a second living room area and see Axel step in front of his sister just as his father goes to backhand her.

Axel flinches beside me at the same time his father's hand makes contact with his face. My stomach drops thinking this is how they grew up. Julia is crying and Axel looks at his father with such determination that I admire the little boy in front of me. "You would be wise to learn your place, boy. As would you Julia. Your brother won't always be around to take responsibility for your screw ups."

The memory changed again, this time it was in the evening and it shows Axel a few years older. "Axel, I am sorry. I do not know what else to say." He looks at me and then down at his feet again. In this moment I can see his raw, deeply buried pain. I squeeze his hand to show him the only reassurance I can think of. "It is okay, Adalee, no one but Julia knows about our father. Not even our mother. He has a mean temper and that is the day I told myself I would take both mine and my sister's beatings."

"Axel. No one should have to grow up with that burden." His features soften as he starts to talk as if some of the pressure he is holding starts to become released. "He got mad that she wanted to hold her doll during the party. She was showing him the dress she made so that way the doll fit in with all of the ladies at the party. I could feel when she started to feel unsafe and I rushed to make sure she did not get hit." Something so simple for him to lose his temper over.

"You know he is an amazing leader for our people, but he has a temper. It stopped after a few years when we both got old enough to stand our ground a little." I was stunned into silence. I stopped and pulled him into a hug. I did not know what else to do. He finally gave in and I could feel him slump against my hold. We stood there, just holding one another, not wanting to let go. It was not long when I heard the happy birthday song being sung by what seemed like thousands of people. I pulled us through the french doors and was shocked at the gathering before me. There was a massive cake and Julia and Axel stood blowing out candles.

"Ugh Adalee, I don't think you need to see this memory. I don't want you to see this part." He was becoming panicked and I am not sure what was about to happen, but I felt in my core that I should see what was going to take place. He tried to get me to pull away. He kept tugging at my hand. "No Axel, I need to see this. I need to know what is going to happen." I shouted back and pulled us back towards where the twins were walking.

The moment I pulled back, our hands disconnected and then it was just me inside Axel's memory. I was shocked that I was still able to see this piece of history. My curiosity was peaked so I followed the crowed as they made it to a stage just at the edge of the forest. I noticed Axel's father and mother stood at the center with Axel and Julia off to the right. Axel's father held up a hand and the crowed greeted both of Axel's parents with, "Good evening Alpha and Luna" and then silence filled the air. I continued to walk through the crowd, sometimes saying excuse me and sorry to the spectators. Forgetting I was just a spectator and nothing more to the past.

After a long speech from the Alpha and Luna, I heard them each greet the twins. They talked about how proud they were for this moment and how much it was anticipated. I could see both Axel and Julia looked terrified, yet they both held their heads high. I admired how they could stand in front of a crowd this size. "Members of the pack. We will begin the ceremony to welcome both Axel Eli Anderson and Julia Grace Anderson as official wolves."

"I, Axel Eli Anderson, promise to put my pack first above all other things. I promise to be guided by the moon and allow Selene the Moon Goddess to use me as she sees fit. I promise to one day take the role of Alpha to which I will lead to the best of my ability. I promise to keep our pack and way of life secret from all creatures of the sun."

After Axel Julia spoke. "I Julia Grace Anderson, promise to put my pack first above all other things. I promise to be guided by the moon and allow Selene the Moon Goddess to use me as she sees fit. I promise to one day have a mate and that we will join in treaty to keep my pack safe. I promise to keep our pack and way of life secret from all creatures of the sun."

After they spoke their vow both Mr. and Mrs. Anderson slit their palm with a dagger and let it drain into a very old looking chalice. Once they were done Axel and Julia both slit their palm and did the same thing. I heard Mr. Anderson speak in a booming voice and his eyes glowed with a light that was almost the color of the moon itself. "Will the Silver Dawn Pack join me in welcoming both of my children as official wolves to this pack." After Mr. Anderson spoke those words the crowd joined in all saying, "Yes Alpha" and proceeded to howl. Axel took the chalice first and drank from its contents and then Julia followed. Once both had taken a sip they joined hands and both howled in unison.

A mystical force hit the crowd and you could see it continue to spread through the pack members. I was mesmerized into my spot. The crowd went deathly quiet when I heard both Axel and Julia cry out from pain and hit their knees on the stage. I could see Axel grab his sister's hand and tell her everything will be okay. I heard them both scream again, and a few words of encouragement came from the crowd. I noticed they started to arch their backs and it sounded like every bone was breaking in their body. What in the hell was going on?

The crowd started to whoop and holler and I could not believe they would encourage whatever was going on. I ran as fast as I could to the stage and stood between Axel and Julia. Wishing there were something that I could do. Being this close I noticed their hands and feet slowly turned into paws and fur started to sprout from their skin. Their clothes ripped and in a matter of seconds there stood a massive black wolf on my right where Axel was just laying, and a massive white wolf were Julia was laying.

The scene around me began to shift and pivot. What in the world is going on? I felt my head go dizzy and the urge to throw up rise from my stomach. I swallowed hard and blinked a few times. I shook my head and attempted to leave this memory, but still I was stuck.

The next thing I know I am looking at an office. Axel's father sat at a large oak wood desk with Axel behind him who looked slightly older than the last memory. I walked around to catch a glimpse of the voice coming from the wing backed chair in front of me.

"Anderson. Are you sure the boy should be in this meeting?" The questions came from no one other than Principle Allen. I watched the reaction from Axel and noticed he neverblinked. He remained there with a stone-cold expression on his face and it made my blood run cold. The atmosphere was so thick with tension I felt it coat my lungs making it hard to breath.

"The boy knows his place. I have made sure of that. He is the future Alpha, and he should know what must be done to protect our people in the future." As I take in the contents of his desk, I notice a large map with coven locations written all over the world on it. Occasionally, I noticed a set marked out in red.

"Anderson, I feel that the council is unwise about attempting to allow a peace treaty with the witches." Axel's dad takes out a large marker and hands it to his son. "You don't have to worry about the witches causing a problem. By the time the treaty passes there won't be many left." As if to drive out the point, Axel takes and marks a large X through a coven's name in Alaska.

"What if the council gets word? You could be starting the next war." The laugh that Alpha Anderson gave was one harsh enough to send chills down my back. How could they be okay with this? How could Axel know any of this information and still look me in the face knowing what I am? "The council thinks that the hybrids are raging this war. If they get smart enough to suspect us it will be too late, and the witches and half breeds would have done more of the work for us." The guy's words from the party rivets around my mind. I really might be in danger as the word half breed stings me to my core. There is no way this could be real. No way any of this was true. Could Axel's father and Principle Allen really be trying to start a war from the shadows?

Chapter 30

I look up and we are still standing at the base of the stairs. Axel is pacing back and forth, the strain across his face shows me just how apprehensive he is. Once he realizes that I am back from his memory he takes a step towards my direction and the only thing I can think to do is bolt.

I run up the stairs and to my room. Before I could get the door completely closed, Axel's hand pushes against it just enough to not allow the door to shut. Frustrated, I kick the door and it splinters at the bottom. I throw my hands up to my face and I am in complete shock at what I just did.

"Adalee, what did you see to cause you to be this upset?" I can hear his voice almost at the edge of tears. I can tell he really wants to help. I step backwards until I hit my bed and I allow myself to fall back into it. "I think you need to explain a few things to me." My body feels on edge. As if at any moment, danger could present itself. I would like to think that I would listen, but my heart is pushing me to continue with searching for answers.

Axel cautiously walks over to my bed and the first thing he does is grab my hands and pulls me to a sitting position. I feel sparks of electricity where our hands are, and it seems magnified by one hundred compared to what I would feel earlier. I gasp and look at our hands and then back to Axel's. I notice his eyes grow wide. "It has never been this strong." He mutters and the only thing I can respond with is simply, "Axel, you can feel these too? I thought it was just me who felt this when we touch." I look back at our hands and hang my head unsure of what to do.

Axel lifts my chin to where I meet his gaze and it shows nothing but patience and understanding. "Adalee, I am sorry to have left you so confused on what has been going on between us. I was unsure and I will explain why. Can you first answer a few questions?" I look at him and all I can think about is my anxiety starting to rise again. Can I trust him? My mind is telling me to proceed with caution while everything else in me wants to run into his arms.

"Adalee. Can you answer my questions? What did you see?" I did not answer and think about if I should. What did I see? It was as if I was myself, but not completely. "Ads, please talk to me." He comes closer to me after a few minutes, I would move away if it meant me not ending up falling on the floor of my bedroom.

He takes advantage of me being at the edge of the bed and scoots as close as he can and starts talking. "Adalee, you have been asking for the truth, I feel like I can tell you everything now. That is if you want. Or I can walk out of here and you would never have to see my face again. It would physically kill me, but I would allow you that option." I look at him and I see nothing but sincerity in his expression. What do I do? My head feels like it is underwater. I do not move. I cannot speak. I can only focus on breathing. Breathing is the only thing that seems to be constant in my life right now. Making my chest go in and out is all I can seem to handle right now.

Axel takes my silence as a sign to wait. It feels like a lifetime passes as I finally settle on explaining what I saw. "After you left the memory, I saw you and your sister become members of your pack.

Once that was over, I was pushed into a more recent memory. One that involved you, your father and principle Allen." The moment I finish talking, he becomes a different person. He rushes over to the open window and closes it and draws the curtain. After that he rushes over to the door and slams it shut, locking us in my bedroom.

Fear starts to creep in as I watch him become someone I do not recognize. Self-preservation starts to surface as the realization comes together that it is just me and him in this room. "Adalee. I will explain everything about that moment. I know it looks bad. Just trust me when I tell you we are both not safe." When he grabs my hands to pull me closer to him, I can see my own fear flash in the reflection of his icy blue eyes.

The moment everything clicks together is like I got hit by a train at full speed. In the dim light of my bedroom, the moment Axel looks at me, the realization of who's eyes haunt me in my dream's surfaces. I double over and grip my head as memory after memory comes flooding in like the dam broke at Niagara Falls. "Adalee, what is wrong? What is going on? I think I need to call your mother or Mrs. Eva." Axel starts to panic, and I hold my hand up to shut him up and hopefully calm him down.

As the memories fly by a few stick out in my mind. I see my dad and I out playing in a field. I see my mother practicing spells. I see Brina's parents and my father going on pack runs. I see that my father was an Alpha. A damn good one at that. I see memories of learning to defend myself with hand-to-hand combat and magic.

I see myself controlling the weather and learning how to perform spells with Mrs. Eva. I learn how to disguise myself as a witch heeding my mother's warnings about letting the wrong people know the truth. Veronica, Brina and I playing as little girls and then growing up to have her shun us a few years later. Multiple memories of my father and principle Allen as best friends until one day they were not.

I see my mother the day of the funeral talking to a few different people and she looked terrified. Ten years of memories come flooding back and it is like I finally feel whole. It is like watching my life come across a TV screen as highlight reels. The most important memory I learn is that I, Adalee Ebony Rosewood, am half witch and half wolf.

Chapter 31

"Adalee, what is wrong? Please talk to me." I look over at Axel. Someone who is supposed to be this big strong alpha and laugh. I genuinely laugh because that is what a normal person does right? I feel like I am just now waking up from a nap and remembering where I put the remote that has been lost for a week. I feel like déjà vu has actually been proven to be real. I feel like I finally know who I am. Like I have been missing.

It does not take but a moment and Axel shows up behind me and stops me mid spin. "Adalee, what is wrong with you?" I look up at him and when our eyes meet it is like we are the only two people in the world. Is this what being mates mean? Before I could stop myself, I pulled him near and kissed him. My emotions were at an all new high. I felt whole and as fast as my emotions peaked, I remembered Veronica, and they crashed. I felt this insane amount of jealousy and it was not long before the wind picked up and lightning strike. "Tell me the truth. Tell me why you choose Veronica over me? Over your mate?" The thoughts of them together made me feel things that I never wanted to feel in my life. I felt my power grow stronger each second that passes. Feeling myself get lost in its magnitude.

As if he could read my mind, Axel starts to speak cautiously. "You know, I truthfully want nothing to do with Veronica. My hands are tied by a contract. A contract my father made me sign if I wanted to take over the pack. It is nothing more than a power move." He should really watch the hole he is digging himself. As he took a pause to see my reaction, I continued to stare at him with a look full of raging jealously. I promised him at one point I could handle all of this and I am determined to keep that promise.

He looked broken. He looked like he just lost his best friend. "Adalee, I am bound by oath and legalities to have someone at my side who makes me feel empty in my soul. The only reason she is okay with our arrangement is because of the power she is promised, it will be enough to keep her happy for a little while. In this life, that is a long time to remain empty." I know he can feel me seething. "To think I care about any of that. What I want to know is if you refuse to be with me because I come from mixed blood." He stops mid stride.

"You think I would care about that Adalee? If that were the case, I would have killed you the moment you moved back like my father ordered." The air leaves my lungs in such a rush the blackness that crowds my vision feels like a punch to the gut. "Explain yourself Axel."

"I was hoping that if I stayed away, the bond would not be strong enough for you to notice. Yet no matter what I did, I ended up around you. You had no clue about any of this." Another truth revealed that knocks the wind out of me. "So, you knew what we were, but decided that because I was… let me see ,a half breed mutt like Veronica called me, you would have been okay with ending my life after not knowing a thing about me?"

I can tell Axel is uneasy. The guilt he must be feeling is deeper than the ocean itself because I can feel it too. It feels as if someone has sat a weight on my chest. "No, you don't understand.

The moment I met you I had no clue you were my mate. That you were destined to be mine." The way his voice deepens as he states I was his causes my cheeks to flush pink. I shake the feeling away because now is not the time. "So, when did you know? All the times you walked away from me?"

Hitting a nerve on Axel almost causes me as much pain as it does him. "The night of your birthday when you finally turned eighteen. I knew when you disappeared, and my wolf went nuts knowing we had hurt you. I tried to stay away from you. Over and over again, but I was not strong enough. Adalee, I put you in danger." Axel walked over to the front steps and sat down burying his head in his hands.

"The night you woke up from your comatose state, I had a discussion about you with my father. My father has spent years convincing the council that there should only be true breeds mated. Mixing breeds can be dangerous, their powers way too strong. My father feels that individuals like yourself threaten his control." I walk over. Standing above him and I offer him my hand. He takes it and I pull him along. Not sure where we are going, just knowing if we are hand in hand, it will all be okay.

At first there is nothing but silence as I process how much danger I really am in. "My father told me that your mother had your memories hidden and that I needed to stay away. I should have stayed away. It would have made your life easier." He turned his back towards me, and I could tell he was struggling with something internal. "What made it easier when I did not know your father wants me dead? Made it simple for him to continue to execute innocent people because he is too small minded to see nothing but his power?" I stood there for a few minutes and waited. I felt my heart become heavy with anticipation. "Axel, can you face me so we can talk about this? Please?" The moment Axel turns around I can tell he is regretting whatever he is about to do.

Axel comes to me and pulls me into a hug. He hugs me like if he squeezes hard enough everything will be okay. I want it to be okay. He pulls back and plants a small kiss on my forehead. I want to live in this moment. I want to remain beside him. I want to keep us together. I pull back and before I could start to speak, he stops me. With his finger still pressed to my lips he looks down in shame. "Adalee, I placed a target on your back. I cannot undo what I have done, but I can try to place distance between us. You know how my father can be, and right now a target is placed on you. My father has

strong connections to the council and I cannot protect you from them

both."

A million questions race to my mind. "Axel we can stand up

to your father together." All we did was find out that we are mates.

"What will that do Adalee? Put the council on our backs. They

would see it as another reason my father was right." Is that not what

the beloved moon goddess wanted for us as creatures of the night?

To have someone that completes us. I need more answers but before

I could get my question out Axel takes a few steps back. What I hear

next ends my world.

"I, Axel Eli Anderson, reject you…" My heart shatters and I

fall to my knees. The pain in my heart feels like it is getting ripped

out of my chest. My body starts to throb. Axel stops momentarily

and then continues through jagged breaths. "Reject you, Adalee

Ebony Rosewood, as my mate."

My world stopped spinning as soon as he finished what he

was saying. I sat in the dirt outside on my knees gripping my chest.

Unsure of how to become balanced again. It felt as if I was thrown

into a jar and tossed around. How could he do that to me? Did this hurt him like it hurt me? I made myself stand up. No man humiliates me like he has and gets the chance to get away with it.

I look him square in the eye and utter one word with all the authority I have to offer. "LEAVE." The earth shook and the wind picked up and I stared at my former mate in the eyes. His expression was nothing but pain and regret, but I did not care how he felt at this moment. He lost the right when he rejected me. How dare he do this to me after all that I have had to go through to learn the truth.

I watch as Axel fights with my command. I remember that I may not have the physical capability to turn into a wolf, but I have alpha blood running through my veins. Once again, I give my command. "LEAVE, AXEL." I watch as he struggles. His eyes begin to glow a silver that is breathtaking. Watching as I challenge another Alpha with my will.

Where Axel once stood is now where a massive black wolf that is as tall as me stands. The wolf lowers its massive head and whimpers towards me. I stand tall and this time yell my command, not afraid to use my authority at full power. "I said to LEAVE AXEL. GO NOW. I hate you. I want nothing to do with you. Run back to Veronica because in this moment you are no better than she is. You were made for each other." As soon as his wolf form turns away from me the tears fall. The sky cries with me as a down pour soaked the earth where we stood. Axel paused for a moment, but never turned around, as if he wanted to come back.

I wished at the pit of my soul that he would come back for me. That he would choose me. He broke what was left of my heart when he finally walked into the night. I fell to my knees and wonder what I have done to deserve this. I look up at the moon goddess and all I can do is yell why. I hear a howl off in the distance and I know it is Axel. I hope he feels the pain he put me through.

I did not move from my spot and let the rain wash away what it could. I wanted it to wash away the feeling of his touch that still lingered on my skin. How could he give this up? How could he give us up? I do not know much about mates, but I know enough to know they are your other half. You will never find someone who can complete you like your mate can.

I will never know how it feels to be an alpha of a pack, I may have alpha blood in me but that does not mean I will ever hold such a position. That should not matter. I think back to my father's story and knowing what I do, I can almost guess his story was of him and mother. He told me that story almost every night before bed, until he died. I know that an Alpha will never be as strong as he needs to without a true Luna at his side. In the middle of my internal rant, Cameron's car drives up in the driveway. About time, I have a bone to pick with my best friend.

Chapter 32

"How dare you lie to me, Brina. I am your best friend. Correction, I was your best friend." I yell at her as I walk through the house sending objects flying left and right. I purposely aim for her and she dodges just like I know she can. She kept the biggest secret of her life from me for the past eight years. How dare she think I would just go on my way and forget that she kept this from me.

She may think this was something small, like it should be forgiven as easy as if someone accidently bumped into you at the mall. She acts like this was something as minor as eating the last piece of candy from the jar and not getting more. "How dare you keep this from me? Then you keep from me that you and Cameron are mates. What the hell Brina?" I throw a plate from the kitchen into the wall with a flick of my wrist. We argue for several minutes and the longer we argue the worse my control over my powers becomes with the sting of betrayal.

I can hear the thunder and lightning outside, and I know it is because of me. "Is this my mother's big secret? That I come from mixed blood?" The look on Brina's face says everything I need to know. I should calm down, but how can I when she kept something this big from me? How can I not be angry when my true soulmate rejected me just moments ago? I pick up another plate and send it flying. "Watch it Adalee. You're going to hit me with something." I know Brina is talking to me, but do you think I listen to her? No. I send a drinking glass flying and then a book off the shelf back-to-back. Listening to them shatter when they hit the wall. She hits the ground and in a matter of seconds is standing right in front of me.

How dare her? I push her back with a gust of wind and she hits the wall. Brina yells out in frustration. I guess Cameron had enough of our fight because he bursted through the door and let out a howl. "Brina, Adalee. Stop this. You guys are going to tear the house apart." I momentarily think about what he says and fling a couple more books in their direction. They both dodge and I kind of hate that they avoided them both. In the middle of me getting ready to throw another object in their direction, I get hit with this pain in my stomach. It is so intense that if I had food in my stomach, I would have thrown up. I double over into the fetal position.

Brina runs over to me and places my head in her lap. I become covered in sweat and start to shake. "Shhh. Shhh. Sugar pie it will be over soon. It is okay. I love you, Adalee. I am right here. Focus on my words. Focus on my voice. Breath in and out." I try to focus on her voice, but the pain was unbearable and caused me to writher on the floor. I do not know what the cause of this pain is, but I hope it will be over soon. I need it to be over, I am not sure I can survive this much longer.

After about ten minutes the pain slowly started to subside, and I was left with a dull ache at the pit of my stomach. My breathing was extremely labored, and I had a hard time trying to stand. Brina picked me up and carried me to the couch and laid me down. "Now let me get you a glass of water. I will be right back sweetie." She grabs Cameron by the hand and drags him into the kitchen. I try to tune out what they are discussing, but it became hard when I overheard Cameron mention Veronica's name.

I struggle to sit up and walk over to where Cameron and Brina are standing still discussing what just happened. I look at my best friend and tears spring to my eyes. "Just tell me what happened. I know you know what caused that pain. Tell me. Please Brina. I can handle it. Look what I have had to handle in the last twenty-four hours." I compose myself and give her my best smile. It was forced, but I think I pulled it off. "Okay Ads. This is not going to make any of this better though. Come sit down and I will explain the mating bond and how everything works." She leads me to the couch and helps me sit down. My stomach still feels on the verge of emptying its contents once again, but I swallow hard and force myself to keep a smile on my face.

"Okay. Where to begin." She taps her fingers together and is trying to gather her thoughts. I wish she would come out with it; the anticipation is killing me. "So, mates. Let's begin with what they are. Mates are two souls destined to be together. A mate complements you and makes you stronger in a sense. Selene the Moon Goddess hand picks each werewolf to have a mate. You are half werewolf which is why you feel the pull. Werewolf's can be mated to anyone; it is just rare that a wolf is mated to someone who is not full werewolf. If you had been just full witch and Axel was still mated to you, you would not feel anything you are feeling at this moment. You would not feel any part of the bond like he does. It would be like a normal human partnership. A mate bond increases your emotions as a wolf. It makes everything tenfold."

Brina paused for a moment and her head dropped as she continued on to what I was really needing to know. "It is very rare for mates to reject one another. It is said to bring on the wrath of Selene herself. Axel rejected you, but it is only one sided. You did not sever the bond because you did not reject him back. Once mates have acknowledged each other a bond is formed and then through the mating process and marking it becomes an unbreakable bond. With the start of the bond, you can feel things from your mate on an emotional level if the emotions are strong enough. When your mate betrays you, you will feel the pain you felt only minutes ago."

She paused and fiddled with her hands as what she said sunk in. It took me a minute to process and when it did, I was not sure what I should say. "Brina. Let me get this straight. So, Axel and I still have a bond? You are telling me he felt what I felt when he attempted to go through with the rejection? You are also telling me he is more than likely with Veronica at this moment? That is the pain that I felt. That is from the betrayal, more than likely with Veronica?" As if my night could not get any worse. "Yet, Axel can feel what I felt. He knows what he did, he also knows that the rejection did not take. Am I getting this right?" I look at Brina and Cameron and they both give me a slow nod.

"Okay." I say nothing more as I get up and stagger to my bedroom. The betrayal burned through me like a wildfire in an untouched forest. I burned with a rage that felt it would eat me alive. My veins scorching with the need to let my powers flow. The need to destroy something, anything.

I get in the shower and let the water get as hot as I can physically stand and then turn it up a tad bit more. With my skin burning, I begin to scrub. I want to feel new. I need to feel new. I need to go to sleep and wake up from this nightmare.

I sit down at the base of the tub and put my head between my knees. Lost, I imagine this is what a sailor lost at sea feels like. Drifting along, knowing eventually I have to end up hitting shore, but unsure of when that might be. How long can I wander until I lose my sanity? I eventually lay down in the shower, curling up into the fetal position, and letting the water wash away everything. The water runs long enough that it starts to turn cold and I know it is my time to get out. I told myself as I gather my towel that the moment I walk out of this bathroom, I am a new woman.

I hold my head up high and look at myself in the mirror. My skin is red from the heat of the water. My curls flattened against my shoulders. The weight of being wet causing it to stick to my back.

My eyes are red rimmed with mascara running from where I allowed Axel to get the better of me in thinking he was different. My shoulders seemed slumped with the pressure of what has changed between Brina and I as the lies continue to build up like a wall. My lips are in a thin line from the anger I feel towards my mother for thinking I couldn't handle the danger she placed us in.

I look at myself, really look at myself and think of my father's memory. He did not raise me this way. He told me repeatedly that "Queens hold their crown up. They do not back down. Queens only allow people to slow them, not stop them. They run this world. You my dear Adalee Ebony, are a Queen and do not allow anyone to tell you different."

As I continue to stare at the mirror, I straighten my shoulders and wipe away the black under my eyes. I force my lips to curve into a smile and I repeat what my father told me. "I, Adalee Ebony, am a queen. No one will tell me any different." I continue saying this over and over again. "I, Adalee Ebony, am a queen. No one will tell me any different."

Each time I say this it becomes easier. "I, Adalee Ebony am a queen. No one will tell me any different." Each time I get louder until I am shouting at the mirror. "I, Adalee Ebony am a queen. No one will tell me any different." I slam my fist into the mirror on the last time and the glass shatters. I look at my hands, bloody and covered in glass. I run my hands under water in the sink to wash the glass away. I notice my hands slowly start to heal. I think about who I am and who I want to be. I know that I am Adalee Ebony Rosewood. I will come back from this better and stronger than before.

Chapter 33

I walk to my room and can feel the weight of today begging me to sleep. It was about four in the morning and so if I were able to fall asleep right away, I could wake up at around eleven and hopefully get things done before mom made it home. I am not sure what to do about my mother just yet, but I know I will have to confront her head on tomorrow. I get dressed in my best pajamas and braided my hair.

I pull my blanket up over my head and think positive thoughts regardless of how my mind continues to think of Axel. I think about the memories that used to be a blank void and how they now can come to life. It takes some time, but I slowly drift off to sleep. The darkness settles over my mind and consumes me.

I hear howling coming from my right. I hear panting up ahead. I hear paws turning against the earth as fast as they can go behind me. I feel panicked but comforted at where I am located. I can only see darkness, but it allows my other senses to take control. I hear whining and growling coming from somewhere to my left.

After a few moments they fade, and I am left at a pond. The same pond located near the Anderson's house. I remember running here the night I caught Axel and Veronica in his office. I made it to this pond, it seems odd that I would dream of this place. Had I been here before I started having my dreams? I think back and I cannot remember if I had ever stepped foot here before the night of the bonfire.

I walk to the dock like I have done a dozen times in my dream and sit to let my feet dangle. This time it is daylight in my dream. Most of the time when I dream of this place, the moon is shining above me at full force. I wonder if my wolf will be around to see me this time. I wonder about my wolf and think that maybe that was my self-conscious trying to get me to see the truth of the situation I was living in. Just as I am thinking if my wolf would show, I realize I finally have the courage to look at it in the flesh and demand who it could be.

As I was taking in the beauty around me, I heard steps behind me. Odd, usually they are almost silent as the wolf in my dreams walks up in caution. Maybe this time my self-conscious knows I can handle the truth and so it does not need to sneak something into my dreams. "I am shocked to see you are still in my dreams, wolf." I throw out behind me.

What is the worst that can happen, it is my dream after all. The thing behind me stops. I would turn around, but I figured the mystery being would reveal itself eventually. Right now, I was enjoying the view in front of me. Utter peace settling over me.

The lake looked beautiful in the daytime. It was a deep blue that seemed to be as deep as the ocean. There were lily pads and cat tails along its banks; they put a nice green contrast to the dark water. The trees danced in a soft breeze that somehow found its way to this clearing deep in the forest. Colors of orange, yellow and red danced in the background as the trees swayed back and forth. I thought it might be nice to have long sleeves or a jacket seeing as it was October, but then again, I was pretty accustomed to the cold seasons.

"Are you just going to stand there?" I casually state as I lean forward and twirl one of my hands in the water. Still, nothing comes from behind me. I hear nothing but the rustling of leaves from the trees deep in the forest and the heavy uneven breathing that brushes my neck. "Adalee, I don't know why we are still meeting here."

I nearly fell into the water, he startled me so badly. Had it not been for Axel wrapping his arms around me to save me, I would have ended up soaked from the pond. I picked myself up and turned to face him. Just mere inches away from his face and shoved him backwards with all of my strength. He stumbled backwards. "What was that for Adalee?" He yelped out.

"How dare you sneak up on me like that and scare me by yelling at me. I nearly had a heart attack. Come to think of it, I think I would rather have one than face you right now." I turn my back to him and place my hands to my temple. "Go away. Go away. Go away." I whisper to myself, but loud enough he would hear it and get the idea.

He laughs at me and I whip my head around. "Adalee, I am not going anywhere, and I didn't yell." I start pacing as the overwhelming feelings that seeing him brings starts threatening to pull me under. "This is as much my dream as it is yours. We are bonded." Great. That is just what I wanted to hear. I refused to give way to the yearning in my heart.

"Have you been the one in my dreams this whole time?" Axel pulls his arm up over his head and scratches at the back of his neck. His face showing a sheepish grin. I watch the way his bicep strains and pops in the movement of his arm. "That look of guilt is unbecoming on you."

"I didn't realize you cared what looked good on me Adalee. I am touched." I sure hope the amount of disdain that is seeping from my pours shows Axel just how wrong, but so right, he might be about that statement. "If I recall, I am not the one who tried to reject you." The pain that flashes in his eyes is one mirrored in my own.

He shuffles back and forth slightly unsure of how to proceed. Awkward tension filling the air. "We have actually shared a dream together for weeks now. I stayed in my wolf form during the other ones because I was afraid I would startle you. I was honestly freaked out when the first dreamed happened the night before school started." Good to know this is just as shocking to him as it is to me.

"I remember thinking how life-like it was. I tracked you in the woods once I heard you run. I may not have known who you were, but I could feel the connection we had. It was strong even through the dream." He looked over at me and his shoulders dropped as he admitted all of this to me. All this time I thought I was alone, that the wolf in my dreams was nothing more than what my subconscious had decided to make up. Is anything in my life what it seems?

"Then I went to school and saw you and became curious about you Adalee, but I didn't want to let anyone in on the secret. I know Julia got suspicious, but she made sure not to do anything that tipped me off to how much she did know." I think back to my friend. To this girl who has grown so close to me but the betrayal from Brina has me doubting if she has been completely honest with me.

"At first, I thought you were a human at school. You mother did a great job of covering not only your memories but your scent also. Each species has a distinct scent to a wolf. Yours is definitely unique and I can see why she masked it." I start to walk away from him again. Needing to clear my mind and being so close to him just jumbled everything up. I could feel the sparks and electricity of

Axel's touch as it laced around my skin at my wrist. Such a small gesture had me wanting to run into his arms, but the pain of last night tainted it all. Like placing paint into the clear water that was us. It will never really be removed; the pain will always be present.

"It was not until you walked into my office the night of the party that I could actually smell what you were and then the dreams made sense with you being a witch. Well, half witch." The world seems to spin out of control as I think about what I should even feel. It is as if all I can do is succumb to the raging storm inside of me.

"So, what you're saying, Axel? Is this is another lie to add to your pile?" I gave back in a snarky tone because I could not think of anything else that sounded fitting. His expression turns to one of stone. "Adalee, I promise I do not want to fight. Honestly, I want nothing more than to take you and make you mine. I cannot do that without starting a war and putting you in harm's way."

The way his words bound against me makes them seem hallow. "How am I supposed to believe another meaningless promise?" I become torn. I can see the internal struggle he is having as if I am front row to the picture show. "I know at your house I was a coward. I took the easy way out and attempted a rejection, not knowing you had to repeat the phrase back at me. I thought it would allow you to be free from me."

I stop. My jaw hitting the floor. "Is that what you think I wanted Axel? To be free of you?" This time he takes both of his hands and drags them down his face. "I thought what I was doing was keeping you safe. Yet, the moment I felt what kind of pain you were in because of me I ran. I felt your heart break at what I told you while we were outside your house. I relished in the pain I caused because I knew I deserved whatever was given to me." He paused and looked down in what I would like to think is shame.

Serves him right. He should feel shame and guilt, but do I really want him to feel this way? I know he is my mate, and we have a bond, but I also do not know what position he was put in by his father. Maybe he thought what he was doing was right. "How can you think that a rej… rejec… rejection would fix this? We are past the point of trying to fix this."

I had a hard time getting that word to come out without feeling like I am suffocating. "You may have felt the rejection was justified, but that does not excuse what happened after Axel. Why run to Veronica when I know you felt what I did because we are still bonded." I see him look up like he was shocked I wanted to discuss this topic.

Why would I not want to know why he betrayed me with another? "Truthfully, I was hoping that if you knew I betrayed you then you would go through with the rejection. I knew once I left it was not completed because I could feel the pain and rage through the bond. I had forgotten that we both have to say it in order for it to work." The anger in me started to overcome my thoughts. It sat there at the pit of my soul festering and bubbling. "So, I ran straight to Veronica and she had no problem going along with what I wanted. Even though it is not what I wanted at all. I wanted to run back to you and never let you go. To take you and let us leave my father and the council behind."

He paused for a moment and the thought of him and Veronica was enough to make me see red. I do not know if it is because I am part wolf, but I have this newfound raging jealously and I wish it would stop. "Adalee. Please. I need you to believe me. I went to Veronica for a messed up reason, but I could not go through with any of it. I went to her and the moment our lips met I could feel the pain you felt through the bond."

I don't know why I was expecting his confession to make this better. All it did was make me step back clutching my stomach. "I was revolted just looking at her. I could not take the guilt. You know I ran straight back to your house. I caught Cameron leaving and he hit me square in the jaw." A small glint of satisfaction creeps in thinking of how that went down. "He practically laid me out in the front yard. I could not be mad. My beta thought so low of me that he hit me as hard as he could and walked away only saying that I better get in his car."

I take in his words. One by one judging if I could trust them. "I had the hardest time leaving your house knowing I was the reason you were sobbing. I could hear it. It tore at me. The drive to our house was a long one. I went to bed hoping that I could talk to you and try to mend everything. I was such an idiot." I pinch the bridge to my nose. Hoping it would give me some clarity.

He attempted to walk closer to me, and I held my hand out to stop him. I could not believe what he was saying. He needed to know I was not weak, that I have a purpose besides what our life could have been. "Axel, I am your other half. The one made for you and you decide to take it into your own hands and just decide what I can handle."

The clouds in the sky slowly starts to gather. Casting a shadow over what should be a beautiful day. "Axel, you just made the choice regarding both of us and did not even think to ask if I might have wanted to fight beside you. You would know enough about me if you had spent some time actually getting to know me instead of pushing me away, that I am always up for a challenge. I am stronger than you give me credit."

I was beginning to have enough of him in this moment. I was really hating that he was ruining this small piece of normal in my life. It was like he was all consuming and taking over every inch of my life. I was trying to put myself first. I was attempting to see my worth and he was not making that easy.

"Adalee, I know that I jumped in and didn't ask you what we should have done. It should have been a decision between us, and I made it a decision solely based on my judgement. I will regret it for the rest of my life, but I felt that my back was against the wall." He slowly makes his way towards me. The wind swirling from my fingers pushing us together instead of apart.

"Veronica went to her father and they are bringing this up to the council. There is a reason there are not many hybrids roaming the earth." I think about what that could possibly mean for me. Words of caution flowing through me at a whisper. "Axel, I am more worried about what my mother is going to do when she gets home from her business trip. Not whatever this council business entails."

Axel stands inches away from me. Our emotions swirling like the snow in a blizzard. Our bodies hum a tune together that is as unique as a snowflake. "Adalee. I am sorry for this, but I can't fight it anymore." Before I could ask what, he meant, his lips were on mine. My body giving in to his as I knew I wanted this more than anything else. My anger and rage melting away because I knew Axel would be mine from here on out.

As I start to become lost in the moment, my memories of the night before come in full force like a slap in the face. This house. Our house. My mother. I sat up in bed and looked around my room and threw myself back against my mattress. This was going to be a lot of work.

Chapter 34

It took me a good twenty minutes to get up and get my feet moving.
I feel rested physically. Pretty shocked that Axel had to interrupt my
dream. However, I feel drained mentally with everything that is
going on. Is running away an option? No, that is right because as dad
used to say, "I, Adalee Ebony, am a queen. No one will tell me any
different." I finally get dressed and head downstairs hoping that
Brina is up already. There is so much to do and so little time.
Practically no time to consider all that happened between Brina and
I. I walk to the kitchen and look at the clock. 11:45 is what the
microwave reads, and my mother will be home in four hours if we
are lucky.

I look around and realize the house is destroyed. It would be easier to just tear it down and build a new one. I make some coffee and sit on a bar stool not knowing where to start cleaning. At around twelve Brina makes her way downstairs and stops once she hits the bottom. "Adalee, we are going to be dead when mom gets home." I look over at her and just sip my coffee. I honestly have no idea what we are going to do.

I finally put my coffee down and look back at my best friend. "You think this is bad, you should see the jeep. We are beyond dead." The prick of treachery hitting my heart every time I look at her and act like everything is okay. I walk to the pantry and pull out a box of trash bags and grab the broom. "Hey Brina, I think we should start in the kitchen. It might be the easiest. It is also mom's favorite area in the house." Brina walks over and grabs the broom from my hand. She lingers looking at me as if she needed to say something. I turn away from her, never giving her the chance.

We turn on some music and get busy. About thirty minutes into cleaning, we hear honking coming from outside and we both look at each other. We are so dead. We have not made a dent in what needs to be done. We walk over to the door and just stand by it closed, "Brina, why is she here so early? She told us this afternoon." I got pretty squeaky on the last part and my voice hit a few octaves higher than I thought it could reach.

Brina takes in a deep breath and opens the door about the same time that Cameron reaches for the handle. Cameron falls through the door and hits Brina. The pure weight of his six-foot five frame causing her to be thrown off balance. Before Brina had time to process she had him flipped over and pinned down on the floor in less than ten seconds. I was super impressed with her fighting skills and I think I need her to brush me up on mine, it has only been about ten years.

Brina notices that it is Cameron and immediately gets off of him and starts apologizing. "OMG honey britches, why would you scare me like that? Are you okay? Did I hurt you? Oh, Cameron I am so sorry." He gets up and starts laughing. "You are such a feisty one, B. I have my work cut out for me, don't I?" Brina becomes the shade of a stop sign and I could not help but join in on Cameron's laughing. It was pretty funny.

"Shut up y'all. Now Cameron, what are you doing here? You gave Brina and I a heart attack. I told you this morning I had my work cut out for me." He pulls her in for a quick kiss and then steps

inside the house and picks up the broom. "You thought I was going

to let you do all this by yourself? Also, I brought company, Adalee.

Hope you do not mind." I look over at him and my eyes narrow.

About the time I turn around to step around the door frame

and look outside I hear him outside talking on the phone. Axel

sounds like he is in a heated conversation, but it does not last long. I

step out on the porch and my heart hurts because the last time he was

here, he tried to reject me. "I am a queen." I repeat more to myself.

"Yes, you are babe." I hear come from beside me. I was so in tune to

Axel I had missed Julia and Carter were walking up on the porch. I

was so happy to see her that the second it registered who was beside

me I flew to her and gave her huge hug that almost knocked both of

us down. I think we might have hit the ground had Carter not held up

Julia from the back. He was always so protective of her.

Tears sprung to my eyes when I looked at this girl. I refused

to allow the suspicion that started creeping become more than a

simple second of a thought. I had missed her and when I needed a

friend most, she was here. I mean Axel was here also, but he looked

like he got dragged into coming where Julia volunteered.

Still embraced in our hug she casually whispered in my ear, "I know he messed up. Just don't be too hard on him. He does deserve it though." I pull back and roll my eyes. "Okay Ads, we are going to get to work. I figured you and Axel could get your jeep and tow it back. It is like six or seven miles up the road." Julia was always one to take charge. I think she might have been better at it than Axel.

"Once we get it back here, we will call a repair shop and have them tow it. Also, here catch these." I reach out my hands and catch a set of keys. "What are these for Julia?" She laughs and just points outside. At the same time Brina comes running outside and yells a huge heck yeah and does some kind of dance to herself. Cameron comes behind her and busted out laughing. "Ugh, I still don't get it!" Before anyone could answer Axel walks next to two brand new identical Jeeps and opens the door. "Adalee, one is yours and one is Brina's Jeep."

Axel starts to give me that sheepish boy grin and goes to scratch the back of his neck. "I felt bad seeing as the night you wrecked was really because of me and so I got you one and Cameron got Brina one. We can't have our girls stranded."

I looked at him and became pissed. Happy, but pissed at him because he just admitted he lied about my wreck last night. I knew I was not crazy, and he had me imagining that I was seeing and believing what did not exist. As if he could read my mind, he butts in really quick with another apology. He is full of those lately. "Look Adalee, I am sorry about lying last night. I just was afraid you would run if I admitted I was coming to check on you. I will not tell another lie from here on out."

He gave me his best set of puppy dog eyes and I could not help but roll mine. I might not give him hell forever, but he deserves some of it. "These are a nice jester, but I cannot accept mine. I can get my own vehicle. You did not owe me anything, Axel." Brina looks over at me and her jaw hits the floor. "Speak for yourself sugar, I love mine. Thanks pumpkin!" she says as she turns to Cameron and gives him an uncomfortable, awkward kiss.

"Adalee, please accept this small gift from me. I really only got it because I caused you to wreck last night. I do not know why I stopped in the middle of the road; it was like I was forced to stop moving. I know it sounds weird, right? It was like I was mesmerized by your jeep lights." I look down at the keys in my hands. The metal feeling hot and heavy against my skin. "Please. I feel bad. If you want, just drive it until your old car gets fixed and then I will take it back and let it sit in the garage until it rots." I look at him, really look at him and I feel like he is telling the truth. I sigh and just nod my head in his direction. It was a super nice gesture.

"So, let us all get inside, and we will come up with a plan to get everything in order before mom comes home. After that, Axel and I will get the jeep and tow it back." We all stand around what should be our living room. Guilt starts to eat at me when I think about the destruction I caused.

We come up with a plan for Julia and Carter to tackle the kitchen while Brina and Cameron start on the living room. Axel called a few people from the pack to bring over some tools and fix some of the things that got broken like the door that is splintered. Julia comes over and shoos me outside. "Do not worry Ads, we will have this place in tip top shape. Just go get your jeep so you can come back and help" I shake my head at her and walk towards Axel's truck. I walk to the passenger side and he runs around and opens the door for me and then he proceeds to buckle my seat belt across me.

When our skin touches, it is like fire is dancing through my veins. Melting away all the animosity I might be feeling. My natural response is to take in a deep breath of air and I notice Axel freezes with his hand just over my lap. He looks up at me and I slightly flinch hearing the click of the buckle. When he gets back inside the truck, I am not sure what to say, so I pop off some smart comment. "You know I could have buckled my own seatbelt. I am not incompetent."

He looks over at me and never misses a beat. "Adalee, I did not do that to show you were incompetent. I did that to give me peace of mind to know you are safe while riding with me." Speechless. He is really laying the charm on thick. He starts driving and he gets about halfway between the house and the scene of the wreck when he looks at me and does not stop.

His gaze burning into me. Like light in the darkness. I squirm in my seat a little and turn my attention to the trees outside the passenger window. Beautiful colors of yellow, orange, and red with an occasional stubborn leaf that is still green. It may not be a stubborn leaf, but a late bloomer. That is how I feel right now, like I am super late to my own life.

I am that person who comes in after the first five minutes of the movie with popcorn spilling everywhere and my drink sloshing around on people. Interrupting the movie and then having to ask the people next to me why something is happening because I missed the beginning of the movie. Everyone knows that is the most important part. The whole thing is ruined if you miss it, yet there are still people who show up late and are an inconvenience throughout the rest of the movie. Is that what I am destined to be? An inconvenience to everyone for the rest of my life?

Axel pulls up to the where my jeep laid mangled. I am actually shocked I walked away from such a bad wreck. Most people would have been seriously injured, then I remembered I am not like everyone else. The front end was completely smashed and it caused the whole frame to shift around the tree. I was not sure it was even movable. The airbags deployed and it left a white dust everywhere.

The driver side door was thrown on the ground right where I left it. I marveled at my own strength for a moment and then turned to Axel. "So, how do you want to go about getting my jeep untangled from that tree? It looks pretty bad." He sits back in his seat and looks like he is pondering life at the moment.

"You know we will figure that out in a moment. We need to discuss something bigger than your jeep right now. The phone call I was on earlier was with a friend I have that works closely with the council and…" I stopped him abruptly. I was tired of hearing about the council and not knowing a thing about what they could possibly want with me other than I have mixed blood.

"Okay. You want to discuss all of this, that is fine. I am honestly not sure that my mind can handle that at the moment but go ahead and let's see if it will. What makes me so important that they might come for me?" I used my fingers and did the whole over dramatic air quotations on the they might come for me part. I had no clue about any of this so how could I fear the unknown?

After a few moments he starts at the very beginning and fills me in on every detail. "Okay Adalee, we will start from the beginning. I am sure you do not know about them, given your mother has kept you a secret from this life for the last eleven years. I want to start with your family first." I lean my head against the glass. Watching as it fogs up over and over again with each of my breath.

"Your father was an Alpha when he was alive. He was a strong leader and led his people with an iron fist. He was looked at to be one of the greatest Alphas of this generation. His pack held a large portion of the land that is to the South of what my pack has acquired." Unknown emotions stir in me now that I have memories to go along with what I am being told.

"The story goes that your father went years without finding his mate, your mother. He searched and searched but came up with nothing. It is said that he started to grow restless, impatient, and weak. A rouge Alpha came in and tried to wage war on your father's pack. He prevailed but lost many good men." I think of my father. Unable to see him as weak. In my memories he was massive in every part of his life. His size, personality and how kind he was to others. "He had determined that he could not allow his pack to suffer because other alphas looked down on him. He traveled deep into Northern Canada and asked the River Ash Pack for an alliance."

My memory of my father telling me this story played along with what Axel was telling me. "While on his way to visit them, he came under attack and that is when he found his mate. Your mother took off with a pack of warrior women before he could stop her. He continued on his travels and met with the Alpha of the River Ash

Pack. During his stay, there he was able to finally meet your mother. She was one of the daughters of the Alpha of the River Ash Pack."

I don't know why I feel I need to ask because I feel like this story might be common knowledge to someone of the wolf community. "Axel, how do you know this? How do you know this about my family? I don't even know this information about my parents, yet here you are spitting facts at me like you read an entire novel about my life." The air in the truck became thick with discomfort. How would he know this information?

"Well, after you called me your mate and then passed out, I knew that something was not right. I got super close with Mrs. Evanora. Out of everyone who might have been able to help, it would have been her." I chuckle thinking about Mrs. Eva in a nurse's outfit. Then I start thinking back into my memories and how she has always sort of been there.

"Tell me about why you feel as if you put me in even more danger?" Axel paused. Getting out of the jeep, I watched as he walked slowly to my side. His movement slow, but deliberate as he unbuckled my seat belt. Intense focus showing in every ounce of his being. Once my feet were on the ground Axel turned and went to walk past me. My question still unanswered.

"Are you going to answer me?" I was blunt enough to stop him. Slowly walking around him I grabbed his face with both hands. Showing him deep down how it was okay. Whatever he needed to say was going to be okay. "You can tell me. I can handle the truth Axel."

"It is not you who I am worried about, Adalee. Admitting what I did or really what I couldn't do. Just shows you how selfish I can be." He pushes away from me, but I am not letting him get off that easily. "Axel Anderson, just spit it out already." The seconds that tick by seem like an eternity. "Adalee. My father made a deal with me. In order to keep you alive I have to have Veronica as my wife. If I went against my father's orders, the arrangement was he would kill you and strip me of my title."

Chapter 35

For what seemed like an eternity we just stood. Staring at each other. As if moving would cause this moment to shatter. As if either of us dared to breath too hard we would lose everything. I could not take it any longer. "Axel, I don't care that you went against your father. I really doubt your father would actually go through with what you say. I mean that is just crazy."

This entire last twenty-four hours has come to be an absolute nightmare. I am sure of it; I will open my eyes any moment and all of this will go away. "Adalee, I am sorry I could not stay away from you. I fear your mother and Brina are also in danger."

A person can only have so much in her life she cannot control until she decides to do something about it. "Why don't we just go talk to your father? I bet we can clear all of this up." The laugh following that sentence was not the reaction I was expecting, and it rubbed my ego the wrong way.

"That can never happen, Adalee. Right now, I am positive my father doesn't know about us and I need to get you out of this city and into safety before he does." I pulled away from his embrace. I could see the pain it caused come across his face. His body reacted to mine without him even knowing. "I am not running away, Axel. I just found out that I am home. For the first time in years and I refuse to let some tyrant think he can scare me away."

I watched from the side as he stepped toward me almost automatically. I decide to put some distance between us as I walk over to the jeep. I needed a distraction, something to get my mind off of all the talk of me dying. Looking at this vehicle I have a hard time thinking my mother will let me live past tonight.

The front was almost unrecognizable and with the air bags out it was hard to see what the dash looked like from where I stood. "Hey Axel, why don't you swing the truck around, and we will hook up the wench and see if we can get it away from the tree." I hollered at him from the base of the ditch. I hope his truck has enough power to pull it free. I guess we will figure some way for it to come lose.

Axel walks down the ditch and stands next to me and looked for the best angle to park the truck. It was kind of steep and going to put the truck in an awkward position to use the wench. After talking about a few different options, we settled on the spot that would be best for the truck to get maximum traction.

Axel puts it in place and then walks down the cable and lays on the ground to figure out the best place to hook the jeep. Watching Axel underneath my jeep caused my stomach to flip and a rosy tint to hit my cheeks. My palms became sweaty and I could feel the hum of my body being pulled towards his. I needed to step away and cool off. "Hey, Axel, mind if I use your phone to call Brina or Julia? I want to make sure they are okay at the house." Still under the jeep he hollers out an okay and I walk back up the ditch.

As I am pulling out Axel's cell phone, I hear a commotion coming from behind me. It causes the hairs on the back my neck to stand up. Before I have the chance to turn around, panic rises up through my body. A terrifying and immobilizing fear grounds me to my spot.

I hear shouting and grunting coming from the direction of my wrecked jeep. In a matter of seconds, I run around the truck and look down to see Axel struggling with three huge men. He makes eye contact with me as he pushes off one of the intruders. "Run Adalee, NOW. Take the truck" is all he can holler out before they plunge a needle deep in his neck and I watch him go limp. I run back to the truck and before I could get the door closed one of the large men that was struggling with Axel rips the door from its hinges.

I kick the guy in the face and use magic to push him back as far as I can, thankful to have the natural elements at my disposal. Just as I am about to start the engine one of the men jump on the hood of the truck denting it in with the weight of his pounce. Startled, I drop the keys and start scrambling. With the flick of my wrist, I pick the guy up and toss him to the side.

I hear thunder booming ahead as my body goes into full flight or fight mode. Panicked is an understatement as to what I am feeling at this moment. What do these guys want with me? I find the keys and finally get the truck started. I throw it into gear and hit to gas. The truck launches forward and then the tires start to spin. The truck only moved forward a few feet and I curse under my breath realizing it is connected to the jeep.

Off in the distance I notice the guys get up and while I am focused on the two in front of me, the third guy grabs me from the driver's side. I kick and scream as loud as I could. Lightning strikes the ground a few feet in front of me and the wind whips around us causing dirt and debris to form a vortex around us. I attempt to use any magic that I can remember, but before I can compose myself to throw a blast in their direction, my hands are twisted behind my back. I am pinned to the ground and handcuffs are thrown around my wrist.

I try anything I can think of to get away and the three guys and stand up. A familiar voice cuts through their laughter. "Okay guys, load her up and make sure that you put the bag over her eyes." As I am trying to place the voice, I get picked up and I shudder when I see who the voice belongs to. It is Demetri, the same guy who tried to grab me from the bonfire. He notices the look on my face and laughs. "Told you I like to play rough. Don't worry, I did not extend my invitation to Axel this time." Before I could say anything, they place a bag over me and then something hits the back of my head

and my world goes dark.

Chapter 36

I can tell we are driving down a bumpy road. My back hitting against the metal truck sending a dull pain down my spine. I sit still and listen as best I can over the blaring radio. I and can hear the guys talking but cannot make out what they are saying.

I attempt to open my eyes in order to see anything and realize they kept my face covered. Terrified, I try to slow my heartbeat. It is racing out of my chest. I bend my body forward and try to wiggle the bag off my face. The feeling of the bag, the darkness, and being handcuffed makes me feel like I am suffocating. As if I have been lost to all of the air around me. My lungs burning as my breathing becomes faster.

My mind becomes foggy as I think about suffocating and what that would feel like. Would it be like falling to sleep? It can't be that way, not with the way my lungs are screaming at me from inside saying they need to take a deep breath. I feel my head begin to get woozy and my brow has sweat running down it. I can feel the sting in my eyes as the sweat makes its way down my face.

I finally get the bag off of my face and take in a deep refreshing breath. My heart calms down a little and I can feel my head start to clear. I look around and notice that it is dark outside. Was I passed out that long? My mind starts to race as I think of Axel and how the last thing I saw was his body being tossed to the side like a rag doll. I feel tears spring to my eyes, and I blink them back. No time to cry. I force myself to push Axel out of my mind and focus on the task in front of me. Right now, it is time to try to escape. I think back to the training my father gave me and I come up with nothing useful in this moment. Having the handcuffs secured behind my back puts me at a disadvantage.

I slowly work the handcuffs to the front of my body, making sure to be as quiet as I can. As I am trying to get myself in a position to possibly jump out of the back of the SUV, I hear Demetri tell one of the guys in the second row of seats to check on me. I push myself as close as I can to his seat in hopes he does not notice I am awake and with the bag off my face I can feel this guy's eyes on me as he does a quick once over and then turns back around. It was not but a minute or two later that I notice we are slowing down. I think that if I ready myself in the back to be able to spring forward once they open the door, I might surprise them and put some distance between us.

We come to a complete stop and I notice out the window that we are parked near a huge house. It was a beautiful home, but I had no time to admire anything about this place if I was to try to escape. I positioned myself once the guys left the SUV at the back, crouched down, to where when they opened the hatch I could jump out and hopefully make a break for it. I hear the guys at the back of the vehicle and my heart drops. "I can do this. I have people counting on me. I need to make it home. I have got this." I say to myself barely above a whisper. I see more movement at the back of the SUV, and I try my best to sit there patiently.

Fear was attempting to consume me. To drag me down beneath it's dark and overpowering waters. The suspense was killing my confidence, but finally I hear them press the button to open the back hatch. Once the hatch was halfway open, I sprang from the back and took off as fast as my legs would carry me. I was impressed with how fast my legs would go. I made it about two hundred feet to the edge of the woods. I felt like I was really going to make it and the moment I broke past the tree line I felt someone grab the back of my neck and slam me down.

When I hit the hard ground, spots filled my vision. The wind gets knocked out of my lungs. I look like a fish stranded out of water trying to gulp for air. The pain in my back lashing out down my arms and legs. My vision clears after a little time and I see Demetri standing above me with a sadistic grin on his face. "You thought you could get away from me, my little pet? I do not think so. We have got plans for you."

"Demetri, it is not kind to play with our prisoners." The raspy voice that just spoke sent a shiver down my spine. "Who made you the boss, Hunter?" The way he looks at me makes me feel as if I am no larger than an ant. His piercing black eyes makes me feel hallow inside. As if they could suck my soul right out of my body.

Demetri picks me up by the shirt high enough that my feet do not touch the ground, breaking me from Hunters gaze. I thrash around, panic filling me to the brim as I struggle to breath against his hand around my throat. "Are you sure we have to give her over? I kind of like how spirited she can be." He throws me back down at an odd angle. I hit the earth hard enough that I can hear a crack and I am pretty sure it was my shoulder.

"We have orders from the council Demetri." They walk over to me and I become pinned in my position. "You think I gave a damn what the council wants?" He spat his words out so harsh I could see the venom dripping off his lips.

In a flash Hunter has Demetri in the air without ever lifting a finger. "It would serve you well to watch your tone and temper with me, brother." The night of the party comes back to me. My body is tense like a tightrope walker trying to get to the safety of her platform. Every nerve screaming at me how much danger I am in. Hunter let go of Demetri. His coughing and sputtering made me happy. To see him struggle while I lie here at their mercy.

I finally get enough of my senses to me that I throw my hands up in an attempt to use magic. Nothing happens. No, no, no, why is nothing happening? Demetri sees what I am doing, and he

rests his back against a tree. "Not so tough without your magic, huh,

witch? Those handcuffs are designed specifically to keep your magic

at bay." He lets a chilling laugh ring through the air.

The tension in the air becomes unbearable, he walks over and

grabs my legs. I attempt to kick but all it does is anger him more. He

tightens down and it feel as if he will break my foot at any moment

if I am not careful. What little strength I do have is no match for

him.

I feel vulnerable. What is he going to do with me? I was told

the council only banishes mixed breeds. Does banishment mean

death? It is all I can do to not fight against his hold. As he drags me

out of the woods I look down and my clothes are torn to shreds and I

am bleeding from multiple cuts and scrapes along my torso. Demetri

looks over at me and then a sick grin comes across his face. "Do not

worry little pet. Nothing is going to happen right now. The fun

begins tomorrow." He leans down and picks me up by my hair and

then hits me one time in the nose and I black out almost instantly.

I get woken up by ice cold water being dumped on me. My

teeth chatter instantly. I try to move away from the miserable downspout of unbearable cold liquid but my hands and feet meet pain and resistance. I can feel the sting of my wrists and ankles after a few moments and it causes me to cry out. "Aw little pet, are you okay? Ha, just kidding. Do not think about trying to go anywhere. The more you wiggle around, the quicker the silver will eat at your flesh."

The smell of charred hair and flesh hits my nostrils and I feel as if I am going to throw up. "The more silver there is in your flesh, the weaker you will feel. They are also magic resistance, pretty nice touch, huh?" He steps closer to me and I flinch. "You know pet, you may have hated the water, but it did clean that face of yours. I can see what Axel finds so intriguing about you. Now that the blood is gone, you really are a looker." He reaches to caress my cheek and I pull away. Any movement I make seems to cause my wrists and ankles to burn and makes me writhe under the pain.

"I better go before Hunter decides to blow his top. Don't worry. I will see you later." Guilt burns through me as he grabs my chin, turning my head towards him with force. Shame follows his touch. He was looking at me like a dog looks at a steak. His laugh echoed throughout the room and then he got up and walked away.

After some time, some random guy comes and drops off a tray of food. It looked to be some sort of runny mashed potatoes with random vegetables floating in them and a glass of water. Nothing else. I am looking down at the tray when a soft voice seems to break my concentration. "I know this situation is not ideal, but it is best to keep your strength up my dear. I am sorry you are here." No sooner than those words were spoken, the guy who brought my food left. Making me question why I should eat this and what makes him think I would listen to someone like him. Look who he works for and the conditions I am living under.

I lean back against the stone and finally stop to take in my surroundings. The dull ache of my wrist and ankles are an unbearable reminder that I am trapped. The grey stone is riddled with mold and slime and the occasional scuff marks. I have some slack in my chains and I notice a commode in one corner. Guess they plan on keeping me here for a while. I look ahead of me and notice there is a cell on the other side of mine but I do not see anyone inside. The room is dark with just a single light above me.

I look down to see that my clothes are torn to shreds and I am nasty. There is blood down most of my shirt and I have dirt covering what is left of my pants. I figured my nose would bleed but I did not think it would bleed this much. I am soaked from head to toe and I begin quivering.

It is cold and damp down here and being dowsed in ice water does not help. I can hear my teeth begin to clang against one another so forcefully that I fear they might break. The shivering causes my muscles to cramp and my wrists and ankles to burn constantly.

I inspect my ankles and notice that the skin is starting to sluff off. That is going to leave a nasty scar. My nose is sore, and although my shoulder seems healed it still has some pain. Finally noticing my legs and arms I run my hand over where my scrapes are now healed. A bright, shiny pink tint to my skin and dried blood there where the scrapes use to be.

I sink even lower into the wall behind me praying I might melt into it. That I might blend in to where they will never find me. I am terrified about what is to come and what Demetri or Hunter might do to me. I think to what my mother must be feeling right now. A small tear spills over my cheek when I picture her face. She must be devastated. All those years she spent protecting me to finally be able to let her guard down and within a few months I get captured. Some daughter I am I just hope she is strong enough to pull through and find me before it is too late.

In this tiny prison everything seems to come into context. The pain and anger I felt towards Brina and my mother seem almost small at the thought I might never get to see them again. All the animosity and bitterness I felt at their betray of my trust seem silly.

I do not know how long I have been here, but I sat as calmly as I could. I finally gave in and decided to drink the water. It felt good going down my throat, hitting my stomach and sending a wave of relief over me. My body begged me for more, but I was unsuccessful. I tried to eat but the moment the spoon hit my tongue my insides threatened to spill out. I refused to throw up anything and waste the water that was sloshing like a metal weight in my belly.

After what seemed like an eternity the same soft voice from earlier came for the shadows. "Oh miss, you were supposed to eat. My boss will not be happy that you did not eat. I brought lunch, please try to get this one down." An older man makes his way in hesitantly and swaps the trays out. I notice this time it looks to be some kind of clear broth with water. At least I might be able to keep this down. I look up at the man standing before me and I cannot help but ask before he returns to the darkness. "Excuse me, sir, may I know your name? It might give me a little comfort to know something about this place."

The guy looks at me with a puzzled look. He comes a little closer and acts like he is going to speak, but then turns and hurries into the darkness. Maybe I can get him to warm up to me to where I might get some information as to where I am located. Not that it would do me any good. Who would I tell? I look at the water and the broth, thinking about if I should try it.

My stomach gives a rumble loud enough that it sounds like a monster in the dark. I tried the broth and the moment it hit my tongue, I turned up the bowl and proceeded to drink every drop. I downed the water and then sat back and waited.

I noticed how ghostly this place seemed to be. You could almost hear a pin drop it was so quiet. The solitude was enough to drive someone mad. Occasionally, you could hear a rattle of chains, but they seemed miles away. I figured it would be loud with hollering and screaming. I think I could have handled that better than the silence that fell on this place.

Demetri came and visited me for dinner and attempted to make conversation. I tried to keep my head turned away from his repulsive face, but every time I did, it gave him an excuse to grab my chin and pull my face towards his. My skin crawled everywhere his fingers touched. It caused a shudder deep in my bones with waves of indignity drowning me.

When he finally left my cell, the lights went out. Total darkness. Complete silence. It was maddening, how long would I have to endure this? I finally found a position that allowed me to sleep, but every few minutes my heart would jump, and my eyes would shoot open with the thought that someone was watching me. I begged Selene to allow me to meet Axel in our dream, but I was not so lucky. Nothing came from the attempt to sleep.

The next day after breakfast I was dragged out of my cell and into a bright white room. I was chained to a chair and left it there for what seemed like hours. No one came in to see me. I was left to stare at white walls while this bright light was beaming down on my skin. The light was so hot that had it been closer, I think it would have burned my skin.

I was pouring sweat by the time Hunter and Demetri dragged me to my cell. This routine happened for a week. I would get breakfast. Then I would be dragged to the white room. Then dragged back into my cell. Get a visit from Demetri and then darkness. Become submerged in my own self-loathing. Repeat.

I was starting to feel the mental weight of being isolated. I figured Demetri came and visited me for about an hour. He never touched me except for when I looked away while he was talking. He normally just chatted about off the wall topics without missing a beat. I was not sure if I would not have been better off not seeing him.

His chattering was almost enough to drive me insane by itself. After a week of that routine, they started adding in things while I was chained to my chair in the white room. He brought in a table and laid knives on it for a few days. Then added other torture devices in slowly. After a week and a half of that routine, I was becoming overwhelmed with the anticipation. The expectation of what was to come and the pain it might bring.

The mental struggle of waiting on the edge of my seat every minute was exhausting. It made me realize this was a form of torture in itself. To wait, staring at the objects that could inflict who knows what kind of agony day in and day out. Waiting for someone to come demand anything of me. Waiting to figure out why I was locked up to begin with. So far, I had tried to keep track of the days I had been captured. I believe it was about seventeen days. Seventeen days I have been here waiting for something to change.

My clothes looked to be a size too big on me. My hands and wrists were almost numb to the pain of the chains. The never-ending cycle of my skin being burned and my body healing itself was starting to slow. I now kept open sores on my wrist and ankles.

I was starting to get other marks on my legs and arms where they had me strapped to the chair. I have not spoken a word in over a week. Unsure if I could still form words. In my cell clumps of my hair scattered the floor like confetti. My cheeks were chapped where my tears never stopped and my skin so transparent that you could practically see the blood running underneath.

I felt lost. Unsure of what my future would bring. I was fed up with waiting around for something to happen. Before they could come to pick me up and drag me out of this cell, I stood on my feet and began yelling. I took my tray and started hitting the walls with it. I was tired of being silent. I was going to be silent no more.

They would hear my voice. It was not long after when they rushed in and I started making an even bigger scene. When they undid my chains, I let them have it to the best of my ability. There truly was no use in what I was doing. All I did was wear myself out. I did not care at this point. The dragged me kicking and screaming to the white room and tied me up once again. I was fed up with this and started yelling until my voice could not yell any more. When I finally stopped, I heard a familiar chuckle as the door came open. It was none other than Veronica Allen.

Chapter 37

I am sure if my jaw could have physically hit the floor, it would have been there when I watched her sashay in the room and over to the table that held the torture devices. "You know half breed, I have been waiting for an outburst like the one you displayed earlier. Most people have one within the first week of the silent treatment." She picks up each item on the table to inspects it like an interior decorator looking over paintings.

"I was kind of impressed you lasted eighteen days before deciding to make a little fuss. What is sad is that I felt like we could have been friends, you and I." She picks up and knife and walks over to me and places its blade to my cheek. I sit as still as I can manage.

"I felt like if you would have listened to my warnings, that we would have learned to get along. Well maybe not get along, but you would at least know your place." I can hear the anger in her tone. The pitching of each syllable becoming higher.

"But no, you have to stick your nose in my business and get yourself mixed up with Axel. Not that he was my only shot for power, but he was the easiest." She pulls the knife away and I released a breath I did not know I was holding. I watch as she pulls up a chair beside me. The scraping of the metal legs ringing in my ears. "Answer me this one question and maybe I will let you go. What makes you think you can come and try to ruin my life? What gives you that right?"

"Excuse me? What could I have possibly done to you?" I look at her and I think she has lost her mind. Is she really doing this because of Axel? She takes the blade across my cheek and makes a pretty deep cut. I can feel the warm liquid trickle down my face and the smell of metal makes my nose crinkle. "What the hell Veronica? What was that for?"

"Just because you may be mated to Axel does not mean you will take my place." She really has lost her mind. I watch her walk back to the table and grab a different knife. My left cheek still

burning. "I think this one. This one has serrations on the blade. What

do you think?" She comes over and holds it to my throat. I can feel

the coolness of the metal attempting to dig itself into my skin with

each breath I take.

"I want to know how you plan on getting the council on your

side. You will not take what is rightfully mine." My head spins with

possible scenarios of how this could go. I really am unsure what her

question even means at this point. "Veronica, I honestly have no idea

what you mean about the council."

I look down and the knife and she takes the hint and removes

it from my neck. She then proceeds to prop her feet up on my lap

and twirls the knife in her hand. The way the blade catches the light

and bounces it off of her features makes her seem like she is

enjoying this way too much. "Adalee, do you think Axel would like

you if you didn't have any of your fingers?"

"Veronica, all I am trying to do is figure out why you took

me in the first place. Let me go and no one will know it was you."

She lets out a sinister chuckle that puts a chill in the air. "It is funny

how he isn't even looking for you." It feels as if she stuck that knife right through my heart. It is like she is delivering one blow after another.

"Such a dilemma you have, Adalee. The council will not approve of you being mated together. Axel would not leave his alpha position to be with you. What will you do?" I honestly cannot answer her question. Demetri walks in the room and for a moment I think maybe he will distract her enough to where she can leave me alone, but luck is not on my side. "I was going to let the council banish you, but what fun would that be?" She twists off the chair and Demetri grabbed my hair hard enough for my head to be pulled back and she comes right next to my ear. "Why don't you answer some of my questions. We can come to an agreement and I might let you live until maybe tomorrow. Huh?"

With my life on the line all I can do is squeak out a yes. "So, pet. You know Demetri I like that nickname; I think it suits her." Demetri who still has my hair in his hands pulls me back to where I can see him staring down on me, "You know Veronica, I think it does." He lets me go momentarily and I can feel my head pounding. My eyes start watering from how bad my scalp is stinging. "What do you want with me, Veronica? What have I done to you?" I shouted back; I was sick of this twisted game she was trying to play.

"You don't even know do you?" I stare back at her. Unable to answer that question. At this point, I know nothing about anything. "You know Demetri, I am about tired of her for today. Why don't you put her back and we can pick up where we left off tomorrow?" Veronica puts her knife down and walks out of the door. Demetri takes me to my cell where he proceeds to tell me about his day. After about an hour of having to listen to him talk, he goes to leave, but before he does, he grabs me by the neck, picks me up and places a kiss on my cheek. "What the hell are you doing?"

He handles me as if I am rag doll and proceeds to drop me and I hit the ground with a thud. I land funny on my hip and I cry out in pain. He gives off a laugh and then walks out of the cell. Darkness finally falls and I am still squirming on what Demetri did before he left my cell. How much longer will he wait until he does something that cannot be forgiven?

I look up and imagine it is a full moon tonight. Something makes me think that it might be. I sit and wonder what tomorrow will bring. I close my eyes and I find myself falling asleep. It is a restless night as my body waits for what tomorrow might bring. Before I know it, my cell's dim light comes on and my breakfast is dropped off. I push it away and think about my best friend. I never did get to ask her about her wolf. I wanted to get to see what she looked like. Did she continue training to be a warrior like her parents were? What about her and Cameron? How are they in their relationship? I need my best friend near me, I feel isolated.

My lonely feeling does not last long before a guy comes in and grabs me to take me to the white room. Usually, it is a couple of guys who come and take me, but I guess they thought one would suffice. He drags me and chains me to the chair I have become accustom to spending the majority of time in lately. It is not long when Veronica makes her way in, hanging on Demetri's arm.

I look at them and just stare my way into the soul she apparently does not have. She goes over and picks up some kind of ice pick looking object and sits in her seat, feet up on my lap. "So pet, can you tell me what you know about your father's death?"

"Veronica, why are you bringing him into this? I thought this was about Axel." She looks over at me and then takes the ice pick and shoves it into my shoulder. I double over in pain and my breathing becomes heavy. It's on fire. "What the hell." She pulls it out and the laughs. "You know pet, say I believe you. Say you know absolutely nothing. How bad would it look for me to let you go and then what happened with your father go to the council? They already have a soft spot for you and your mother because of Mrs. Evanora."

"What do you mean what happened to my father?" I look over her and shake my head. Demetri comes around and grabs my hair making me look directly at her. "What can I say other than his car wreck was not an accident." She laughs in my face and then brings the heel of her stilettos down on my toes. Tears escape my eyes as I hear the sickening crunch of my bones. The discomfort in my shoulder dulling as my body takes in the agony of my foot. "You know Veronica, this is pathetic to think you can bully your way into anything. You want to know why I was mated to Axel? I have alpha blood running through my veins. Both of my parents have alpha blood."

"You are nothing more than a freak." I could tell I hit a nerve, so I kept fishing. "You think just because you have a title people will respect you? They won't. They will see you for what you really are. A coward." Not a second later, she threw her right fist forward and I could hear my nose break. My vision went cloudy. I spit the blood out that was running into my mouth and happened to make it fly in her direction. She hated that and hit me again, this time it was a hard-enough hit to knock me out.

I woke up sometime later to someone washing my face with a rag. I slowly opened my eyes and could tell I was in my cell and it was dark. I felt the water run down my face and hit my chest. A cool breeze then came from the door of my cell and it brought awareness to just how much of my skin was exposed.

"I am sorry miss. I could not stand to see you covered in blood like they left you. I hope you do not mind." I flinched at first and the realized after a little time he had no intentions of hurting me. I let him wash my face off and when he was done, he offered me a sweet smile and then scurried off into the darkness. Listening to Veronica talk about my father lit a fire under me. The passion to find out what I was missing fed my soul. I was fed up and was going to plan my escape. I needed to get free before something happens and I never have the option to leave. Never have the option to find the truth.

I thought about what I had learned in the last several weeks. It had to be close to the end of November at this point. I know that I hear no guards at night. I know that when they drag me to the white room it is in a different building. I hardly see any guards roaming the grounds in the forty feet they drag me from my cell to the white room.

The white room is kind of off by itself and closer to the forest than the cells. I remember that we drove for hours when they first captured me. I know Veronica has to be smart enough to know that she must keep up appearances. I have a hard time seeing any of this being legal, even for wolf law. I do not think she wants to get caught so I know I am probably away somewhere far. Julia did mention that Alpha Allen had almost ten thousand acres in his territory. If I can manage to escape, I am not sure where I would end up going but I know it will be away from here.

The next couple of days is much the same. They use one guard to take me to the white room. One guard to bring me back. Veronica and Demetri visit me the first day and ask me off the wall questions which I cannot answer. On the second day they take me to the white room and let me sit. The third day is the same, no Demetri or Veronica. On my way to the white room on the fourth day I notice there are no guards roaming around outside. I determine at this time that right now might be the best time to escape. I can practically pull my hands through my cuffs and once I do I can knock out the one guard and get away as fast as my legs will take me.

I determine the best time to plan an escape would be on the way back. Right at dusk when I could use night to help aid in my running. I may not see like a wolf does in the dark but I might find a better place to hide. I sit patiently waiting to see if Veronica or Demetri show up today and thankfully, they do not make their presence known. I am unsure if they are on the grounds, but I have to take that chance.

The longer I sit and wait, the antsier I become in my chair. I try to remain calm on the surface and hope it does not give anything away. Finally, the guard comes to take me away, he undoes my chains to switch me into hand cuffs and that is when I take my chance. With my hands freed I used all the magic I could muster and throw him into a wall and take off without looking back.

Chapter 38

As I make it out of the building I look around in quick haste and notice that the sun is setting over the back of the building I just ran out of. I quickly think, sun rises in the east and sets in the west. I remember Julia saying that the Allen's pack property was to the west, so I need to run straight ahead. Problem was that put me running across the lawn in the open. In a split second I think I could take off in the woods and circle back around, but I was not sure I could trust myself to stay on the right path in the woods. I only had another second to think about it. I chose to run in the woods and then I would turn to the east before the sun went completely down.

I took off and used everything I had to put some distance between me and the property. It was chilly during this time of the year and it made my teeth chatter as I made my legs push me faster and faster. I know I was not going full speed, simply due to the fact I had not moved in the last twenty something days and I was not given a proper meal.

I basically drank my food in the form of broth. I did not care; I pushed and pushed my body until I was forced to stop. I looked up and noticed that the sky had gone completely dark. I used my better than normal hearing and could hear howling in a distance. I had to continue going forward. I needed to find somewhere to hide. I thought about a cave or someplace dark, but then thought it would be to obvious. Maybe I could climb a tree? I needed to focus on one thing right now. They could smell me if I'm not careful. I first needed to find a body of water to try to disguise my scent.

I quivered thinking about having to dip myself in water. Yet, in order to truly get away I was willing to do whatever I needed. I focused on trying to find water. I put all of my concentration into finding some source of water and after a few minutes, I could hear the faint trickle of drops. It was all I needed. I followed the noise and after some time came to a cave.

I went inside being careful to make sure that I did not slip on the rocks beneath my feet. I went deep inside the cave and froze when I heard movements. I used my hand and created a soft glow of fire. I still remembered a little bit of my training and hoped it was enough magic to help me get through all of this. Most of the time my magic seemed to fluctuate with my moods. If I ever make it home I am going to need to take a crash course on all things witchy.

With a soft glow coming from my palm, I looked around and noticed several bats fly over head the same time I looked up. They must have been what made the noise, or that is what I told myself. I walked further in following the sound of the water. Towards the back of the cave was a small area filled with water. It looked like it was fed from a small trickle of water that came down from the ceiling of the cave.

I took a moment to catch my breath and then waded into the water. It came about chest high and was so cold that my teeth instantly started chattering. The lungs felt rigid, but the cool water made the ache in my legs a little better. I washed my main areas in the water as best I could to try to disguise my scent as best I could and finally felt that I made a little progress. I got out and felt how truly cold my body was at that moment. It was a chill that hurt down to my bones.

I looked around the cave and noticed I was pretty far back so I slowly made my way to the front and gathered some sticks. Hoping I could make a fire, somehow. I know at one point my mother taught me basic skills with magic for situations just like this, but those memories have been locked away for so long I am not sure I would know how to access them. I walk far enough into the cave that I felt it would be safe if I made a fire.

I wanted to make sure no one would be able to see the glow from the entrance. I put my sticks in a pile and tried to start a fire. No luck on my part. I tried everything that I could remember, but it was beginning to be hard to think of anything other than how cold I was. Finally, I threw my hands up in frustration and a fire broke out in the logs. I thanked the moon goddess herself, because I was sure I would be found frozen to death if I did not warm up soon. The fire was nice, and I warmed up rather quickly.

Within a few hours I was warmed up and rested enough to continue my journey. I put out my fire and walked towards the entrance of the cave. Looking for anything that I could use to deter my scent. I let my scent guide me, thinking that anything I could smell would confuse their senses. I came across a white looking flower and it looked like it would do the trick.

Before I took off, I listened for a few minutes and it was not long before I heard a howl probably a hundred feet from where I was standing. I hurried back inside the cave and cursed myself for getting comfortable. I should have moved on sooner.

I looked around inside the cave and found a group of rocks to hide behind. About the time I got hunkered down I hear steps walking in the cave. I held my breath and cursed myself silently. If I did all of this just to get caught within the first twelve hours of fleeing, I deserved to be brought back.

The steps paused a few feet from me and there was no way the wolf did not smell me. I would be shocked if they actually could not see me. I barely fit behind these rocks, but it was the only option I had on such a short notice. I tucked my head as far between my knees as I could and hoped for the best. I sat as still as I could, but I was sure if you listened closely enough, you could heart my heart beating out of my chest.

I heard the steps come a little closer. Then they stopped. I knew my heart was going to give out as fast as it was racing. I held my breath and waited for what my death would mean, I knew it was coming. Just when I thought the person would grab me, I heard them turn around and walk out of the cave.

Off in the distance I heard, "No, sir. I have no idea where the miss might be but she could not have gotten far. I checked the cave and there is no sign of her." I am sure my mouth hit the floor. I know who that was, it was the older gentleman who would bring my food while I was locked up. The one I tried to get to tell me his name.

"Are you sure? I am positive I smelt her stench. She must have been here at some point." The other voice shouted from what seemed like the front of the cave. "No, Hunter. I did not see a sign of her. I think we should go back and rest and pick it up in the daylight." My savior calmly said as he walked towards the front of the cage. "You are right, Scott. We should continue in the morning. We will probably find her dead tomorrow anyways. Boss won't be very happy, but that brat is not really my main concern."

Knowing Hunter was so close to where I was, halted me from making any movements. The fear of what he could do to me seemed to have a paralyzing effect. Beads of sweat lined my forehead and hands became clammy. I sat for what seemed like hours listening to the natural sounds of the forest around me.

I took off out of the cave a few hours later. I was starving, cold and exhausted, but if I stayed, they would surely find me in the morning. I continued walking in the opposite direction of the way the guards came in order to put distance between me and Veronica's property.

I walked until I could not walk anymore physically due to the pain that ran through my legs. It felt as if you took my legs and ran them through a meat grinder. Each step brought tears to my eyes and I knew I had to stop soon. I told myself I needed to find somewhere to rest and try to get a few minutes of sleep. If I were going to continue on my journey, I needed to be smart and try to rest when I could.

I found an area that was thick with underbrush. The underbrush stood about as tall as I did, and I figured this might give me a chance to not be seen. I got on my hands and knees and crawled my way to the center. By the time I reached the center, I was scraped from head to toe and my arms felt like they would come off

if I tried to move them.

I wiggled my way into the underbrush, enough to lay down

and close my eyes hoping for just an hour nap. The moment I closed

my eyes I was hit with a brightness. I blinked a few times and when

my eyes adjusted, I noticed I was at the pond behind Axel's house. I

looked around and my heart dropped when I noticed he was not

around. I went to the dock and sat down, wishing to see him if not

for just a short second. I needed to feel okay. I wished to see my

mother or Brina. I needed someone to tell me it was okay. I was

exhausted.

"You have managed to make me quite surprised. It took you

longer to get here than I thought it would. I figured the daughter of

the great Alpha Rosewood would be capable of more." My back

straightened and the hairs on my neck stood tall. "Should have

known that with your mother's blood in you it would weaken

whatever legacy your father thought he was leaving behind." The

sound of his voice was not a pleasant sound and it ruined this

sanctuary. I turned around and got into a defensive position. He

laughed when he saw what I did, and it only made me tremble. I was in no shape to attempt a fight and he knew it. "What can I do for you, Alpha Anderson? Any particular reason you are invading my dreams?"

"You think I would waste my time with you girl? I just want to chat." I looked around expecting to see Alpha Allen, but there stood Alpha Anderson in a business suit alone. Flashbacks of Axel and Julia as a little kid flashed before my eyes and I winced as I heard the sound of him smacking Axel in my mind. "You know my son told me all about you being his mate. Begging that we make a deal to where I would spare your life." He spat at the last part as if saying it put a bad taste in his mouth. "I mean, I do like my life and would like to be around a little longer."

"I honestly could not believe Selene, the great and powerful Goddess of the Moon, would do that to this family. How dare she think my son deserve a disgrace like yourself after all the work I did to secure this pack's future." I watch as his black business suit shimmers in the sun. "May I ask what you possibly could have done to secure your packs future?"

He looked around and admired the scenery for a moment before his voice came again like a deep thundering boom. "Not sure why this is the place you and my son chose to meet at. There are such prettier places on the property." Honestly, I could not answer that question. "Okay, time to get to business. You need to leave if you know what is good for you."

I looked at him confused and he just stared at me like he was scolding the help he had around his house. "If you want to continue breathing, I advise you to leave and disappear before my son finds you. He is destined to do great things and I will not have your tainted blood spilling on this family's name. Your father made the biggest mistake of his life allowing himself to get attached to that thing you call your mother." I could feel myself beginning to get angry.

"Are you trying to avoid my question, Mr. Anderson?" How dare he talk about my family like we were gum at the bottom of someone's shoe. He stopped me before I could say anything more. "You will be wise to remember your place and call me by my title, Alpha." I looked over at him and setting defiance in all my features. "As I was saying, Mr. Anderson. I do not know who you think you are, but you have nothing above me. You are not better than me and never will be. A person is not defined by a title someone gives them if they have not earned it."

I can tell he is not used to someone going against his orders. The way his jaw tightens and he clenches his fists. "Where I am looking, both you and I will be buried in the same sized hole in the ground. You have no right to judge me or my family. It does not take status to be a good person. I will not vanish, and I will not disappear because you think your word holds something over me. Your words hold no threat. As for Axel, he has that right to determine his life. He can decide who he wants to be with."

I stopped for just a moment and noticed he was fuming. "Also, Mr. Anderson, you cannot stop destiny. What is meant to happen will happen." If he was not angry before, he was definitely angry now. Had he been in a cartoon, smoke would have come from his ears.

"You ungrateful little brat. How dare you think you can talk to me that way." He walks closer to me and I notice I am in a terrible position. "The arrogance your mother instilled in you. I can see why she fell for my letter from the council stating that her family was finally safe." With my back at the end of the dock, I was stuck unless I turned around and dove into the water. I thought about it and it actually was not a terrible plan. "She fell right into my trap." I had a hard time seeing Mr. Anderson wanting to get wet. Yet knowing him, he would walk across the water in my dream. Not sure how he got here to begin with. I notice he is slowly walking to me and mumbling under his breath.

"Ugh, that damn Allen, cannot even finish the simplest jobs he was given. He was a terrible beta and even more so as an Alpha. That daughter walks all over him. He failed the first time and here I am to clean up his mess eleven years later." He is slow to walk in my direction at first. Nothing but complete concentration as he stalks forward. "What do you mean you have to clean up Allen's mess?"

Before I got my question answered, he is suddenly in front of me with lightning speed and grabs me by the neck. He throws me in the water and proceeds to try to drown me. I try to wake myself up, but I cannot seem to open my eyes. I need to wake up. I need to wake up I continue to tell myself. I am struggling against his grip around my neck and about the time my lungs fill with air and I hear a muffled growl and his hand release its grip.

He momentarily brings me up to the surface. His voice cutting in and out as the water drains from my ears. "Oh, sweet child. I had Allen kill your father with the plan of taking over his pack. I would then be the Alpha of the largest pack in the world and could rid this planet of every disgrace such as yourself." His hand tightens around my throat. My vision blurs just as I notice the black fur of the wolf running at us.

Anderson is too busy with me to notice until the wolf is right on top of him. A sickening grin makes its way onto his face as he throws out his free hand. I cannot seem to find the strength to break the water's surface and I start to sink. I feel like I am falling into the liquid's depth for hours. I look up and see the sun dancing through the water and then I notice a figure swimming towards me. My vision goes dark just before Axel can reach me.

Chapter 39

I jolt awake coughing and struggling to breath. Alpha Anderson's words playing over and over. "I had Allen kill your father." I sit in silence hidden from the world. Allowing myself to understand the gravity of the situation. Knowing the truth about my father does not feel as I imagined it.

My insides feel hallow. A barren land with no sign of hope. The realization that Alpha Anderson and Allen killed my father means they also killed Brina's parents. The guilty thought that she might also know this information passes through me so quickly, I almost misread my own emotions. There is no way she could know about that. How could she act halfway okay around Veronica and know the truth?

I come to the conclusion that she cannot. There is no way. My inner demons come to the surface when I contemplate whether it is even worth it to get up. I could lay here until they found me and then I would not have to live with this crippling sadness. The grief that I never fully processed comes flooding into me. The dam I did not even know I had, breaks fully.

I think about my mother and how strong she must have been to know she had to flee her home and everything she had worked for was stripped away by a power-hungry low life. How strong Brina has had to be to live with this grief I now feel, for most of her life. After wallowing in my own self-pity, I realize this is not who I was meant to be. This was not the end of my journey.

Silence surrounds me and feel like it is safe to crawl out of where I was hiding. I make my way out and I feel that physically body is rested. My arms and legs are a tad sore, but it was manageable. My stomach growls louder than I have ever heard and my clothes feel a little wet, causing me to freeze.

I break from the thicket and notice the sky has lightened some. I have got to get a move on if I am to put some more distance between me and the wolves hunting me. I start walking and after a little time, I can tell which way the sun is rising, and I start to walk that direction. I am walking with a hastened pace as I to try and conserve my energy.

Thankfully, it has warmed up a little bit but it is still freezing out here with almost no clothing. I stop after what seems like a few hours and start a fire using as little magic as I could. I warm myself up and then stomp the fire out and continue in the right direction. I crossed groves of trees and streams. I climb over and around large rocks and ravines. I see multiple forest creatures on my travels and eventually when the sun is at its peak, I come to the edge of a road.

I have never been so excited to come across a piece of civility before. Where there is a road, there must be a town somewhere close. I decide to stay about forty feet from the road in the trees and continue walking along the path of the road. I alternate walking and resting to warm up.

My stomach is cramping, I am so hungry and I have a splitting headache, but for the first time I feel like I have a possibility of making it home. With it almost being dark, I struggle with finding somewhere to rest or continuing on my journey. I decided to walk until I cannot physically see anymore and then hopefully, I will find somewhere safe to rest. I needed to find somewhere fast, it has been two days since I have eaten. I have found running water throughout my journey, so for that I am thankful.

As I struggle with walking in the dark, I think to myself just a little while longer. I walk to the road and decide it would be faster to walk along the edge. I also have less of a chance to lose it. With it being so dark I should see a car coming before they can see me. I walk for what feels like hours when I round a corner and see a small glimpse of light ahead of me.

My heart soars with joy and a new sense of determination hits me like wind carrying a sailor home the last couple of miles from shore. I feel a newfound freshness in thinking that maybe, just maybe, I can find a phone. I pick up the pace in which I am walking and make it to the edge of town.

I look at what I am wearing and notice that I need some new clothes. How will I be able to get something though? I walk around the shadows of town and notice it must be late enough that most people are home. I walk around the back of a convenience store and notice a row of buildings. I run across the street and down the alley, hoping to find something that could help me.

Finally, I come to the end of the alley and across the street was a laundromat. I noticed the lights were on and there was a girl about my size, or what was my size, sitting with a small child reading a book. It seemed she was waiting on clothes to finish washing. I watched her for a moment to see if she were someone I could trust.

I felt like I was far enough from Veronica's property that I was safe, yet I was not sure how far I really was. I felt like I had walked hundreds of miles when it was probably closer to twenty, maybe. I turned my attention back to the girl and continued watching her through the giant windows. She was kind to the child and seemed to really care for him. I think she may have been an older sister because when the child did something wrong, she corrected him but not in the way a mother would have. I finally calm my nerves and realize this girl might be my last chance at going home.

I think back to what Alpha Anderson had mentioned about needing to disappear. Could I go home after all of this? I was not sure what would happen to me if I went back and faced the people I loved again. I think back to how threating Alpha Anderson was and I would have no doubt that he would make good on his treat to kill me next time. Could I afford to put my mother and Brina in danger like that?

Maybe I can go home long enough to gather things and the make a break for it. I think that maybe I could go to the council because there is no way this is all legal. Is this what the council stood for? They found it easier to get rid of problems permanently instead of trying to see what was just. I shook my head and thought about how twisted this all was. More than likely Anderson had them in his pocket.

I noticed the girl was getting up to take the child to the bathroom and possibly change him. I took this as my opportunity to get inside the laundromat and then I would figure out a way to approach her. I decide to hide behind the first row of machines and after a few minutes I hear this girl come out from the bathroom and go back to where she was sitting.

I am trying to calm my breathing so I can approach her when I hear her speak. "Excuse me, you can come out." I am unsure of what to do. I sit in the same spot, frozen. How did she know I was here? "I can smell you. You reek."

I slowly come out from behind the rows of washing machines and show myself to the girl. I hear her take a deep breath in and I know that I must look terrible. I am about fifteen pounds under weight and my hair is frail, thin, and matted. I am dirty with torn clothes that barely fit. My legs and arms are dirty and have dried blood on them.

"What happened to you?" Was all she could get out to ask. Can I tell her the truth? How do I know I can trust her? "Let's just say, long story short, it has been a rough couple of weeks." She looks at me suspiciously. I notice the way her eyes become more focused and how she looks me up and down. "I just need to borrow a phone. Do you have one I could use?"

"Just promise me you won't steal it." She slowly hands it over to me. As understandable as that comment is, it makes my heart ache to know how hard it is to trust people. To allow yourself to be placed in a vulnerable position such as this one.

I call Brina's number and it does not even finish the first ring when I hear her southern draw across the phone. "Hello?" I burst into ugly tears immediately. "B- B- Brina. It is me. I need you to come and get me now. Please. I am in a little town called…" I paused still unsure of what town I am in, pleading silently with the girl in front of me who still doesn't quite trust me.

"Where are you? Adalee, I need to know the exact address. Are you okay? Did they hurt you? Do you know who took you? Do you know how sick we have been? We have looked for you every day. Axel even has a team of his men searching for you. Adalee, answer me damnit."

I go from crying to laughing and then back to crying. "Hold on, B. You are talking so fast I can't answer all of your questions. I am in Northport, Washington. Please come get me in a hurry. I will fill you in once you get here."

I hear that Brina is talking to someone and then before I could tell her the address, I feel a rush of wind behind me. I go into defense mode and whip my body around and was met with a flash of pale blonde hair as I go tumbling to the ground. "ADALEE EBONY ROSEWOOD YOU ARE OKAY!!! You are really here." The largest smile I could muster comes across my face. Brina had me tackled on the ground and in a huge hug. The tile floor in the laundromat breaking my fall. The pain that course through my body didn't have a chance to dull the pure happiness of that moment.

Chapter 40

Brina kept me in a soul crushing hug until my mother began to speak. "Oh, my baby. Brina get off of her and let her breath. Oh Adalee, I was so worried." Brina climbs off of me and pulls me to a standing position. Before Brina can let go of me completely, my mother grabs me and pulls me into a crushing hug.

I let the tears fall and can feel her shirt becoming soaked. I pull back and look at my mother and best friend. The joy in my heart was like a kid at the fair finally getting cotton candy after being told no all night. All the stress was lifted off of my shoulders. I felt so light I swear I could fly to Neverland. After several hugs and even more tears, I heard someone clear their throat and I instantly became defensive. I threw my hands up and used all the magic I could muster and sent a blast in the direction of the mystery person.

When my mind processed who was standing there, I regretted it instantly. "Oh, Mrs. Eva, I am so sorry. Are you okay?" I rushed to her side and noticed she laughed it off. Thank goodness. I was worried that I had severely messed up. "Oh, sweet child. I want to say I am so thankful that you have made it to safety. My heart has been heavy the past twenty-six days."

"I know a certain young man who has been in a tizzy since you were taken." I blush at her comment about Axel and wonder where he is at right now. Would he really want me after his father's threat? "Now child. We need to sit down and have a little chat. I recently took over the seat for witches on the council and I would like to bring this up to them. This will not go unpunished."

I become zoned out as I watch the three women in front of me. All three of them playing some of the most important roles in my life. "I am sorry. What were you saying?" I looked away from Brina to focus and was a little embarrassed. "Do not fret child. I have a feeling this journey is far from over."

I looked at Mrs. Eva and silently nodded. I picked up where I left off at the moment I was taken. As I told my story, I could see how the expressions of my mother went from concerned to downright angry. She was not a woman to be trifled with. When I was done with my story everyone was silent. My mother got up and just held me. I am sure my story was nothing a mother ever wanted to hear that their child went through.

"So, you are telling me Adalee, that Veronica Allen and Demetri Green kidnapped you?" It was Mrs. Eva who finally spoke and brought it all back to reality. "Did you say Demetri Green, Mrs. Eva? Is he related to nerdy math teacher Green?" I never did think to ask his last name. "Why yes Adalee, that is his father who also has a seat on the council. Who else was there? Did you say a Hunter?"

I still couldn't get past that Mr. Green, nerdy calculus teaching Mr. Green, was an important vampire on the council. "Yes. His name was Hunter. Do you know him? Also, why do you think that Veronica and Demetri were working together?" Mrs. Eva gets up from the table and walks over to the window of the living room. "I thought Hunter was dead. I guess he has been hiding."

"What do you mean you thought he was dead?" I think back to how Hunter looked. How pale and cold his skin was compared to Demetri's. "That my child, is a story for another day. Back to the topic at hand." I was still unsure what that was. "Well, Adalee, I think it has something to do with influence. Allen is a terrible Alpha, but he has influential people that owe him favors. I think the council is worried about upsetting him and the retaliation that could bring. He is known to have information on several tightly kept secrets." Right. Why I would be kidnapped? I felt to sleepy it was hard to keep track of each veering subject.

I walk over to the window where Mrs. Eva is standing and look out into the empty street. "Mrs. Eva, what am I to do? Alpha Anderson will not rest until I am dead. He tried to kill me in my dream." The laundromat walls seem to be closing in.

"I know that anything Veronica wants, she gets, and she wants me dead. Now you are saying Demetri has ties to the council and what do you know, he wants me as a pet. Is love even worth this? I wanted a love that would bring about change. A love so strong stories would be told for generations. Now I think it would be better to walk away and allow Axel to live his life."

Before Mrs. Eva could speak, my mother comes over. "You know my dear, I had the same doubts with your father. Your father when we met begged me to leave Canada and I was madly in love, so I followed. When we got back to his territory, I was worried. Your father made arrangements that we would spend the first five years in the house we live in now. We spent five beautiful years there." I think back to my memories and even though I have those intact now, I still can't seem to remember him.

"I was worried about your father. He seemed lost at times although he tried to hide it. He needed his pack; it was in his blood. Running it from afar was not the same as being there for his people. His pack loved him, yet we still took precautions. I hid our scent and helped you control your powers until Allen found out and confronted your father." I realize I have no clue what my mother went through.

"Your father refused to give in to his treats and it was not but a year later when he died in a car accident and Allen took over as Alpha. We cannot tell you what to do." My mother paused and pulled me into another hug. "I know what I would do if it came to Axel." I looked over at my best friend and she was wiggling her eyebrows at me. She was ridiculous. My mother clears her throat and it causes Brina to turn red. I bust out laughing and my mother rolls her eyes.

"Adalee, I can tell you that boy loves you with all of his heart. I know that you think you have to make this decision on your own, but he should have a say in it. A wolf having to live without their mate leads to a long, miserable life. I do not know what he would pick. I would be happy for the two of you if you both decided to stay together." Is that really an option like my mother thinks? What will happen when they come looking for me?

"The two of you could have a love most dream of wanting. I can tell you a life on the run is not for the weak. It will test you at every turn. I do not see another option until we get the council straightened out and a few rules changed with the help of Mrs. Eva other than for you to go on the run. Your safety is my biggest priority. I promised your father that I would always protect you and clearly, I cannot do that in this town." What Alpha Anderson says sticks out about leading us home to finish the job.

"I thought it had been long enough that old issues were forgotten and that we could be home, but I was mistaken. I will not be fooled again." I think about what my mother is saying and I am unsure of what to do. Even more torn. We cannot fight the council on our own. By now Veronica and Demetri would have informed them of my escape and they could be looking for me now.

I know I must go on the run, but what about Axel? What about Brina? Could she come with me? "What about Brina? What would I do without you?" I ask as tears start to form. I have not had to live without my best friend, how would I now? "Oh honey, I promise we would find a safe way to communicate and see each other. I think I need to be here and to try to help with the mission at hand. I want you safe and I think this would be the best way for me to help with that."

She comes over and wipes my tears away. She lifts my chin up and smiles at me. Goodness, how will I do this without her? I know I must leave for my own safety, but not having either my mother or Brina in my life is going to prove to be difficult. How can I be so selfish as to think that if Axel comes with me at least I will not be alone? I cannot ask him to abandon his pack or sister. How could he even want to come with me? I think I should just pack my stuff and head out on my own.

"Okay you guys. I think I need to get home and pack a bag. I need to put some distance between me and my enemies. How do I do this mom?" She looks at me and I would almost think she has a sense of pride to her. "Well, Adalee. First, we will get you home and then we will pack your things. You must pack light at first, but do not fret. Once we get you set up, we will make sure you have enough cash to get started with a new life. If you play it smart you can stay in one place for up to a year. How does being a college exchange student sound? We will need to get you a new name and everything that goes with that. Let me make a few phone calls once we get back home." I think about going back home. Will I be in danger even in the few hours I am gone? "How do we get home? I mean you all appeared out of thin air." They all laughed, and Mrs. Eva just waved her arms in a bowing motion. "Do not worry child. I will be the one to get us home. Now let's gather all around."

"Is this how you seemed to vanish into thin air at school?" With a twinkle of mischief in her eyes, Mrs. Eva asked if we were ready and then with a nod of her head when transported right into my bedroom. I went to run through a shower and while I was in the shower, Mrs. Eva and Brina packed me two bags and my mother made arrangements to get me out of the country safely and discreetly. I came down the stairs and went into my mother's study while Brina finished up a few things in my room.

"Momma, I am scared. How do I know I will be okay?" She stops what she is doing and comes over and picks up both of my hands in hers. She looks me in the eyes and calmly states, "because I raised you to be okay." She lets go of my hands and then proceeds to make a few more phone calls. Brina comes downstairs and sets a duffle bag and a backpack down. "Do not worry sugar.

I packed all the essentials and the cutest clothes I could find. You also have several practical outfits. I made sure to think of everything." I cannot help but giggle thinking of Brina picking out my clothes. She always loved to pick my outfits for important events. Mrs. Eva shows up behind Brina and hands me a small fanny pack. "You will know what to do when the time is right. I also got you a new cell phone and your new ID. Hope the name is okay. I open it up and look at the ID. It is me, but my hair is altered to be almost blonde and my name reads Rosie Michelle Woods and I smile at what Mrs. Eva did with the play on the new name. Rosie Woods has a nice ring to it.

UNKNOWN

My mother gets off the phone and joins in on the group discussion about the new name. "My little Rosie. I love it. Okay, back to the business at hand. I have secured you a private plane to the Northern Territories of Canada and then from there you will take a few different airplanes to end up in New Zealand. It is beautiful there." I look around at these strong women in my presence. I can do this.

My mother continues to talk, and I hang on every word afraid I might miss the most important part. "You should be safe for your first year. So, to get to the private plane I am going to drive you to the edge of the land where banished creatures live and then it is a small five-mile hike through the woods to get to a private air strip. I want to warn you, once you get to New Zealand, do not stay where the plane drops you off. Find a small off the beaten path town or a super large city. Either one will do. Keep your head down and you will be fine."

"How are you going to keep yourself out of trouble? That part of the equation still not figured out." My mother and Mrs. Eva just look at each other with dread. "Well, I will have to go underground myself. I just will not be leaving here until I have solid proof Anderson killed your father." She gives me a kiss on the cheek and the starts to walk to her car. I guess that is all to say. I feel like a spectator to my own life.

"Okay Ads, this is the last time I will see you or speak to you for a while. Know I love you and this will all pass. You will be okay. I promise." Brina gives me a huge hug and then grabs my bags and walks out of the house behind my mother. I turn to Mrs. Eva and smile at her. It was a half-hearted effort, but it was all I could muster. "Mrs. Eva, I want to thank you for everything you have done for me. Will you promise me something?"

I watch as her expression becomes puzzled. "Sure child, what might that promise be?" I look back at the door that Brina just walked out of and sigh. "I want you to promise to keep an eye out for Brina. She means the world to me." Mrs. Eva looks towards the door and just nods hear head. I give her a quick hug and walk towards the car. This is it. Here is to the start of a new chapter.

The drive was a rather long one and the car ride was filled with awkward silence. No music was playing and no banter was happening. Brina, my mother and I all sat and stared ahead at the dark winding road. After about two hours we reach a rest stop and my mother pulls over. "Okay Adalee, the plane is straight through the woods in that direction." She points into the darkness and flashes from my escape come creeping back.

I calm myself and try to focus on what she is saying, but it feels like I have water in my ears. It is hard to make out what she is saying. "Adalee, we love you and I promise you will be okay. You must get going if you are to remain safe." I finally hear as she starts to get out of the car. She goes to the trunk to grab my bags and then comes to my door and opens it. Waiting for me to get out, but I feel like my body is made of concrete. Unable to move and stuck in one place like a gargoyle.

My mother pulls me out of the car, and I stand looking at the forest. It looks uninviting and I dread having to go back into it when I clawed my way out of it just hours ago. My mother and best friend give me a few more words of advice and then push me towards the tree line. Such stillness around me and it makes me tremble. I know I must go for my safety as well as my family's safety, but it does not make it any easier. Finally, I step into the tree line and freeze.

Blackness. That is what surrounds me while my eyes adjust to what is directly in front. The forest is hauntingly beautiful. Trees so close to one another it seems they support the ones directly next in line. As if one tree would fall, they all would fall soon after. The tops creating the canopy of darkness I stand under.

Branches hang down with a sense of sadness while their dead leaves create a musty, wet layer of debris underneath my feet. My bare toes crinkle at the slimy feeling of mush comes up between my toes. Where are my shoes? The silence I hear is almost inviting as I start to take a step forward. Why am I going towards something that looks as if it will swallow me whole? The darkness, as eerie as it seems pulls me in like the tide of the ocean. Back to safety and into the unknown. The moment I move forward birds come rushing near me, beckoning me with a warning to not to move. It is like I am compelled to not listen, my feet shifting even though in the back of my mind I know that it is not a good idea.

As I make my way into the grove of trees, I notice that I have no idea where I am going. My body seems to work on autopilot. Like this is just a normal stroll in a park I have spent years with. What is my destination if I do not even know where I am? A feeling of dread with a handful of knots forms at the pit of my stomach, and I push down the urge to throw up.

The hairs on the back of my neck stand tall and goosebumps raise along my arms. Before I know what my own body will do, I take off into a dead sprint. Running. Faster than I thought humanly possible. Why am I running? Pushing past trees and underbrush not caring that my clothes are being ripped. My arms and legs feel like they have been torn to shreds. The stinging in my skin begging me to stop, if only for a moment. Do you think I listen? No. I run for what seems like miles when my body betrays me and stops suddenly. I double over and fling my hands above my head trying to catch my breath. I need to continue to the plane.

All of a sudden, I hear what apparently caused me to start running. I look around frantically as twigs snap and brush rustles with movement. This strange sense of foreboding comes to me when I notice just as the figure starts to step out of the night.

I feel the rush of wind and my view turns sideways. I try to catch myself from falling but my arms betray the rest of my body and all I expect to hear is the whack my head makes when it hits the ground, but it never comes. A pair of arms catch me mid fall. Defining silence in the air. Nothing stirring, the stillness almost unnerving when at last I see movement ahead.

I try to speak but my voice betrays me. I want to scream, but no even air makes it way out of my throat. A strange sense of calmness comes over me while my body tries to go into flight or fight, and I want to continue my running. I feel thousands of tiny of sparks run up and down my body. I feel the electricity surge through me. I want to go back to the start of it all before our life became complicated. I want to curse my legs for shuffling their way into the vast forest, should I have stayed and stood my ground?

My breathing catches in my lungs and my heart skips a beat when I catch myself staring into the most gorgeous pair of icy blue eyes I have ever seen. Once I catch my breath, I manage to find my voice. "Axel Eli Anderson, fancy meeting you here." I say as seductively as I could and all it does is make me laugh. "That sounded terrible huh?"

My laughter fills the silent forest. I look at him sideways and notice his stone-cold expression turn into one with a huge grin. It amazed me how one touch from him instantly calms me. I was amazed that he found me. After all this time he found me. Our relationship, if you even want to call it that, was so rocky that is made Mount Everest look like a speed bump.

We went through so much to end up having to face leaving

behind what we love. I was okay with it seeing as I have moved

around my entire life, but was Axel? How can he be so sure of us to

want to leave his entire family and pack behind? Was he making a

mistake on me? I turned my head away and looked into the forest. I

was unsure of everything in my life at this moment. I finally faced

him after a few moments and my expression was one of torment.

Torment in thinking I was ruining his life.

His happy expression turned back into stone after a few

moments. "Ads, you know we cannot run like this forever. They will

find us eventually. I do know this is the best way to keep you safe." I

look at the growing forest and then back to my mate. "Are you sure

you want to do this with me? I would not blame you for wanting to

stay with your pack.

"I know for me, that so long as I have you beside me, I can

face whatever or whoever stands in our way. I know we are destined

to be together, but this is a huge risk to follow me into the unknown

with potential danger at every corner." Axel pulls me in for a kiss

and when he pulls away my body begs for more. My body reacts to

his every touch. When he leans away, I automatically lean towards him. I do not want this to end. To finally know we are where we should be, with each other.

He looks down at me and laughs in my face. How dare he, he knows I am sensitive. Or at least he should know I am sensitive after everything we have been through. "You know Axel, I have legs and can walk right. You can set me down at any time." A little bit of my bratty side comes out seeing as he laughed at me. He pulls me closer and buries his head in my neck, taking long, deep breaths. "Rainwater and roses. Mmmm. I have waited so long for this moment, let me live in it. Let me have my Luna in my arms for just a little bit longer. I do not know what tomorrow will bring. The last image I have is of you sinking in water. I thought I lost you." He whispered the last words.

"Adalee Ebony, you have no idea what that did to me when I thought you were gone forever. I showed up in our little piece of heaven hoping to see you. I went twenty-eight days hoping every night just to hold you once more. When I showed up that night it seemed different. That is when I saw him. I saw my father holding you down in the water and I could have killed him for you. I still have no idea how he managed to get in our dream."

"That moment though I knew, I knew that he would never be considered my father again. He lost his son that night and he did it to himself." He finally sets me down and we continue into the darkness. "So, you are the one who saved me from your father? Very brave of you. If you continue saving me, I might just have to call you prince charming." I smile my biggest smile up at him and he leans in to kiss my forehead.

He stops us walking and grabs the side of my face. "Adalee, I will do my best to always protect you. I am sorry that I let you down the day you were taken. I can tell you each minute that passed by while you were gone, I did not rest trying to find you. I searched under every stone and behind every tree and still I failed in my job to defend you. You are my life. I cannot live without you beside me. I know it took me longer than it should to admit that, but I am here now trying to make up for it." I pull him in for a kiss.

When his lips meet mine it is like the outside world melts away. It is only the two of us in this vast forest with the earth at our fingertips. That first kiss was soft and beautiful, but when Axel pulled me closer the rest of the kisses had an air of hunger to them.

We melted into each other. I had no idea two people could be so close to one another, yet still feel worlds apart. I pulled him closer and the moment I do, we go toppling backwards.

Axel laid on top of me and my body ached for him. He slowed his kisses, and his breath came out rough. "Do not worry love. We have the rest of our lives. We need to get going before our plane leaves us stranded. We have a couple miles left to walk." I stare at the only thing I can really see in this vast obscurity, and it is his blue ice-colored eyes. They seem to glow in the night, and it is stunning. They make me think of when you see snow for the first time in the winter. They are magical.

I beg for just one more kiss and Axel obliges with no issue. He pulls me up from the ground by my waist. I look into the forest once more and guilt hits me. I do not want our time to end but is that selfish of me? How can I be sure this is what he really wants? I cannot help but give him one more chance to turn away. With my heart feeling like it will rip in two, I ask him as casually as I can manage even though my voice broke in a few places showing my lack of strength. "Axel, are you sure you want to do this? There is no turning back once we make it to that plane."

UNKNOWN

He looks at me and then grabs my bag in one hand and holds out his other for me to take. I look at it and a smile stretches across my face. Hand in hand, we start walking to our new destiny, ready to take on whatever is thrown our way. I know so long as we are together, nothing can stand in our way. We may have had a rocky start, but somehow, we found each other when it mattered the most. I am unsure of what tomorrow might bring, but right now all I can think about are how those icy blue eyes will be beside me.

Acknowledgments

Have you ever dreamed of something so BIG that when it happens it feels too good to be true? This book is my dream. My family is extremely important to me. They are in short, my everything! For the unmeasurable love and unending support with this journey, I thank you.

A personal thank you to my editor Chersti Nieveen, for transforming my rough vision into something I can truly be proud of, Doug Hoppes for creating a stunning cover and Halleigh Thompson for the help to buff out the rough spots.

What more can I say other than, I DID IT!

Jordan, Kova, Leeland, Nana, Papa, Giddy, Dad, Niese, JoNana, Jimmy, Tristen, Grace, Delaney, Dylon, Elizabeth, and Staci.

Thank you for everything!

Made in the USA
Las Vegas, NV
06 March 2021